Lucretia

a novel by

NOEL BARTON

Cover design by Poppa Tudor
Editing SKYWriters
Special final editing Bobbie Falin and Gerry Brown

Dedication

For Juanita and her family

Table of Contents

Praises for Lucretia

"Noel Barton has done it again. If you liked her previous books, "Watch for the Whirlwinds," and "Meryl Jean Another Whirlwind," you will absolutely love "Lucretia," her latest contribution to the literary pantheon. Much more than a coming-of-age story and a slice of Americana that readers of all ages will be able to relate to, Barton's latest foray into our collective psyche will have you laughing, crying – but most of all reflecting on your own life and experiences. I instantly saw myself and my family in many of the interactions Barton so eloquently describes in such exquisite detail. Her writing style is fluid and conversational; you feel like you are actually in the room where everything is taking place. And, unlike many works these days, there is an underlying strength and spiritual dimension to the book that will leave you feeling uplifted and encouraged by the time you make your way to the final page. Highly recommended."

—Dr. Aaron Hughey
Professor, Student Affairs Program Coordinator
Western Kentucky University

Once again, Noel Barton has achieved success in writing a beautiful read of historical fiction. This story produces background to her previous two books: "*Watch for the Whirlwinds*," and "*Meryl Jean Another Whirlwind.*" The book is easy to read, unencumbered with foul language and not complicated with impossible to follow action. It contains a story that one will be caught up in reading a chapter and "remembering the good "ole" days as you reflect upon what you just read. The story is not only enjoyable, but also a book one will want to read over again, and it would benefit sharing with the old, who have experienced the "historical," and the young teen who can learn and benefit the "historical."

—Joe Causey
Retired Pastor
Hospital Chaplain

Love and loss, great challenges, and wrenching heartbreaks, then at last love again for a girl who finds she has no choice other than become a woman overnight. Lucretia is an uplifting story of will and determination, of a young woman's belief in her ability to not only survive, but to grow.

—Gerry Harlan Brown
Author of *White Squirrels and Other Monsters* and
Ring the Bell

A story of a girl struggling to find her place in the harsh environment of the Missouri Bootheel from an author who specializes in writing strong women. Life was not easy around the middle of the last century for Lucretia, but there are still moments of joy and laughter amid the pain. The secret delight to the knowing reader is encountering characters from Noel's other books in various other stages of their lives.

—Bobbie Falin
Author of Flashing Dark and the Star Child series

Noel Barton has done it again!

Lucretia is a wonderfully written novel that will make you laugh as well as shed a few tears. Barton pulls in characters and locations from her other books and intertwines them with some new characters with which the reader will surely form an instant connection. You will root for the main character from the beginning to the end as she shows us that it is possible to rise above poor choices from the past, and that determination and courage will always triumph.

This inspiring novel has a down-home feel and is very hard to put down. It has the reader hooked from the very first page. It's definitely a must read!!

—Karen Treece
Reading Teacher
Edmonson County Middle School

I couldn't be more pleased that Noel Barton chose to write my mother's story. Although parts of this account were fiction, the parts that were fact made me so very proud of the determination and unwavering courage she had to not allow her youthful choices to define the rest of her life. I would only hope anyone after reading Lucretia, would decide to do the same. Just reading about her life and beautiful love stories made me appreciate and miss my sweet mother even more.

—Marta Denham Brumley
Daughter of Lucretia

Illinois
To St. Louis
Cairo
Sikeston
Kentucky
Bootheel
of
Missouri
Tennessee
*Pemiscot
County
Mississippi River
To Jonesboro
Union City
Kennett
Muddy Ox
Doodlum Switch
Hayti
Caruthersville
Steele
Dyersburg
Caraway
Blytheville
Arkansas
Memphis
Mississippi

Foreword

Good literature, not necessarily popular literature, should be a good story, with a "moral" lesson that is fun and enjoyable to read. Once again, Noel Barton has achieved success in writing a beautiful read of historical fiction. This story produces background to her previous two books: *Watch for the Whirlwinds* and *Meryl Jean Another Whirlwind*. The book is easy to read, unencumbered with foul language and not complicated with impossible to follow action. It contains a story that one will be caught up in reading a chapter and "remembering the good "ole" days as you reflect upon what you just read. The story is not only enjoyable, but also educational; Do you know how to drive "stick shift" with a clutch? The story teaches you. It's not just practical, it becomes educational.

Lucretia encounters crisis after crisis. Raised in a strict matronly environment, she faces an unwed pregnancy, marriage to an older man, death of a husband she has learned to love, and incapacitating injuries to her parents. Throughout her struggles, she demonstrates an unwavering faith in God, and support from her family, who have come around to accept her faith and confidence. She accepts her condition and grows immensely by realizing (in her mother's words) that, "the only thing I knew for sure was-I didn't know anything for sure."

Out of her struggles to "grow up fast after suffering the consequences of bad choices," comes a family relationship which starts out unfair and overly protective and moves to one of "humility and peace." The family grows in love, the community (church) grows in love and ministry and God is recognized as, "the only one who loves you more than your Mama and Daddy."

The final word (from God) comes from Meryl Jean's grandmother, "Find your vision. Pray about it. And let God be who helps you decide your path-not a bunch of waggin' tongues."

Once again, Barton has written a book that one will want to read over again; and it would prove beneficial in sharing with the old, who have experienced the "historical," and the young teen who can learn to appreciate the "historical."

"It is sad, that people don't carry on traditions like they used to."

The "moral," beautifully illustrated, is found in the Bible verse quoted at the end.

Proverbs 3:5-6

—Joe Causey
Retired Pastor
Hospital Chaplain

Prologue

"HERE'S YER BABY doll and its blanket, Lucretia. Stay here and play. I'll be right over there picking the ends of the rows until someone comes to the scales," Mama said as she spread a quilt on the ground for me under the shade of the cotton wagon.

After my parents got their farm, Daddy's job was to plant, plow, and harvest the crops. Mama was the field boss, weighing the sacks, and keeping up with everyone's daily totals. Until I was big enough to swing a hoe or pull a cotton sack, my job was to stay out of their way and mind every word they said. Even at age four, I had learned my job very well.

Some field bosses were content to lean back and wait for the next sack to be weighed. Not Mama. She wasn't one to sit very long anywhere. As soon as the last weight was recorded, she strapped on her sack and started picking the ends of the rows until the next person appeared.

"It's just too hot for you out there in the field today. Here, take your trucks and sit there in the shade with that little girl," a lady said to her son.

The little boy sat several feet from me and started to

play with his trucks. It was fine until he started making motor sounds.

"You're gonna wake my baby," I shushed.

"Sorry," he said and continued to quietly make roads in the dirt.

Suddenly, I bolted from beneath the wagon and did what probably looked like a war dance. A huge grasshopper had crawled under my shirt.

"Get it—get it off of me!" I screamed.

The boy jumped up, raised the back of my shirt, knocked the culprit to the ground and stomped it into the dirt.

"What are you doin' to my little girl?" Mama yelled. My shirt, still in his hands when Mama arrived.

"Nothin.' I was helpin' her. I wasn't doin' nothin' to her," he stumbled backwards several feet.

"You—you get away from her. Where's yer Mama? Lucretia, you come over here with me."

"He was killin' that grasshopper," I whined, pointing to the dead insect on the ground. "He wasn't hurting me."

"What's goin' on here?" the boy's mother asked as she walked quickly toward us after hearing the commotion.

"Yer boy here was pullin' up my little girl's clothes." Mama was red-faced and angry.

"No Mommy. I wasn't. I was getting' a grasshopper off her." By now, he and I both were crying.

"I'm sure this is a big misunderstandin'. If you want to pay us for the day, we will leave now." The lady was polite but stern.

Mama sullenly added up what she owed them, and they left. He turned and looked at me with tears in his eyes as his mother led him away.

"He wasn't hurting me, Mama. He wasn't."

"Lucretia, you don't need to be around kids like that. Matter of fact. You stay away from boys altogether. I say good riddens' to the likes of them."

From that day on, Mama forbade me to be around or even talk to a boy. It became worse the older I got.

"OKAY NOW, AFTER you strip your bed and get the scarves off the dresser and side tables, remember to pull the bed out from the wall to clean under it. Hurry up now, I don't want it to take us all day to get this washin' over with. And I better not see a smidgen of dust on those baseboards when you're done either. You hear me, Lucretia?" Mama was already training me, at the age of ten to spit-shine every inch of my room to equal the sterility of the rest of our house.

My mother, Emerald Bertram was obsessed with cleanliness. It was religion to her. However, in the same way she would have chosen certain foods for her plate, prepared by only a select few at a potluck dinner, she culled and tweaked Bible scriptures to make them apply to her purpose. She would have argued until her tongue fell out that *cleanliness is next to Godliness, beauty is as beauty does and a scraggly picked row of cotton is an abomination in the eyes of God,* were actual Bible verses. Each Monday morning, weather permitting, every sheet, blanket, pillowcase, table scarf, and throw rug we owned was washed and hung uniformly across our clotheslines. The mop dangling to dry from its perch on the back porch was a sure sign that we could have eaten dinner off our floors.

As long as her house was spotless, her cotton crop was prosperous, Daddy pulled his shoes off at the door, and I succumbed completely to her will, all was right in Mama's world, and we were allowed to live in it. My friends had to also measure up to her self-imposed standards. And Heaven help me if I spoke to a boy without her permission after I reached puberty. I was not Lucretia Bertram. I was Emerald Bertram's daughter. I sometimes felt as though it was not my face, but hers, staring back at me when I looked into a mirror. People often called me the town's beauty. She took full credit for that too, although I hardly resembled either of my parents.

Some said I was a root out of dry ground.

Chapter One

"MAMA, BILLIE KAY wants to come over after supper so we can study together for tomorrow's test. Can she?" I asked as I finished ironing my sheets and pillowcases.

"I don't care for her comin' over as long as y'all study on the porch or out there under the willow tree. I don't want that girl trackin' in my house. But you need to get those linens ironed and put back on your bed before she gets here."

I tucked the bedspread tightly for Mama's inspection, before grabbing my books and heading to the back porch to wait for Billie Kay Brown to arrive. She and I rose to the top of the class when it came to grade point average after we started studying together. Just a few weeks left of our sophomore year, and we'd be sixteen and juniors. Both our birthdays were in June. Billie Kay would see sixteen three days before me.

Billie's parents officially allowed her to have boyfriends and double date at age fifteen. Although, I knew she had boyfriends long before that. Mama let us be friends since there was only a fence between our back yard and the Brown's and she could see nearly every move Billie's family made. However, Billie was a sly one. Mama just thought she knew and saw all.

"Can I get us each a glass of sweet tea when she gets here?" I asked beyond the screen door.

"I'll hand it to you. I don't want you trackin' in either. Not 'til you're ready to come in for the night."

Without fail, I knew a pan of water, a rag and a clean pair of socks would be waiting for me by the door for washing my feet before coming inside. Also, our shoes had to be wiped clean and neatly lined just inside our door. Her rules were that only socked-feet, never shoes walked on her floors—her sanctuary—our house.

"Hey Cretia, are you ready to crack some books?" Billie Kay asked as she balanced on the plank that bridged the road ditch and our yard.

"I'm ready. Want to study here on the porch or go sit on the stumps out under the willow tree?"

"Under the tree is fine with me," Billie Kay said cunningly. She was up to something. Her face gave her away.

"Mama, you can hand me our tea now. We'll be out by the tree."

"Here you go. Y'all got 'bout two hours 'fore supper's ready and your daddy gets home," Mama warned.

As soon as we got to the stumps and out of earshot of Mama, Billie Kay lowered her voice to a whisper. "I got a note from Gil today. He and his friend Ben want to walk us home tomorrow after school."

"Billie Kay, you know Mama won't let me walk home with a boy. She gets mad if she even sees me talking to one."

"Aw Cretia, your Mama will never know. She'll be too busy polishing y'all's doorknobs to notice," Billie Kay laughed.

"I don't know. I'd be in some real kind of trouble if she caught me."

"Look at it like this. They're on the road. We're on the road. Girl, it's just a road. Your Mama can't say who can or can't walk on the road. Now, can she?"

"Well…" I pondered.

"Lucretia, Gil said Ben told him you were about the prettiest thing he'd ever laid eyes on. He's crazy to meet you."

"He did? I don't think I know this Ben. What's his last name? Is he new at school?"

"He don't exactly go to school. His family just moved to these parts from the Ozark Mountains area. They're living on the Tulley farm. He and his dad are doing odd jobs for Mr. Tulley until the cotton's ready to chop."

"Billie Kay, are you saying he's a drop out?"

"I don't know if he's dropped out or just don't want to start school here with only a few weeks to go before the end of the year. Anyway, he's not asking you to marry him. He just wants to walk you home from school. GOOD GRACIOUS!"

"Well…I guess if he just happens to be with Gil and they're walking behind us, Mama can't say anything about that…right? But they can't walk us all the way home. We'll have to part ways when we get to the gravel road in case Mama's out on the porch watching for us."

"Your Mama might think she does, but she don't own the road."

"No, but she owns me."

"Cretia…" Billie Kay gave me that I can't believe you said that look.

"Okay, I guess. What can it hurt? We'll be in broad daylight."

"Now you're talking. Let's get to studying before she calls you in to clean the baseboards and windowsills if she happens to think about it."

"Nope. I already cleaned them all today."

"Girl, are you serious? I was just funnin' ya. I never seen anyone so bent on keeping things clean as your Mama is. I mean my mom cleans the baseboards and windowsills too. But not like clockwork every single week."

"I know. But we're talking about Emerald Bertram here. What can I say?"

"You and Billie Kay better get to yer studyin' Lucretia," a yell came from the kitchen.

"We are, Mama."

"Seems to me like you're doin' more talkin' and messin' 'round than studyin'. You better get on with it.

It'll be time to stop 'fore long."

"Okay, we will," I replied.

"Cretia, you go first. Who wrote the poem, Abou Ben Adhem?"

"James Henry Leigh Hunt," I was quick to answer. "Now, it's your turn. Who wrote How Do I Love Thee?"

"Elizabeth Barrett Brown," Billie Kay retorted.

"Try again."

"Elizabeth Barrett Brown. Isn't that right? It's Brown like my last name."

"ing…Browning. It's Elizabeth Barrett Browning," I corrected.

"Oh, I forgot. Think Mrs. Tyree would count it wrong if I forgot the ing?"

"Yes, Billie Kay. I think she would. Now tell me again. Who wrote How Do I Love Thee?"

"Elizabeth Barrett Brown…ING," Billie Kay mocked.

"Well, that's why we're studying together. If you want to make a good grade, you have to get it right. Let's try it this way. You ask me the questions first. Then I'll ask you. We can learn easier that way, I think."

After we'd gone through all the poems and their authors twice, we both knew the answers frontwards, backwards, and sideways.

"Lucretia, come on in now and set the table. Your daddy'll be here d'rectly," Mama yelled.

"I think we're ready for the test. See you in the morning." Billie Kay took Mama's unsubtle hint and gathered her books to leave.

"I'll be ready." I definitely would be ready and waiting on the porch. Even though Billie Kay wasn't welcome to come inside our house I knew if given the opportunity, she would. Billie Kay had a defiant nature. If she had been a bird, she would have always been the one to break formation.

"Wear something real cute tomorrow. Bet you'll like Ben. Did I tell you he's a couple of years older than us?" Billie Kay whispered as I walked with her toward the cross plank.

"No, you didn't. Mama sure wouldn't like me hanging around an eighteen-year-old. I don't know about this, Billie Kay." I whispered back.

"Don't be a baby, Cretia. Surely your Mama will let you talk to boys after you turn sixteen. And that's just about a month from now."

Her whisper became louder, and I feared Mama might have an ear to the door. I wanted this conversation to end. "Okay, see you in the morning," I said in a loud voice to fill the silence of our whispering. She bounced playfully on the plank as she crossed the road ditch.

I sat on the steps to remove and clean my shoes. Just as I'd finished, I heard his old Ford truck crunching the gravel road as daddy turned down our lane and pulled it to a halt by the shed. Mama met him on the porch promptly with another pan of water and rags for his cleaning ritual. I had the table set and tea poured by the time he came into the kitchen. A towel had been placed across the seat of his chair before he sat down. His hands and feet were clean but the rest of him still had the cotton field on him.

After supper, I helped with the dishes while daddy finished cleaning up. Clad in a clean pair of overalls, he positioned his chair on the kitchen side of the door leading into the living room. Dizzy Dean's voice blared from the old Philco radio positioned just inside the door so he could adjust the volume. The St. Louis Cardinals, a favorite of most everyone in our part of the world, were hammering the Chicago Cubs—again.

We were allowed to walk through the living room to get to our bedrooms but were never permitted to sit in there. No one else was either. I passed by our perfectly lined shoes on the way to my room.

Mama didn't care for baseball, so she got a pan of beans and sat at the table to snap them before bed. That scene was replayed nightly, with the exception of whatever else Mama did other than interact with my father or me.

I was nervous but excited about walking home with Ben the next day. I just hoped Mama never saw me or found out.

"Lucretia, you come straight home after school. I'm

going to wash all the window curtains today and I need you to iron 'them so I can get 'em back up before supper."

"Okay, Mama." I couldn't believe she was going to wash our curtains again. We'd just washed them a few weeks prior. I often wondered why she was so driven to keep things clean. The other women in our neighborhood were clean house keepers, maybe with the exception of one or two, but no one cleaned as much or as often as Mama. Also, it wasn't like we ever had company. No one was allowed to come past our doors—front or back.

We studied about compulsive disorders in our psychology class earlier in the year. Our teacher said some people have a mild disorder and some have a more severe case. I think Mama would kick someone until their nose bled if they tried to hang any kind of disorder label on her. I sure wouldn't want to be the one who did it. But because of her need for cleanliness, she could wear that label honestly.

"Hey girl, you look cute today. 'Course you're cute every day," Billie Kay said as she approached.

"You always look nice too," I returned.

"Thanks. I'll see Gil third period and find out when he and Ben plan to meet up with us."

"I thought they were just going to casually be walking behind or with us on the way home," I replied.

"Well, yeah, but…I don't know if they will be waiting at the end of the sidewalk or in front of the Green Fly Diner or where. Cretia, we're not runnin away with these guys. They're going to walk beside us on the way home. It's nothing. Trust me."

"Well, Mama just told me she was washing all our curtains today. So maybe that will keep her busy until I get home."

Billie Kay and I aced the test. I knew we would since we had prepared so well. We only had two more class periods to go. I had convinced myself that Mama wouldn't ever know I had let a boy walk me home, which sort of calmed the big knot in my stomach. Billie Kay was right. We weren't really doing anything wrong. We were both almost sixteen years old. Mama was being unfair and overly protective as always.

Ben was very much a gentleman when Gil introduced us. A flutter flopped inside my stomach when our eyes met. Gosh…he was cute. Gil strode next to Billie Kay and Ben fell in step with me. He never touched me, said anything out of the way, or made me feel uncomfortable at all. When we reached the gravel road, I politely thanked him and said good-bye.

He got the message and he and Gil went their own way. As if planned, Ben and I looked back simultaneously. His smile warmed me to my toes.

"See, I told you he was nice. I told you there was nothing wrong with those guys walking with us part of the way home," Billie Kay was looking for confirmation that I agreed with her.

"You're right. I can't see how we were wrong. He didn't even balk when I told him good-bye. Did you see how cute he was?"

"Well, I couldn't look at him too long or Gil would have been jealous but yes… sure I saw how cute he was. I'm not blind."

I laughed. Billie Kay was so funny.

"Gil said they could meet us again tomorrow."

"I have to admit. I'd like to see Ben again. He is really nice," I replied.

Billie Kay and I parted at the cross plank. I donned my socks, took my books to my room, and quickly set up the ironing board. Mama hung the curtains she had already ironed while I pressed the remaining ones. We were able to get them all back on the windows and finish fixing supper before my dad arrived home from the field.

Gil and Ben walked us part of the way home for the next three days. As before, we said our good-byes when we reached the gravel road. It was now Friday, and they were sitting on the steps of the Big Store waiting for us as usual.

I don't know if I was blinded by the stars in my eyes or just so deep in conversation with Ben that I didn't notice Mama waiting at the corner.

I'm sure Ben got nervous when he saw all the blood drain from my face and the switch in Mama's hand. This time, he and Gil stopped short of the gravel to part ways with us. Mama grabbed my right hand and switched my legs the entire length of the road home. I had never been so embarrassed in my life. Not only did Ben and Gil witness my switching, every eye on two school buses that passed by was centered on me. The pain from my striped legs matched the knotted pain in my stomach. My throat tightened until I could no longer cry out. I was humiliated and wanted to die.

That was May 10, 1942. I was not yet sixteen. I never went to school another day.

FROM THAT DAY on, I was a different girl. Mama's switch had beaten so much more out of me than the blood running down my legs. I never saw Ben again but the desire to please her and fit into the mold she had made for me was gone. I felt raw and rebellious. Me being the good girl with test scores as high as Mama's unending expectations had not been enough. She had never planned to loosen the chains she had around me. I would have to free myself. I was beaten and made to look like a harlot who had displeased her master. I decided to live up to the new reputation Mama had given me. By the time mine and Billie Kay's sixteenth birthdays finally arrived, we had become experts at sneaking out of the house, lying to cover up, where we had been, and who we had been with.

Mama didn't like the new me, but her power was diminished, and she knew it. Her house and dominion over my father remained the same but her bragging rights of being a perfect mother with a perfect daughter were gone. She destroyed them that day by her own hand and a willow switch—where the blacktop and gravel roads meet.

Billie Kay and I had plenty of time to plan all our escapades, since she dropped out of school soon after I did. One night, we slipped out to go to the dance barn in Muddy Ox. I loved to dance. Billie Kay loved flirting and the attention it got her. That particular night, the dance barn was packed with many soldiers on leave, in addition to the regular Friday night locals. It didn't take Billie long to find a guy. I sat at a corner table to survey the crowd.

A few minutes later, the most handsome fellow in uniform I think I'd ever seen, locked eyes with me. The next thing I knew he was walking toward me carrying a cup of spiced cider.

"I decided I'd bring a cup of cider to the prettiest girl in this place tonight and here she sits," said my handsome suitor.

"Thank you for the cider sir—and the compliment too."

"I'm Theodore Dalton. But you can call me Theo."

"I'm Lucretia Bertram. My friends sometimes call me Cretia,"

"Well, I have every intention of being your friend but if it's okay with you, I'd love to call you Lucretia. That's a beautiful name. It's almost as beautiful as you."

"Yes, you can call me Lucretia. I'd like that. I love to hear you say it."

"Lucretia," Theo leaned close and whispered.

That was how it began. Theo had a week before he had to report back to base. We saw each other every night. Every time he whispered my name, I fell a little deeper for him. Some would say it was fascination; others might call it pure lust. It was all of that. But most of all—it felt like love.

His departure date came too soon for both of us. We planned to marry when he returned in six months. We kissed and held each other until the last call came for him to board the train. He left with an envelope that had my picture, address and a lock of my hair tucked inside his shirt pocket. He promised to write every chance he got. I promised to write him every day.

It had been six weeks since we'd kissed good-bye and I'd waved to him until the train disappeared in the sun's haze, I arose early to add a few more lines to his letter before placing it in the mailbox for the post man.

After scripting good morning, I love you, hurry home, and kissing the stamp, I started toward the mailbox. The next thing I knew was I was lying on my bed with a cold washcloth on my forehead.

"Are you alright, Lucretia?" Mama asked.

"I think so. What happened?"

"Doug McCormick saw you fall and ran over to bring you in the house," Mama sounded part scared and part disgusted.

"You let him bring me inside?"

"Well, I couldn't let you lay out there on the ground for all the neighbors to see and I couldn't carry you myself."

"Thank you, Mama," I groaned realizing her dilemma of allowing a shoe-clad intruder to enter her sanctuary.

"Yer Daddy went to the Big Store, but I expect him back in a few minutes. We'll take you to Doc McFarnz to see what's wrong with you."

"I feel weak. My head is swimming. I could throw up any minute."

"Let me run and get you something before that happens." I knew the last thing Mama wanted was for me to throw up on the floor.

"I guess I ate something that didn't agree with me," I told her when she returned with a bucket and a couple of towels.

A few hours later, every emotion possible fled over me, after Doctor McFarnz told me I was pregnant. I was thrilled to be carrying Theo's baby. But because I was unwed, I was embarrassed and knew the good ladies of Muddy Ox would have plenty to say about me when word got out. I could only imagine the looming reaction once we got home.

"Well, Lucretia," Mama began. "You've managed to disgrace me to the bone."

I should have known Mama would be worried about herself and how my condition would reflect onto her. However, I wasn't prepared for what she said next.

"Do you know who the father is?"

"Mama, of course I know who the father is. I've only been with one man. He's a soldier. We planned to get married when he came back on leave in six months. I'm not one of those girls who sleeps around with anybody and everybody."

"Maybe you can go live with my sister in St. Louis until your soldier can get back and make an honest woman out of you."

"I am an honest woman, Mama. I always have been."

Chapter Two

"A HONEST WOMAN thinks enough of her family not to bring disgrace down on 'them." By the disgust in her eyes, I felt like Mama could spit on me for real instead of spewing insults from her pursed lips.

"Maybe Theo can come home sooner than six months so we can get married right away."

"That all sounds well and good but you don't even know how yer THEO is gonna' take this news. You may never hear from him again." Mama spoke his name like venom could drip from her lips.

"We love each other. Theo will love me even more to know I am carrying his baby. He's not like that."

"How long you known this man? A month? There aint no way you can know what he's like. After men like him get a girl in-the-family-way, all they have to do is zip up their pants and move on."

"You can't throw him in a pile with other men you know of. He's different. Just wait and see, Mama. Just wait and see."

"You caint afford to do much waitin'. Not with a bastard baby growin' inside your belly."

"My baby won't be a bastard," I whispered.

Mama never heard me because she had already stomped out of my room and shut the door hard. I pushed her insults and my nausea as far away as I could. With trembling hands, I reached for the pen and paper I kept by my bed and began my nightly letter to Theo.

Mama was wrong. I was not just some girl he had met at a barn dance. I was sure Theo's love for me was real. The pen and letter were lying on the floor the next morning when I was awoken to voices coming from the kitchen. Who dared to darken the door to Mama's sanctuary so early in the day?

"Lucretia, get on up now. Try to make yerself presentable. You got a visitor," Mama's voice was cold and snarly coming through the partially opened door.

I had never met the distinguished, older gentleman standing just inside our kitchen, still wearing his shoes. However, something about him warmed my soul. When he was finally invited to sit, Mama and I joined him at our table.

"Lucretia, I presume?" His voice was as smooth as his demeanor.

"Yes, have we met?" I asked. Mama huffed sarcastically. Was she thinking I had been promiscuous with this man too?

"No, we haven't. But we have a mutual acquaintance."

"I don't understand," I replied.

Mama huffed again.

"You are as beautiful as my son, Theodore said you were."

"You're Theo's father?"

"Yes. And I regret meeting you like this."

"Well, I'm glad to meet you under any conditions. Theo and I…"

"Lucretia, my regret is to tell you that I was notified two days ago that…" He folded his hands tightly and his countenance fell. "That Theodore was killed in combat."

I heard his words, but they shattered against my mind's door. My lips parted but I couldn't muster a sound.

"Now what are we gonna do? You got to get to St. Louis as soon as we can get you there 'fore this scandal gets out. If it does, I won't be able to hold my head up in this town ever again."

Theo's father looked at Mama with confusion. The voice I found was one of a heartbroken, outraged, terrified, now gutsy young woman. "Stop it, Mama! Just stop! This man has lost a son. One who was fighting for you and our country. And I lost the man I love. A man I dreamed of having a future with. The father of my unborn child. And all you can think of is yourself and what people will think of you? Shame on you, Mama."

"Shame on me? You have the nerve to shame me when you are the one who disgraced yourself while actin' like a hot-to-trot harlot?"

"You beat me like a trashy harlot just because I let a boy walk me part of the way home from school one day. You embarrassed me in front of him and half the school. If you want to call me a harlot, well then guess in your eyes, I've finally earned the title."

Mama was without words. I'd never spoken to her in such a way. Theo's father sat stunned and silent. My dad, after hearing all the commotion, was standing mutely on the sidelines. Devastation was not a strong enough word to describe how I felt, as my sobs filled the room.

"You…you are carrying Theodore's child?" Mr. Dalton finally reacted.

"I only found out yesterday. I was going to send Theo a letter telling him today." His soft hands cupped mine. If my eyes had been closed, I could have imagined Theo cradling my hand and not his father.

I'm not sure how long we all were frozen in time but surprisingly, Daddy who was usually a man of few words, broke the ice.

"We'll figure this out. I'm not sure what we'll do yet. But she's our daughter."

Mama started to interject but daddy stopped her.

"Emerald, I said she's our daughter. We'll take care of it," he repeated sharply. It was as though when I found the gall to stand up to her, some of it spilled out on him as well.

After another long silence in the room, Mr. Dalton

stood to his feet. "I will do my part also. That's my grandchild too. You'll be hearing from me again."

He left quietly without a good-bye from either of us.

"I don't know what he thinks he can do. It was his boy, not him who made this mess. Besides, nobody's goin' to come at him with a bunch of stares and questions." Mama snatched her writing tablet and a pen from the cabinet drawer and began composing a letter at the kitchen table, I supposed to my aunt in St. Louis.

Although I'd stood up for myself, I knew Mama's plan was to get me gone before rumors could ripen. Still feeling unleashed by speaking his mind, my dad found the fortitude to amble over and sit in the overstuffed chair in our living room. That was a first for the chair and him.

However, he didn't sit long after feeling the daggers from Mama's eyes. He was positioning his cane bottom chair inside the kitchen door to avoid the edge of Mama's sharp tongue as I left the room.

What a mortifying turn of events. Our future together had been shot down along with Theo in a foreign land. I placed my hand on my, for now, flat stomach, to promise the little beginning within me that his or her life would be better than mine had been so far. In comparison to my first sixteen years, that promise wouldn't be too hard to keep.

It was out of character for Mama to let me sleep past breakfast, but I was grateful for my temporary escape from reality. I dreamt I was back in Theo's arms swaying on the dance floor to the Andrew Sisters singing, *I'll Be With You In Apple Blossom Time*. We planned to be married and living happily ever after by spring of 1943, when the apple blossoms were blooming and everything in our life was fresh and new.

Now the only thing fresh and new was the baby growing inside me. A baby Theo would never see. I cried myself back to sleep. Normally, the smell of food from Mama's kitchen would have lured me there. This time, it brought gut-wrenching waves of sickness.

"Think she's awake? Should we let her know she has a letter from that soldier?" I awoke to hear my dad ask.

A letter from Theo. I had a letter from Theo. After throwing on a robe, I rushed to the kitchen, despite the smell and my nausea.

"There's a letter for me?" I snatched the envelope from my dad's hands, clutched it to my chest and ran out to the stump by the willow tree to read it. I wanted as far from the smell of food and the ears, eyes, and mouth of Mama, as possible.

My dearest Lucretia,

I don't have much time to write. Things are getting worse here all the time. I can't give you details. Just keep us in your prayers. Your beautiful face and our getting married as soon as I can get back home is all that keeps me going these days. I love getting your letters. Keep them coming baby. I read them over and over. I love you my sweet Lucretia. Can't wait to hold you in my arms again

Forever yours,
Theo

I brushed my fingers across his signature and closed my eyes while trying to picture his face as he signed the letter. Theo's hands folded the paper and held the pen that wrote every word. I kissed the seal where his lips had touched the envelope.

My parents sat at the table as I passed through the kitchen back to my bedroom. I was grateful that neither of them spoke. I'm not sure how many times I reread Theo's letter while rocking back and forth in the middle of my bed and before crying myself to sleep once more.

"That boy's daddy is here again, Lucretia. Says he needs to speak with you some more." Mama was shaking my foot to wake me.

With a tear-streaked face, tousled hair and the letter still clutched in my hand, I followed her back through the kitchen. I hadn't bothered to make myself presentable this time. Mr. Dalton stood just beyond the screen door.

"He wanted to wait for you out on the porch instead of coming inside," Mama spouted.

"Is there somewhere we can speak privately?" he asked.

"Yes, we can sit out by the willow tree if you like." I knew Mama would try to listen if she could. But a slight breeze rustled the limbs of the willow just enough to muffle our voices.

"I got a letter from Theo today. Would you like to read it?" I offered once we were seated.

"I'd love to. Thank you for sharing," Mr. Dalton was so polite, a true gentlemen.

He sat quietly for a moment then brushed his fingers across Theo's signature as I had earlier. He teared up before briefly looking away.

"My son clearly loved you very much. It's evident that you loved him too. He would have been thrilled about the baby and I have no doubt he would have made an excellent father.

I smiled to hear him say how he felt about mine and Theo's feelings for one another and how he thought Theo would feel about the baby.

"I wish Mama could see things as you do. But she grew up in Muddy Ox and knows how gossip gets around. She mostly sees this as being about her and how the town will judge her."

"I'm sorry about any distress this has caused your parents, but you and my son's child are my first concern right now. Lucretia, I say this reluctantly but please know I have the baby's and your best interest in mind. I mean no disrespect by what I am about to propose. Again, please don't take offense."

"Mr. Dalton, I can't imagine you disrespecting me. What is it?"

"I have always been straightforward. I really don't know how to be any other way. So, I am going to just come out and say what I have on my mind. I hope you will take this in the same way I am presenting it to you.

"Theo's mother died when he was a boy. Because of that, my son and I had a special kind of bond. We've always had one another's backs. That's why I am going to offer to marry you and be a father to your child. I know there is quite an age difference but I'm healthy and I think I have enough years left in me to provide for you and the baby now that my son can't. I've thought this through. Both of you will have the Dalton name. I will love the child as my own. It will be your choice when or if you ever want to tell the baby or anyone else about its real father. Not only will this save your reputation, but your child will also have two living parents. Your mother won't have to be embarrassed or scorned. Neither will you." He took a breath then continued. "The marriage can be on your terms. I won't expect anything from you that you don't want to give, other than letting me be in the baby's and your life to preserve my son's good name.

"You can think about this and talk it over with your family and let me know. However, if we are going to avoid scrutiny, we have to do whatever we are going to do as quickly as possible."

Of all the things I could have guessed that Mr. Dalton would have wanted to talk to me about, a marriage proposal would have never entered my mind. It was the second time that day that my voice failed me. This man. This gentle, distinguished man, not many years younger than my daddy was offering to marry me and be a father to mine and his dead son's baby.

I knew it was to help my relationship with my parents, but I understood he also feared he might lose a grandchild after he'd already lost his son. Plus, he didn't want the Dalton name tarnished any more than my parents wanted the Bertram name dishonored. He patiently waited for my response.

My reply began as a whisper. "I…I don't know what to say. I could never have imagined this to be what you wanted to talk to me about. I'm still shaken after your telling me about Theo's death."

"I understand you must be reeling right now. This is a lot to take on. Especially for a young lady of sixteen. I am not trying to pressure you. I will understand if you can't or don't want to do this. Also, your parents might not agree to it."

"First of all, I don't see it disrespectful or that you're pressuring me."

"I can go and come back after you've talked with your parents," he quickly added.

I suddenly found clarity to consider what Theo might have wanted. How would he feel about me becoming his father's wife to legitimately give our baby the Dalton name? What would Mama and Daddy say? After all, what could they say? I instantly searched my heart and knew the answer to all those what ifs'.

"No—no. I don't want you to leave. We can go together and talk to my parents if you're willing to do this."

"Are you sure?" he asked nervously. I think it shocked him that I became so composed or would readily accept. But he couldn't have known about my life or about the promise I had made to my baby a few hours prior.

"I am," I confirmed, and we headed toward the kitchen.

Mama was so distraught, she forgot that Mr. Dalton still had his shoes on or that I had entered with unwashed, bare feet.

I asked her and my dad to sit to hear what we had to say. My dad was quiet, as usual. Mama's eyes went from big to squinting to big again, after hearing Mr. Dalton's proposal.

"Lucretia, this man has to be near the age of yer own daddy!" Mama exclaimed.

"Are you sure you want to do this, Lucretia?" my

dad questioned.

"I've thought about it. And yes, I'm sure."

"I...I don't know," Mama hesitated. She didn't like not being in control.

"I'm barely pregnant. If we got married quickly and quietly, the good ladies of Muddy Ox wouldn't know when to start marking off their calendars since they wouldn't know how long we had kept our wedding a secret," I interjected.

"I have a nice place over in Bragg City. People here wouldn't be seeing Lucretia every day to realize she was pregnant," Mr. Dalton added.

"I don't know," Mama hesitated again.

"Well then if you don't agree for us to marry and Mr. Dalton wants me and the baby, I'll just go live with him. You want to send me off to St. Louis anyway."

I looked at Theo's dad and he nodded in agreement. We hadn't talked about me moving in with him as an option. But he caught on quickly and followed my lead.

"Oh no. If yer gonna' go live with a man, you have to marry him. That'd be as bad or worse a scandal as havin' a baby out of wedlock," Mama spouted.

"Then you agree to it?" I caught her off guard.

"Well...ugh...well I guess it's the best of two evils." Mama moaned.

"It's going to be a legal marriage Mama. There's nothing evil about it."

IT TOOK ME less than an hour to pack my necessities with a plan to get the rest later. I hugged Mama and Daddy. Mr. Dalton gave them both a strong handshake. Mama never gave the impression she would have accepted a hug from him.

"I'm sorry that this was so awkward. But I knew if it was going to happen, that time wasn't on our side," Mr. Dalton said after we had left.

"From no longer than you were around my Mama, I think you realize I'm used to awkward. It has actually become a way of life for me. I promised my baby this very morning he or she would not have to live like that. I did not know how I was going to keep that promise. I only knew I had to."

"Yes, I have to admit. I see what you mean. I assume your mother means well; but I see what you mean. I'll help you keep that promise, Lucretia. Maybe before long you can think of he or she as being our baby—yours, Theo's, and mine."

"I think Theo would agree to that Mr. Dalton. By the way, what is your first name? If we are going to be married, I can't keep calling you, Mr. Dalton."

"It's Theodore. Theo was a junior."

Chapter Three

THE CLOUDS GREW lighter after the rain had finally stopped. We had been driving for a couple of hours to set some distance between Muddy Ox and the ideal place for us to pledge our vows.

"Look, a double rainbow!" I exclaimed.

Beautiful strands of pastels arched slightly above a dense orchard of pecan trees ahead.

"And there's a small church right past it. Think it's a sign?" Theodore asked.

"It could be. Maybe by now, we are far enough away from Muddy Ox. I sure don't know anyone in these parts. Do you?" I asked.

"No, and I bet that house by the church is the parsonage. I'll check it out," Theodore said, reaching for the door handle.

My being only sixteen, I needed parental consent to marry. Mama went with us to the Pemiscot County Courthouse in Caruthersville, to get our marriage license and to write her name on the dotted line. She also insisted that we be married in a church by an ordained minister. I think she saw it as her last opportunity to control me. She didn't want any part of the actual wedding, however. That way she could honestly say she didn't know any details in case people asked.

Shortly after entering the parsonage, Theodore reappeared with an elderly couple. The man held a Bible. The woman took off her apron and draped it over a rocking chair before stepping off their front porch. Theodore motioned for me to come, and we followed them inside the small church.

They never commented, but by their expressions, I was sure the preacher and his wife wondered about our age difference. They were sole witnesses to a ceremony that took all of twenty minutes for me to promise to love, honor and obey and to become Mrs. Theodore Xavier Dalton Sr.

The gold bands we shared, according to our officiate, were to seal our promises to one another. I also knew they would help seal a gaggle of gossiping lips along with those promises.

"You know what? I think that rainbow was a sign that somewhere, Theo is happy for what we just did for his child." I smiled.

"Me too," Theodore answered solemnly. We rode in silence for a long while. I was replaying the last two weeks in my mind. I assumed he was doing the same.

"I'm going to stop here for fuel. Are you hungry, wife?" he teased.

"Yes I am, husband," I replied accordingly.

"I'll see what I can do." He smiled.

With a keen pair of eyes, I watched the stranger I had just married as he went inside to pay. He looked much younger than his forty-seven years. I had never looked at him that closely before. After all, we had only known one another for two weeks. Although they had similar features, Theo's father had an allurement about him that by far surpassed his handsome son of twenty. He possessed a charm that I supposed only came with maturity and was strikingly handsome, especially when he smiled. That was nice.

"I hope you like bologna," he said handing me a sandwich and a coke when he returned.

"Bologna will do fine. Thank you." I had not realized just how hungry I was.

"Well, it isn't much of a wedding supper, but it looked better than the liverwurst, headcheese or pickle loaf they had."

"Eww. Give me bologna any day over those choices." I laughed.

"Lucretia, I plan to give you and this baby as good a life as humanly possible. And you don't have to worry about those vows of honor and obedience. The next part of that Bible verse requires me to love you as Christ loved His church. I promise to do exactly that."

"I feel like our baby and I are in good hands."

"Our baby. I love the sound of that."

He lightly kissed my forehead before driving away.

MAMA HADN'T SPENT as much time teaching me to cook as she had teaching me how to keep things meticulously clean. After four months of my attempts at cooking, I am sure Theodore wished she had.

It was easier for her to do the cooking herself than to take the time to show me how to do it. And in all honesty, I had not responded well to her teaching methods. The few sessions we had, usually ended in an argument and me stomping out of the kitchen. I had heard the term oil and vinegar used for people who couldn't work together. Mama and I were more like ice water and lard.

Theodore never complained, although once he asked me what was in the dish nearest to him on the table. He had a perplexed smile as he poured what I informed him were mashed potatoes and never asked about the bowl next to them. I would have happily told him it was gravy.

"Lucretia, want to go with me to Caruthersville? We need a new car battery before winter sets in," Theodore asked.

"I would like that. Can you drop me off at Corbin's Five and Dime while you look for a battery? I need some material and thread so I can work on a quilt for the baby." Luckily, Mama had taught me the bare basics of sewing and quilting.

"Yes, I can. How soon can you be ready to go?"

"I only need to change and run a brush through my hair."

As soon as I found a dress that would accommodate the growth in my waistline and slipped into some comfortable shoes, I announced I was ready.

"It won't take me more than thirty minutes to find what I am looking for," Theodore said after he came around to open the car door for me and slipped some folding money into my hand.

"Take your time. I always loved to look around Corbin's, even as a kid."

To some, I still looked like a kid. But that day, I tried to look like a grown woman. I for sure felt like one.

I filled my shopping basket with several pieces of scrap material and thread to match. I didn't know if I was having a boy or a girl, so I went with yellows and pale green that would work for either. I was on my way to pay when the words, *The Fine Art of Cooking* caught my eye. After thumbing through it, I saw the recipes looked basic and easy to follow. I added the book to my basket and proceeded to the register.

Theodore was standing by the opened car door as I stepped out of the store. I decided not to tell him about the recipe book. I'd surprise him instead.

"Did you find everything you needed?" he asked.

"Yes, I think so. And you got a new battery?"

"I did. Now, winter can come whenever it pleases. We are prepared." He smiled.

I remembered how my dad made sure things were taken care of like that. I hoped my mother appreciated him as much as I had learned to appreciate Theodore. I had never heard her say so if she did.

"Want to drop by Aunt Connie's Boarding House and have supper before going home? You probably don't feel up to cooking tonight now, after shopping."

"That would be nice," I agreed. As much as I was anxious to try out my new cookbook, the offer to have supper prepared for us was more enticing.

We were looking over the menu when I heard a familiar voice from across the room.

"Lucretia, is that really you?" Billie Kay asked walking toward us.

"Oh, my goodness. What a wonderful surprise," I stood to hug her when she reached our table.

"What happened to you? Every time I've gone by your house, your mama just said you moved away. I asked her to tell you I came by, but I didn't feel like she would. Did you really move? Where to?" She had undoubtably felt my rounded belly by her expression.

"Theodore, this is Billie Kay Brown. She was my neighbor and is a friend of mine. Billie Kay, this is Theodore Dalton—my husband."

I'd seen Billie Kay's jaw drop before, but never this far down. The last time I had seen her was when we met Theo and his friend that night at the Dance Barn in Muddy Ox. She moved to Caruthersville not long after we both quit school.

"Your husband? Girl when did you get married? And how come you didn't invite me, your best friend, to your wedding?"

"We obviously have a lot of catching up to do. I…we live in Bragg City now. Maybe you can drop by our house one day soon. Do you eat here often?" I asked.

"Eat here? I work here. I got this job right after I moved in with my cousin, Gail. She and her husband, Billy, live on the other side of Fair Boulevard. Yes, I'd love to come visit you."

"Soon, I hope. I've missed you," I said.

"Hello, Mr. Dalton. Pardon my manners." Billie Kay extended her hand.

"Call me Theodore. Lucretia's best friend is surely a friend of mine." He obliged.

I figured Billie Kay called him Mr. Dalton because of his age. It was a wonder everyone in the room couldn't see the huge question mark hanging over her head. I sure could. I knew her well.

A throat cleared loudly from behind the counter. Billie Kay quickly snapped back into waitress mode. "What can I get y'all to drink?" she asked but had to work at being serious since it was me she was serving.

"I'd like sweet tea," I responded.

"I'll have black coffee," Theodore followed.

Once she trotted off to get our drinks, I let out a sigh. I never expected to see anyone I knew in Caruthersville on a Tuesday evening. Most people came to town on either Fridays or Saturdays. Oh well, if I had to run into someone, Billie Kay was the safest person I could think of. Before we left, I gave her directions to our house and she and I set a time for her to visit. Theodore left her a nice tip.

The next afternoon, I chose a meatloaf recipe from my cookbook, as a supper surprise. The first line read, gather the ingredients, and prepare as directed.

Following directions clearly was not something I had done very well in the past—guess it was time I learned.

Chapter Four

My New Cookbook was a treasure. Our mealtimes became a source of anticipation each time I mastered a new recipe. Reading and following directions at my own speed was much easier than trying to work with impossible-to-please Mama. Since I was now on my own, I took great care to get it right. The rewards were Theodore's smiles and a gratifying sense of self pride. Most rewarding—the book did not yell at me.

However, I hated to admit that while the cookbook bridged the gap in the kitchen, there were voids in my new life that could only be filled with my Mama—yes Mama. She was the one I could ask about what to expect during labor, or after. She would know why lately a nap was more important to me than a peanut butter cookie, like the ones from the school lunchroom. Prior to pregnancy, napping was out of the question. What teenager wasted time on a nap when there was fun to be had? Maybe I just answered my last question. I was still a teenager, but teen years would look a lot different from here on.

A cookbook-perfect blackberry cobbler was cooling on the counter. Billie Kay was to arrive in an hour. I had just enough time to spruce things up a bit and make myself more presentable. Grief over Theo's death, stress of trying to fit into my new role and my clothes, and oh yes, morning sickness, had taken its toll. But lately some of the color had returned to my cheeks and I felt a little more relaxed. Billie Kay had always boosted my confidence. I did not want anything about my appearance today to change that. I needed her encouragement now more than ever. I might be a pregnant, married woman, but I was still me, Lucretia Bertram.

Well, Dalton now.

There was a knock on the door as I returned from powdering my nose. Billie Kay must be arriving early. Guess she couldn't wait to get together again either. I pinched my cheeks to give them a bit more color before opening the door.

"Mama," I gasped.

"Lucretia," she replied.

"Come…come in. I'm surprised to see you." Mama was never free with hugs. Our time apart had not changed that about her.

"I think I have a few things you might need. Since you haven't come to see us since you left, I decided to bring them to you myself." She awkwardly clutched a brown bag. I started to tell her she didn't have to remove her shoes but chose not to challenge her principles. After all, it was not a good sign that she was already frowning.

"Thank you. Mama, I was just thinking about you today."

"Well, a body can't hear another's thoughts. We need to hear words."

"I am glad you came. I thought about coming to see you and Daddy a few times but wasn't sure you wanted me to. I imagine people have had questions by now. I didn't want to bring on more."

"Oh yes. There's been a powerful lot a questions. You can rest assured 'bout that. But I answered everybody with as short a answer as I could. I told 'em you got married and moved to Bragg City. That you had a whirlwind courtship and didn't want to drag it out. Then I stared 'em down until they decided to not ask me anything else."

"Did that seem to satisfy them?"

"Well, it was never a secret about how headstrong you have always been. Most of 'em nodded as though they understood and went on about their business."

"Most of them? Who wouldn't let it go?" I asked while directing Mama to a chair at the kitchen table.

"That friend of yers. That Billie Kay Brown. She came by several times. Kept askin' me to tell you that she came by and to have you get in touch with her. Hadn't seen her in a while now. Guess she finally gave up."

"Funny you mentioned her. Theodore and I went to Caruthersville last week and we ran into Billie Kay at

Aunt Connie's Boarding House. We went there for supper before coming home."

"So, you've become one of 'em women who eats out for supper now? Come to think of it. I'm guessing cookin' is not high on your list of things to do. I'm more surprised that Billie Kay is one of 'em women too. Guess she's moved up in the world since she's dropped out of school," Mama said sarcastically.

"You're doing a lot of guessing, as usual, Mama. We went to Caruthersville on a Tuesday. Theodore needed a new battery before cold weather. I went along to get some material to start a quilt for the baby. I thought for sure I could avoid seeing anyone on a weekday. We ate supper there so I wouldn't have to cook after we got home. It was already late in the day. And no, you guessed wrong again. Billie Kay works there. You probably haven't seen her lately because she moved to Caruthersville to get a job and lives with her sister and brother-in-law now. Billie Kay told me she came over and asked you about me. It was good to see her. She is coming to see me today too. Matter a fact, I thought it was her getting here early when I heard your knock."

"Smart man you married there. He probably grabbed a chance to get a good meal while y'all was out and figured you wouldn't catch on to his fa-nig-a-ling." She ignored the part about Billie Kay so she could dig me about my cooking.

"No, that was not it...he..." I stopped mid-sentence. *Could Mama be right? Maybe I just thought Theodore was being considerate. Was he really trying to avoid another one of my botched meals?*

"You sure 'bout that?" It was as though she could see the doubt she had planted in my mind.

"Yes, I am. Besides, I have a cookbook now and Theodore loves what I fix him out of it." I decided if he really had been fa-nig-a-ling me as Mama said, I would forgive him. He never let on if he hated my cooking. He ate everything I put on the table. Anyway, how could I blame him if he did? I even hated my cooking before getting the cookbook.

"Well, I'll be," Mama exclaimed.

"Look, I made this today. What do you think?" I picked up the cobbler, hoping for a favorable acknowledgement. Instead, she glared mutely at my culinary creation before continuing with her blasting.

"I'd a never thought a girl of mine would be cookin' out of a cookbook. But you done a lot a things I'd never thought a girl of mine would a done."

I could have smarted back to her, and our visit would not have ended well. Instead, I softened my tone and spoke from my heart.

"I'm sorry I've always been so headstrong, Mama. Sorry I've shamed and embarrassed you in front of the ladies of Muddy Ox. And I…I'm sorry I hurt you."

"Lucretia, I think you mean it. I believe you really are sorry." For a split second, I thought she was going to say she was sorry too—but didn't.

"I am. I know it hasn't been that long since I moved out, but I have grown up a lot in that short time. I have changed. Let's not fight anymore. I really need you now, Mama."

Her shoulders relaxed. Her jaw was no longer jutted. Tears pooled in her eyes. All the sarcasm and hostility seem to be replaced with humility and peace. She looked like the mother I always wished for but never had. Her hand felt warm and reassuring when she placed it over mine. It felt good.

"You need me? Are you havin' troubles? You do look a little peaked." She appeared genuinely concerned.

"Morning sickness has been terrible. My legs cramp something awful. What should I expect during delivery? I don't even know what to expect after the baby gets here. I have never been around babies or know how to take care of one. You know that better than anyone. Mama, I'm scared."

"Now, you come on and sit down. We will talk about all this. Let me ask, are you wantin' a boy or a girl?" Maybe me being away caused a change in her too. I think she would have said she was too busy to talk before or that I was being a worry wart. Then again, this was a side of me that was new to both of us.

"I think I would like a little girl." I really had not thought about it very much. But as soon as Mama asked, I knew in my heart I would love to have a girl.

"Well, sounds like yer in luck. If you've been havin' bad mornin' sickness, that usually means a girl. Been havin' lots of heartburn too? Here, I brought you some saltine crackers. They always helped my mornin' sickness and heartburn," she said retrieving a sleeve of saltines from her bag.

"Oh yes. Seems like everything I eat upsets my stomach." It was all I could do to keep from burping once Mama mentioned heartburn.

"That's good too. Heartburn means yer little girl's gonna' have a head full of dark hair."

"Theo had dark hair like mine. I would love for the baby to favor him."

"As far as the birthin,' don't even try to think about it. The Good Lord'll help you get through it like He has every other woman that ever had a baby. And the odd thing is, we women forget all about that pain once the baby comes. Guess it's a good thing we do. If that pain stayed with us, there'd be a lot less babies bein' born in this world."

I wanted to know more about giving birth but was afraid to ask. Besides, she moved right along.

"And listen, don't worry about how yer gonna' take care of that baby. It just comes natural to us women. The good Lord took care of that too. It's called mother's instinct. Why you could have a whole passel a kids and none of 'em would be alike. You learn to take care of each one accordin' to how they are."

"I don't want to think about having more kids right now, a passel for sure. I think I'll do good to get through this one."

"Now, as far as those legs a crampin.' I never had much trouble myself with that. But, Ole Miss Grimsley always said if you put a cork or two under the sheets near yer feet, it will help with them. I just happen to have a few here in my sack." She handed me several corks before continuing. "I've also heard if you put yer husband's shoes upside down just under yer side of the bed at night, you won't have any cramps a'tall. Like I said, I never had to try that one."

"Well, umm, Theodore doesn't sleep in my bed. You think it would work if I put a pair of his shoes there anyway?"

It wasn't often that Mama was without words. This was one of those times, but only briefly. "Why don't he sleep in your bed? Y'all did go through with the weddin' didn't you? Lucretia, please don't tell me yer a livin' here with a man that ain't yer husband."

"Oh, no Mama, we got married. We...Theodore...well, when he asked me to marry him, he said he would give me all the time I needed to decide if...you know...if I wanted to be his wife...you know in every way."

Mama swallowed hard. Her expression was one of shock and disbelief. "Well, I never. I didn't think there was a man in this world that didn't expect a woman to be a wife to him once they were married. You know, sleep with him and all."

There was another knock on the door. Billie Kay arrived just in 'time.

Chapter Five

MY MOTHER NEVER hid her dislike for my best friend. I should not have been surprised when Mama didn't waste any time leaving once Billie Kay arrived. She barely greeted her before dashing out the door.

Billie Kay saved me from anymore discussion about Theodore's and my sleeping arrangements, but I regretted not getting to serve Mama any of my cobbler, even though she never gave me the satisfaction of saying a word about it. Oh well, maybe next time. She said she would come again.

After a long hug, Billie Kay stood back and looked me up and down before patting my rounded belly. "Okay, girl. Start from the beginning and don't leave out a single thing," she said before making herself comfortable on the couch.

"You sure don't waste any time," I said smiling.

"What do you expect? First, you disappear. I went back a couple of times to see you, but Lord knows, your Mama's gonna' stay tight mouthed about what happened to you. Then, the next time I see you, you're married to a man old enough to be your own Daddy and expecting a baby. Can you blame me for needing a few gaps filled in here?"

"Well, if you put it that way," I teased.

"Aint no other way to put it. The last thing I knew, you were swept off your feet by a handsome soldier boy on the dance floor. Y'all looked glued together when…umm…I can't remember the guy's name I was dancing with that night now…but anyway, you and your dreamboat looked pretty serious about one another as I left with him."

"We were serious. Theo and I were very serious."

"Well, you musta' got unserious real quick about your Theo. It takes a while to moved out of your parent's house, get married, pregnant, and…girl, you look ever bit of five or six months."

"Theo, and I were in love. He asked me to marry him before he left. I said yes, and we planned the wedding when he came back on his next leave. But…he…oh Billie Kay, he was killed in combat. I never saw him again. He died before I could tell him we were having a baby. It was awful." The pain, emotion, and tears I had held inside for months released like a flood as soon as her arms wrapped around me.

"I'm so sorry, Cretia. I didn't know all this stuff. You know I would have stood by you if I had."

"Yes, you and I have always been there for one another. I hadn't realized how much I really missed and needed you until now."

"I still have to ask. How did you end up with this older man for a husband?"

"Theodore is Theo's father. I found out I was pregnant the morning of the same day he came to tell me about Theo's death. When he saw Mama's reaction to my being pregnant, he offered to marry me to give the baby a name and us a home. Mama was going to send me off anyway to live with relatives in St. Louis to keep anyone from knowing. You know Mama, she was worried how me being unwed and pregnant would make her look to the town gossips. I decided marrying him would be a good thing for everyone. Mama didn't have to be shamed because of me. The baby would have its father's name and I wouldn't have to move. Theodore is a very, kind, considerate man."

"He aint bad looking either, for an older guy. But remember how we could always talk about everything?

"Yes…"

Billie Kay leaned in and whispered, even though we were the only two people in the room. "Don't you feel a little strange sleeping with the father of a guy you say you are…were…maybe still are in love with? The man who fathered that baby you are carrying?"

"Theodore and I are not sleeping together," I answered.

"Thought you said you all are married."

"We are."

"And you're not sleeping with him?" Billie Kay

almost matched Mama's earlier expression.

"Theodore did the honorable thing to marry me for the baby's sake and save both our family's reputation. But he said the marriage could be on my terms. He wouldn't pressure me in any way."

"So, it's kind of a pretend marriage?"

"No, we are not pretending. We were married by a preacher. Mama signed for me and everything. Our marriage is like everyone else's except we don't sleep together."

"I think it would be hard to be married and live with someone you didn't care about." Billie Kay always had a way of being painfully direct.

Those words hit me hard. At that moment, I realized I did care about Theodore. Maybe not in the same way as I thought I felt about his son, but I did have feelings for him. Feelings that I needed to sort out in my head and heart for this man I married.

"I think maybe I do care about him. And I will get around to dealing with that later. This is all so new to me. But right now, I am worried about this baby I am going to bring into this world in three more months. And scared…Billie Kay, I'm scared about what delivery will be like. I talked to Mama a little about it today before you got here. She said she will come again, and we can talk some more."

"Now, that's new. You and your Mama talking civil to one another?"

"Being pregnant and married has changed me a little. I am the first one to agree that my Mama is a hard woman. But being away from her has caused me to try to see her side of things. I want to teach my child to do good and upright things too, as it grows up. Yes, Mama worries too much about what other people say and think. But maybe there were reasons for that too. I felt like our talk today was between two women and not a woman and a child. I realized I needed Mama in a way that only she could help me. Just like I needed you to help me in ways only a best friend could. Does that make sense to you?" After a brief pause, her face didn't reflect it completely, but she nodded that she understood.

"Hey, with the help of my new cookbook, I've learned to be a pretty good cook. Want to sample some of my cobbler?" I asked, trying to lighten our conversation a bit. Then, I scooped her a generous helping of cobbler and got her a cold glass of milk to go with it. I didn't wait for her to answer. I had never known Billie Kay to turn down dessert of any kind.

"Mmm…you weren't kidding. Why, this is as good as the one we serve at Aunt Connie's," she said after her first bite.

"We've only been talking about me since you arrived. Now, tell me about you. Do you like living with your sister and her husband?"

Billie Kay took a swallow of milk before answering.

"It's all right, I guess. My parents said if I was going to quit school, I needed to get a job. The only job in Muddy Ox was field work and I've had my fill of that. Waitressing is just another kind of hard, but we both know that nothin' compares to picking and chopping cotton."

"You can say that again. Mama was probably getting ready to tell me to get a job too before she found out I was pregnant. After that, all she could think about was to get me gone before anyone found out."

"And look at you now. Married and making cobblers," Billie Kay said with a wide grin.

"Guess we can't much blame our parents. They've worked hard to get us to where we are now. If we are going to stop being kids, then we need to act like adults. Want some more cobbler?" I amazed myself, realizing I sounded just like my Mama.

"Maybe just a little. How did you make this so good?" She slid her plate over for another scoop. I was sure she wondered from where my earlier words of wisdom suddenly appeared. I wondered myself.

"Just followed the recipe step by step. If I can, you can too."

"I think I'll let someone else do the cooking and I'll do the serving for a while. I don't have a man to feed like you do. Maybe someday. Who knows?"

"I hope you find a good man one day, Billie Kay. Are you dating anyone special?"

"You know me. I like to flirt. You can't flirt and have a steady guy too. I might settle on just one eventually, but I am having too much fun right now. Say speaking about your husband, where is he?"

"He's gone to Dyersburg for something. Said he'd be back by suppertime. I don't expect him any time soon. It takes a while to go over into Tennessee and back. I never asked him what he went there after."

"So, what's it like carrying another human being around inside of you?"

"Both strange and amazing. The first time I felt the baby kick, I almost laughed and cried at the same time. It is a feeling like you have never had before. Getting a good night's sleep is tricky though. Sometimes it takes a while to get comfortable. The extra weight I am carrying around is no fun either. I just hope I can find my waistline again after I have this baby. Oh hurry, give me your hand." I placed her hand on my stomach to let her feel the baby kick for herself. Her face lit up and tears brimmed her eyes as she felt the life inside of me. Of course, I cried too.

It was good to have reconnected with Billie Kay. Along with all the other things we best friends had shared, to have her feel my baby's movements was extra special. I needed her in my life again. And my baby would love its Aunt BeeKay, a name she gave herself after feeling the baby kick. Her saying how pregnancy looked good on me and going on about my neat house was the boost my shaken morale craved. I was sad when she stood to leave.

"Promise me you will come again soon. And we will be sure to drop by the diner on our next trip to Caruthersville."

"I'll come any time my sister lets me borrow her car. I'm tryin' to buy one of my own. But savin' money is hard, no more than I make."

"At least you can drive. I have never learned how," I said, mentally adding driving lessons to the many other things I needed to learn for my new adult role.

I lingered at the door to watch her leave and was glad to see her turn in the direction of Muddy Ox instead of back towards Caruthersville. Guess what I said about mine and Mama's talk must have struck a nerve in her. She was surely missing her mother too by now.

Just as I finished washing and drying Billie Kay's glass and saucer, I heard Theodore's truck pull into the driveway. The glimmer of feelings I had admitted having for him briefly crossed my mind but was quickly over-shadowed with curiosity about whatever he had brought home in the bed of his truck.

"Lucretia, open the door wide," Theodore called.

Chapter Six

I HADN'T NOTICED Theodore wasn't alone until I realized someone had to be on the other end of the heavy, bulky object that was challenging their combined strength. The rough, wooden, crate scraped the facing a bit, even though I had opened the door as wide as it would go.

"Don't worry about that Lucretia, those are only surface scratches. I can fix them so you will never know they were there," Theodore promised.

The marks hadn't fazed me at all. Actually, I barely noticed them. My attention was bound to that large, wooden, crate.

"Deke, when I tell you, push as hard as you can," Theodore gritted through clenched teeth.

"Okay, say when, but make it fast. I can't hold this thing much longer."

The man on the most burdensome end of the crate was Deke McCrady. I didn't actually know him but remembered seeing him at the Dance Barn a few times. Come to think of it, he might have even been the fellow Billie Kay left with that night—the one whose name she couldn't remember.

"Lucretia, can you grab that old Army blanket from the closet and lay it under this end of the crate? But be careful. Get back out of the way as soon as you can, so you don't get hurt."

I grabbed the blanket and was able to get it in place seconds before Theodore let their load fall to the floor.

"Now, I'll pull it and you push as hard as you can, Deke," Theodore shouted while tugging the blanket with all the strength he could muster.

The crate jolted through the door, resting inches away from Theodore's body after it flew backward. Luckily, he jerked his foot to the side before it became pinned. Deke collapsed across the crate as soon as his end cleared the threshold.

"You fellas shoulda' yelled. I'd a been glad to help you get that thing in the house." A deep voice boomed from a third person whose shoulders filled the width of the doorway.

"Thanks. I appreciate it. You okay, Deke?" Theodore asked.

"I'm okay, you're the one that almost got pinned under a couple hundred pounds of cook stove. Theodore, this here is Larson Strom. He's a friend of mine from Muddy Ox," Deke replied after catching his breath.

"I was wondering what your mama fed you for supper last night for you to be able to throw me backward like you did."

"Well, I wish I could say it was all me, but I think it was Larson helping me with that last push that threw you back so hard. I've known Larson for a long time now and if he wants something to move, it's gonna' move." Deke smiled.

Theodore extended his hand. "Larson, glad to meet you, man. Let me shake your hand. Since you're here and volunteered, can you help us to get this other stove moved out of the way, so we can put the new one where it was?"

"Sure, be glad to." Larson grinned.

In no time at all, the old stove was setting in the yard, the new one was in place and Larson Strom was gone almost as quickly as he appeared.

"He left before I could offer to pay him for his help."

"Aww, Larson, wasn't expectin' any pay. That's just how he is. He's always been ready and willin' to help a body any time—any place."

"Theodore, I love it," I exclaimed bringing his attention back to our new appliance.

"I decided since you were cooking up such fine meals here lately, you needed a better stove to prepare them with. The salesman assured me that this is the latest and greatest cook stove money can buy. And it uses propane gas, so it won't create the mess that wood stove did," Theodore boasted.

"It's beautiful. Thank you."

"It might be beautiful all right, but one improvement I can see them making on those stoves, is they could come up with a way for them to be a little lighter. If it hadn't a been for Larson, we'd still be trying to get them switched out," Deke added.

"He just showed up from nowhere. But I'm glad he did. I had heard of him before, but this was the first time meeting him." Theodore dropped into a near-by chair. His almost thirty-year difference from the two younger men was evident.

"I've known Larson for years. Me and him's the same age. We was even in school together for a little while. But he had to drop outa' school to help his dad with his fruit peddlin' job. Larson was drivin' them around long before he was anyway near old enough to be behind the wheel of a vehicle. Rumor was, he lied about his age when he was sixteen and joined the Army. Story goes, he coulda' gone far in the Army if he'd a behaved himself."

"What do you mean if he had behaved himself?" Theodore asked.

"Larson's always had a drinkin' problem. Learned it from his dad. And he's got the meanest temper in Muddy Ox. I never seen it in action myself, and I really don't want to. But people have said he's so strong, he can bend a tire tool with his bare hands. And getting' hit by his fist, is like bein' kicked by a Missouri mule. Anyway, he's always been as nice as could be every time

I was around him. He learned to be a pretty dern good mechanic from havin' to keep that old truck of his dad's a goin' all the time. Was a mechanic in the Army too, I hear."

"Sounds like someone it would be good to get to know even better. A good mechanic is hard to find sometimes," Theodore agreed.

"Yeah, just stay on his good side, and you got a friend for life. If I ever got into a fight, I would sure want Larson Strom on my side," Deke added.

"Think I might too," Theodore mused.

"He was nice and was always funny, the few times I was around him," I remarked.

Both men turned to face me. "You know Larson? How would you know him?" Theodore looked puzzled.

"I've seen him a few times at Billie Kay's. He is a good friend of Billie Kay's dad too."

"Billie Kay?" Deke's brow creased.

"Billie Kay Brown. She was my best friend in school."

"Yeah, I remember her now. Aint she the girl that you always hung out with at the Dance Barn in Muddy Ox most Saturday nights, back in the spring?" Deke looked uncomfortable after admitting he saw me at the Dance Barn. No doubt he had seen Theo and me on the dance floor together.

"Yes, that was me. And wasn't it you that left the Dance Barn early that night with Billie Kay?"

Theodore quietly watched the two of us trying to fill in the gaps of our past encounter. I was sure Deke would have been happy to wipe the memory of seeing me swaying to the music in the arms of a much younger man, and his one-night stand with Billie Kay right out of his head. That same memory of the last time Theo and I were together—the night we conceived our child was once blissful—but now, gut-wrenching for me.

Theodore cleared his throat and snapped his helper back to the task at hand. "Hey Deke, didn't you say you knew how to hook up this stove to that propane tank out there?"

"Sure, yeah, let's get some tools and we'll get right on it."

I was amazed at how quickly they had our new stove in working order. Theodore slipped him some money and said something about maybe needing his help again when he went back for that other furniture they were talking about on their way home. Deke said for him to let him know, then told me to enjoy my new stove as he was leaving.

"Oh Theodore, I never dreamed you were going to Dyersburg after a new stove," I said once we were alone.

"I planned for it to be a surprise. That's why I didn't want to take you with me to get it. It worked out just right since you were having your friend stop by today."

"This would have been the very stove I would have

chosen had I been there, I am sure."

"The salesman couldn't say enough about all its features. He definitely sold me when he kept going on about how evenly the oven baked everything."

"Speaking of that, I made a blackberry cobbler today. I wanted to have something for when Billie Kay was here. She had a double helping and said it was as good as the one they serve at Aunt Connie's. But there is plenty left."

"Well, if you will put on a fresh pot of coffee, I'll be glad to be the judge of that as soon as I get washed up."

After getting the coffee started, I grabbed the broom to sweep where they made a mess installing the stove. I smiled to remember one of Mama's sayings, *"Where there's a man—there's a mess."* She surely must have been referring to someone other than my dad. He knew better than to make any mess around her. As for me, I didn't mind at all cleaning up from where Theodore and Deke installed our stove. I wished there were more heartfelt words than just thank you, I love it, and it's beautiful, to let Theodore know how thoughtful he was.

"All right, I'm ready for that coffee and cobbler now."

"Here you go." I poured coffee for both of us and got a helping of cobbler for me too before joining Theodore at the table.

"Billie Kay was right. This is delicious. That new stove has its work cut out for it if it can bake your next cobbler any better than this."

"I think it also has a lot to do with the recipes in that cookbook I bought. Oh, by the way, Billie Kay wasn't the only visitor I had today. Mama came to see me."

Theodore stopped chewing and paused as if he was searching for a reply. "I—I was hoping she would eventually have a change of heart," he finally managed.

"No longer than you were around my mother, I think you know she brought a little attitude with her at first. But I admit, I had also been thinking a lot about her here lately. When she saw me softening a bit, so did she. When I began asking her questions about, you know, things a girl can only talk to her Mama about, I think she felt needed."

"I understand. At least I think I do." He shifted in his chair and his uncertain expression did not match his words.

"I don't mean I needed to talk to her about you. I needed to ask her about the pregnancy and what to expect after the baby gets here."

"Oh okay. And did she help you with that?"

"Actually, she did. At least a little bit, I think. Mama has always been blunt. If I thought she was going to put me at ease about what to expect during delivery, she didn't. But, along with the attitude, she brought a bag of things she knew would be helpful for me right now. That let me know I had also been on her mind. I don't know how she knew to do it, but she brought things I needed even before I told her I needed them. Remedies for some of the problems I've been having."

"Lucretia, I didn't know you were having problems. You never told me about any problems."

"It's nothing to do with the baby. But I am still having morning sickness, a lot of leg cramps and heartburn here lately. Though, I guess, not knowing what to expect during delivery, and how to take care of the baby after it is born have been my worst fears."

"I hope she helped with your concerns about the birthing part. I don't have a clue there. But I can promise you, I will help in any way I can, with taking care of the baby after she comes."

"She? How do you know it will be a girl?"

"I don't really. I just have a strong feeling that we are having a little girl. But if the baby is a boy, I am fine with that too."

"Mama also said she thought I was having a girl. And because I have been having a lot of heartburn, she said the baby will have a head full of dark hair. I'm sure that's an old wives' tale but Mama seemed pretty certain she was right."

"It has been my experience that most of those old wives' tales have merit. Wouldn't you love to have a little girl with dark hair like yours? If it is a girl, I hope she looks just like you. And if she does, she's bound to be a beauty." His soft, calming, voice was so comforting and reassuring. We held our gaze a few seconds before I moved on with my story.

"Mama had a sleeve of saltine crackers in her sack. She knew I needed them even before I told her about my morning sickness and heartburn. And she brought me a handful of corks to put between my sheets at the foot of the bed to help with leg cramps. At least, that is what she had always heard Ole Mrs. Grimsley say would help."

Theodore laughed before he could catch himself. "I've seen Mrs. Grimsley at the Big Store in Muddy Ox before. Actually, I heard her before seeing her. She had this loud, high-pitched voice that carried throughout the entire store. You could hear her greeting people two or three aisles over, saying, 'How you do Miss. Effie?, Aint it a purdy day, Mr. Albert?, And how's yer gout adoin,' Miss Mable Lee?' Most of the time she never waited for them to answer before she walked past them. She's a real character."

"Are you saying you don't think her idea about the corks will work?" I asked.

"I'm not doubting her in the least. If there ever was anyone who knew about old wives' tales, it is Mrs. Grimsley. Anyway, what can it hurt?" Theodore reassured.

"I'll do it then. Also, can I have a pair of your shoes to put under my bed tonight? Mama said she also claims that will help with leg cramps."

"Okay…sure," Theodore might not have laughed at Mrs. Grimsley's shoe theory but looked very confused.

BEFORE BEDTIME THAT night, he handed me a pair of his shoes to put under my bed. I suppose he figured that suggestion couldn't hurt anything either.

"Thank you. I will let you know in the morning if any of Mrs. Grimsley's or Mama's ideas work. Oh, I forgot to ask. What other furniture were you talking about with Deke? Should I be looking for more surprises?"

"It's late. And manhandling that stove wore me out. Can we talk about that in the morning too? Goodnight Lucretia."

"Goodnight Theodore."

Chapter Seven

THERE WAS NEVER a late sleeper at Mama's house. After years of being expected to rise as soon as the rooster crowed, it is no wonder my eyes still pop open by 5:30 each morning. But today, I welcomed my early reveille to fix breakfast on our new cookstove. After reading the user's guide twice, I set the oven. By now, I could whip up a pan of biscuits without even opening my cookbook.

A glint of dawn was trying to part the dark November sky, as the wall clock chimed seven times. Daylight came later and later the closer winter approached. Our meal was ready, all but frying the eggs. And Theodore had yet to make an appearance. My special breakfast would be ruined if I had to serve cold biscuits. Surely the drifting smell of bacon had aroused his appetite by now.

His bedroom door swung open just as I was about to tap. I almost tapped his bare chest instead. An uncomfortable feeling, as though I had been caught with my hand in a cookie jar, swept over me. I found myself in unfamiliar territory, having never approached, let alone, stepped inside his bedroom before. For that matter, nor had he ventured to mine. The layout of his house had been perfect for our situation. Theodore's bedroom was on the complete opposite side of the house from mine with the living, dining, spare bedroom, kitchen, and large pantry between. There had never been reason for me to enter his area before.

"Hmmm…good…good morning," he stuttered, while buttoning his shirt.

"Uh…Good morning. You startled me. I…umm…breakfast is almost ready. I know how you love hot biscuits." Our eyes remained locked while neither of us moved. For a moment, I almost forgot where I was, and why I was there.

"Biscuits…you said biscuits were ready?" He said holding his stare.

"Biscuits…yes…Oh my goodness. The biscuits!"

I am not sure if my hasty about turn or our unexpected close encounter put me into a spin. But had Theodore's strong arms not steadied me, I would have certainly collapsed to the floor. He led me to the living room and eased me onto the couch.

"Are you all right?" he asked.

"I think so. I just suddenly got light-headed."

"Let me get you a cool cloth," he said.

"I'm fine. It was only a little dizzy spell. I've had them before. But this one was… I…I think I just turned around too fast. Maybe if I sit here a few seconds, it will go away."

"Are you sure?"

"Yes. Oh, the biscuits. I need to get them out of the oven before they burn."

I jumped up, standing in place long enough to make sure I had my footing, then proceeded to the kitchen with Theodore trailing closely behind.

"A little longer and they would have been ruined. I am glad I got them out when I did."

"Honestly, I like crusty biscuits. They are just right for me. What can I do to help?"

"You can get the silverware and pour the coffee, while I fry the eggs if you like."

With a little teamwork, we were soon sitting before our first meal cooked on our new stove. He had never said he liked crusty biscuits before, but it was good to know, in case my timing was ever a little off again in the future.

"I've never heard you say anything about having dizzy spells. Have you had them often?" His forehead wrinkled with concerned.

"Only a few times in the beginning. Actually, I fainted by the mailbox the morning of the day you came to our house. That was why Mama took me to the doctor in the first place. And that was when I found out I was pregnant. I've only gotten dizzy a time or two since. Nothing like this morning though."

"When I think of the day when we first met while sitting around your Mama's table, it now seems like a very long time ago. In reality, it has only been a little more than six months. Anyway, I am glad I was there to catch you just now before you fell."

"I'm glad you were there too. And yes, sometimes, it feels like we met a lifetime ago." Our eyes briefly locked again.

"Wh…why were you in your room so long this morning? Why did you sleep so late?" I asked, breaking our gaze.

"I knew I was tired last night. I guess I didn't realize just how tired."

"Oh, and you said you would tell me this morning about the furniture you were talking to Deke McCrady about before he left yesterday."

"Baby furniture. Don't you think we need to get some soon? I also need to clear out that extra room I've been using for a catch-all, so we can turn it into a nursery."

"Yes, I do think we need some baby furniture. I had thought about furniture and that room before but didn't want to ask," I admitted.

"And why would you hesitate to ask me about something like that?" By his expression, I couldn't tell if Theodore was hurt or surprised.

"Well, you've given me a nice room of my own. I've taken over your kitchen and now you've bought this new cookstove. You have been so generous. I didn't want you to think I was expecting more. I guess I imagined we would get a cradle for the baby and put it in my room. I…"

"Lucretia, is that how you see this arrangement of ours? I'm sorry if I gave you that impression. When I married you and brought you here to live, I meant for you to see this as your home too. Your room is the arrangement we agreed upon that day by the willow tree when I asked you to marry me. I want you to think of the entire house as yours, not only the bedroom you occupy and the kitchen where you prepare meals. This is not just my home now. It is our home—yours, mine, and our baby's."

I was sorry for the sadness I had caused in his eyes and didn't actually know how to respond. I definitely hadn't wanted to hurt his feelings or seem ungrateful for what Theodore had done for me and my baby. He never knew how many nights I lay staring at the ceiling in my room and feeling in limbo between the familiar and the unknown.

I didn't want, nor did I have the option to return to a life where my tallest hurdle was reaching Mama's high expectations and where mine and Billie Kay's biggest decision was what to wear to the Barn Dance on a Saturday night.

Although, I managed pretty well to take on my new role of wife and expectant mother, at times, I felt like I was on the sidelines watching me act out my life, but not really living it. Sometimes, I would think, how did I get here? But before I finished that thought, I'd stop and remind myself that no one forced me. I chose here.

"You are right, Theodore. This is my—our home now. I am happy here. I'm sorry if it didn't sound that way."

"That's better. I agree we will need a cradle at first. But our princess will not be able to stay in a cradle forever. She will need a baby bed before we know it." A little light came back into his eyes.

"So, you still think we are having a princess?"

"We won't know for sure until three months from now, but that's my feeling."

"All right then, when you are ready to go shopping for baby furniture, I am ready too." His reaction made me smile.

"Together, we can get this kitchen cleaned up and be on the road to Dyersburg as soon as we're finished."

"Wait a minute, I didn't expect you to want to go so soon. I have to change and make myself presentable first," I said.

"I don't see a need to put it off any longer. Why don't I get the kitchen cleaned while you get ready?" he suggested.

About an hour later we were on our way to Dyersburg. As we rode along, I went over our earlier conversation in my mind. I was truthful. When I honestly thought about it, I was happy living in Theodore's home. And from that day forward, I decided to think of it as home. Our little princess and my home.

I think the store clerk was surprised to see Theodore back so soon and he was equally surprised to see me with him picking out baby furniture. I supposed we might as well get used to the stares when we appeared together in public. The defiance in me rose to think it was really none of his business. To confuse him further, I looped my arm around Theodore's and leaned in close to him as we looked at the long line of baby beds.

"I had no idea it would be this hard to decide on a bed or that there would be so many to choose from," I said.

"Neither did I," Theodore agreed.

"Did you have a particular style in mind?" the clerk asked. By then, we had almost seen them all.

"No, I guess I will just know what I want when I…" The clerk and Theodore stopped and turned to see what made me stop mid-sentence.

"That one. That's the one," I said with surety.

Theodore followed my eyes to see which bed I was so drawn to. "Yes, I agree," he said. "It will be just the thing for our princess."

"So, you like the Jenny Lind? Excellent choice," the clerk said smiling.

I wasn't sure if the man was being truthful about our excellent choice or if he was just pleased that we had finally made a decision. It could have also had to do with the price tag attached to the style we selected. His smile broadened more when we chose a coordinating chest and cradle. And of course, we also had to have a matching set of Jenny Lind sheets for both pieces.

"Deke McCrady's house is on our way home. I will swing by and ask him to follow us and help me unload our things. We can set them inside the spare room for now. We have three months to transform that room into a nursery fit for a princess—or a prince if that's the case."

"If we paint the walls an off-white, we can decorate it accordingly after the baby comes, once we know which it is. Think if we have a prince, he will mind sleeping in a Jenny Lind bed?" I asked.

"If a prince arrives, we can take that bed back and get him one more suitable. But I just don't think we will have to do that." Theodore smiled. Deke was stepping onto his porch as we drove up.

"Going somewhere Deke?" Theodore asked.

"Was headin' to town to meet Larson. We thought we'd do a little messin' around tonight."

"A little extra spending money will be in it for you if you'll follow us home on your way to town. I need help unloading a few more pieces of furniture. Not to worry, none of it is as heavy as that stove was. It's just awkward for one person to handle."

"Sure thing. Lead the way," Deke said and headed toward his truck.

As soon as the furniture was unloaded, Deke was

gone. Guess he didn't want to keep Larson Strom waiting. I changed into my everyday clothes and began fixing our supper.

"We can hold off putting the bed together until after the baby arrives. But don't you think the cradle will do for either a girl or a boy?" Theodore asked.

"Yes, I think it might." I smiled, knowing how anxious he was to get at least something in place for the baby.

The cradle parts were unboxed and lined in order ready to start assembling as soon as we finished with supper. I watched him from the corner of my eye while washing dishes and smiled to see him carefully read and reread the instructions.

Once finished with the kitchen, I joined him on the couch and took over reading the remaining steps for him as he attached each part with care and precision.

"It's taking a little longer than I thought it would. But I should have known. I can't remember a job like this ever taking less time than planned." He frowned.

After darkness fell, he had to finish by lamp light, but was determined to press on. Once he was satisfied with his handiwork, he stood straight, placed his hands on his hips, and leaned back to get the kinks out.

"How do you like it?" he asked proudly.

"It's perfect. I love it," I said rocking the cradle, imagining a sleeping baby inside.

"Okay now, show me where you want it." He lifted

it to follow me to my room.

"I want it right here, as close to my bed as possible."

He set the cradle in place and rocked it gently. I was sure he saw a baby in his imagination too.

"I like what you did with the room. It looks nice." He said, looking around.

"Thank you." I realized it was the first time he had seen the room since we were married.

"Did those help your leg cramps?" He pointed to his shoes on the floor just under the edge of my bedspread as he hesitated by the door.

"I'm not sure if it was your shoes or the corks between the sheets but I haven't had as many cramps since I put both of them there." I grinned, remembering what he said about Mrs. Grimsley's superstitions.

"Whatever works. Let me know if you need a pair of my socks too," he teased.

Chapter Eight

Once in bed, I rolled to my side and gently rocked the cradle again. Why had I feared to ask Theodore about making a room for the baby? He has been nothing but honest, kind, and understanding, from the day we first met. His willingness to dispel my every concern is proof that I can trust him. And I do. I love being protected and provided for. I love being the woman—yes woman of the house. That I am happy living here now is the truth. If I want my baby to feel like this is her home, then I needed to show her I feel at home here as well. Besides, even if I wanted, I couldn't go back and live with my parent's. They certainly wouldn't want me and my child. Well, at least not Mama—Daddy maybe.

Before drifting off, I realized that I had again thought of the baby as a girl.

"Reading? So early in the morning?" I asked

Theodore who was hovered over a book at the kitchen table.

"Out of curiosity, I picked up one of these Farmer's Almanacs while in town the other day. This thing is full of interesting facts," he replied.

"All I know, is my Mama would never be without her copy of The Farmer's Almanac. She wouldn't even think of planting a garden without first checking the signs."

"I've heard others say that works. Having not ever been much of a gardener, I never paid a lot of attention to it before," he said while slowly thumbing the pages.

"Planting isn't the only thing she uses the almanac for. Apparently, the position of the moon has to do with hair growth. In the dark of the moon is the only time she will cut my dad's hair. She and several of her friends were always checking for when the signs were right to set hens, can green beans, wean babies, and prune rose bushes. Daddy even looks at it to know when its favorable to cut his hay."

"I'm glad you and your Mama are sort of back on good terms. Maybe all that knowledge will come in handy after the baby comes." I turned to see if he was making light of our conversation or if he was serious. I saw he was serious, so I went on.

"Next to the Bible, The Farmer's Almanac is Mama's favorite source of information."

"I can see why." he said laying it aside for more

reading material.

"Now what are you reading?"

"I know we don't plan on assembling the bed until after the baby arrives, but I thought, considering how long it took to get that cradle together, I would be smart to study over these instructions ahead of time."

I continued with breakfast while Theodore mulled over the directions. When everything was nearly finished, I broke the silence.

"I'm ready to put the food on the table. Are you almost through reading?" It donned on me I had become my Mama when it came to wanting to serve and eat a meal while it was still hot.

"Yes, I'm sure I'll have to go over it again. But I think the bed will go about the same as the cradle only with several more steps and parts," He ran his hand through his hair and rubbed his forehead.

"I'm sure you will figure it out. And I'll read the steps for you again like last time."

"You were a big help. It definitely went much faster after that. So, how did you sleep last night? Any leg cramps?"

"Not one cramp. I am happy to say."

"Guess my socks can stay in their drawer for the time being then," he teased again.

"Guess they can."

Just as I was taking the biscuits from the oven and we were about to begin breakfast, someone knocked.

"I'll get it," Theodore pushed back from the table.

My annoyance from having our meal interrupted, became instant elation to hear my father's voice.

"Daddy, what a nice surprise. Oh, wait. Is anything wrong?" I said after reaching the door.

"Come in Mr. Bertram," Theodore shut the door behind him.

Daddy started to remove his shoes. I stopped him and assured that removing ones shoes before coming into our house was not a requirement. He kept them on, but his uneasiness was obvious. He stepped awkwardly, as though the floor had been glass.

Theodore pulled up a chair and bid him to join us while I poured him a cup of hot coffee.

"Nothins' wrong. Yer Mama sent me to ask y'all to dinner next Thursday. She said tell you it's not Thanksgivin' without family."

I had forgotten all about Thanksgiving. Mama had always gone above and beyond with her Thanksgiving feast. This invitation was another way of making amends.

"We would love to come, wouldn't we Lucretia?" I think Theodore read my face above my silence, so he was comfortable with accepting.

"Yes…yes, we would love to come."

"That's good. I sure wasn't lookin' forward to tellin' yer Mama if you'd a said no."

Tears rolled as I rushed to him with a hug and

kissed him on his cheek. Unlike Mama, he never raised a wall when it came to hugs. "I've missed you so much, Daddy."

"Yer missed too, Lucretia. That house is way too quiet with you not there."

"I'm sorry. Bet Mama fusses at you even more with me gone."

"No, that's the odd part. Here lately, she's been a heap too quiet. Guess over time it will get better. But you are sorely missed."

"You had to know that I would be leaving home one day, Daddy."

"Didn't think it'd be whilst you was still a little girl though."

"Well, I'm not a little girl any longer but I think I might be having a little girl. Mama said she thought so too from the way I was carrying the baby and because of my morning sickness." I stood back to model for him. He looked me up and down but didn't comment.

"Could be havin' a baby girl around might help wipe the strain off yer Mama's face. Maybe mine too."

"I hope so. I'm sorry this has been so hard on you all, Daddy."

"Mr. Bertram, you should try one of Lucretia's bis-cuits." Theodore handed me a saucer from the cabinet and nodded. He was clearly trying to lighten the conversation.

"Well, I already had break…"

Before he could refuse, I sliced a biscuit, slathered it with butter, dabbled on some sorghum molasses, and pushed it toward him.

"Mmm mmm, yer Mama sure was a good teacher. This here biscuit's ever bit as good as the ones she makes."

"Uh…thank you, Daddy. But…Mama…didn…"

"Your daughter has become a really good cook, sir." Theodore said quickly.

"Well, didn't you always say practice makes perfect? But Daddy, you know how much Mama prides herself in her cooking. It would probably be better if you don't brag on my biscuits too much. At least not to her anyway."

"Come to think of it, yer probably right," he said licking the sorghum off his fingers.

"Mr. Bertram," Theodore began.

"Why don't you call me Asa. It sounds a little funny for you to call me Mr. Bertram and you only bein' a few years younger than me." Daddy always had a way of saying what could have been left unsaid for comfort level—but blurted it out anyway.

"That would be nice, Asa. And of course, you can call me—Theodore." I admired his ability to overlook Daddy's crudeness. Theodore actually had a lot of admirable traits.

"Will do it. Okay then. She'll be havin' dinner on the table at noon, as always. I gotta' get back now, though.

It's the dark of the moon and she's got me lined up for a haircut. See y'all Thursday?"

"You can count on it, Daddy. Tell Mama we will be there a little early so I can set the table." I knew better than to suggest I could help with the meal preparation. Mama was a one-woman-production when it came to holiday meals. However, I decided I could contribute a little by bringing a cobbler. Maybe she would get around to tasting this one.

Daddy asking Theodore to call him Asa and our invitation for Thanksgiving Dinner was a step toward acceptance. Instantly, the baby danced inside me. My heart swelled. We were one step closer to being family again.

I WAS MORE than pleased at how well our first Thanksgiving Dinner went at my parent's house.

"I know you had your doubts about how today might go, but I thought that was a pleasant gathering. And that meal—I think it was one of the best I ever put in my…" Theodore stopped abruptly.

"It's okay, Mama is one of the best cooks in Muddy Ox. You don't have to worry about hurting my feelings."

"You'll be just as good a cook as she is one day. Maybe better. You already make biscuits as good as hers. Your father even said so the other morning."

"I was so afraid Daddy was going to let that slip today. Thankfully, he didn't. The day might not have been as pleasant if he had."

"Well, your Mama's meal was grand, but it didn't take a thing away from that cobbler of yours."

"I finally got her to try it. She didn't say much but I could tell she really liked it by her surprised expression."

"Wonder why she didn't praise you if she really liked it?" Theodore asked.

"She resents that I got the recipe out of a cookbook. She thinks that true southern cooks should create their own dishes, rather than follow other's recipes.

"You're telling me your Mama never used a recipe someone else shared with her?"

"She might start out with their recipe, but she will always find a way to add her personal touch. After that, it is no longer theirs' but hers.' If Mama is anything— she is an original."

"That she is," Theodore agreed.

"Look, it's beginning to snow," I exclaimed.

As children, Billie Kay and I loved to see it snow. We would play for hours making a snowman. I sighed to realize that was another part of my childhood gone.

"Want to tell me what that sigh was about?" Theodore asked.

"I was thinking about all the snowmen and forts Billie Kay, and I made together as children. Now, she has moved to Carthersville and I—I am a married woman about to have a baby in a few months."

"I made my share of snowmen and forts too as a boy. Just think, though. In a few years we can make snow creations with our little girl."

"Yes, you're right."

By the time we arrived home, a heavy blanket of snow had covered everything. "Sit still for a minute while I brush the steps clean. Don't want to take any chances on you falling."

Once he had me safely inside, he brought in all the leftovers Mama sent home with us.

"I won't have to cook for days. That's for sure. I hope I can find room for all of this," I said, starting to arrange things around in the refrigerator.

"I saw you left them a generous serving of your cobbler too."

"It was obvious how much Daddy loved it. I bet Mama won't let her part go to waste either, even if she didn't say a lot about it."

"Do you think we will be invited for Christmas dinner too?"

"We already are. Mama asked me while you went to warm the car before we left."

"It's been years since I've felt like celebrating Christmas or that a tree sat in this living room. If we don't get snowed in, how about I go cut us a Christmas tree tomorrow? Then, we can go into town and get some decorations for it? Just because we will be going to your parents, it doesn't mean we can't be a little festive here ourselves."

"A Christmas tree would be nice. Don't you have decorations?"

"There may be a few tucked away in the closet, but I think we should have our own."

"Me too. And we should start our own traditions—you know for the baby."

"For us too." Theodore had a faraway look in his eyes.

Chapter Nine

"**M**OVE IT UP a little higher and a bit to the left. No, wait. That's too far. Now, back to the right. Okay stop. Hang it right there," I directed.

Luckily, Theodore was a patient man.

He had gotten carried away and cut a tree wider than the door. There were more than enough trimmings to make a wreath after cutting it to size.

"I would like to invite my parents over for Christmas Eve. What do you think?" I asked while adding a bright red bow for a finishing touch.

"I think having them over on Christmas Eve is a great idea. And I do believe, that is as fine of a Christmas wreath as I have ever seen," he bragged as he opened the door for us.

"Thank you. Are you ready to do the tree now?" I asked as we made our way inside.

"I hope you like it there in front of the window. I really didn't see another place to put it."

"That's the perfect place for it," I agreed.

"Do you think we bought enough lights?" Theodore asked as he began unwinding and connecting the many colorful strings.

"I hope so. You sure bought a lot. But you really can't have too many lights for me." I smiled.

"Well, a tree as large as this one calls for a lot of lights and decorations."

After hanging the last of the ornaments and adjusting the garland once more, I handed him a box of silver tinsel and opened a box for myself. "Our tree at home was never complete until it was covered with this tinsel," I said.

"Wait, I have one more thing to add first."

Moments later, he returned with the most beautiful, glistening, golden star I think I had ever seen. "This star is a special memory from my childhood. Our family was never in the same place come Christmas time. But my mother always saw to it that we had a tree. As far back as I can remember, I got to place this star on top of our Christmas tree every year. To continue the tradition, as soon as he was old enough and could do it without toppling it, the placing of this star became Theo's job."

As I watched him carefully position the star, I imagined him doing the same as a little boy. Then I could almost see him lift Theo so he could follow tradition. I immediately understood the faraway look he had the night before. He was remembering happy holiday times when Theo was a child.

Realizing how little I knew about him or his son, I was suddenly filled with curiosity and many questions.

"You have never spoken of your childhood before.

Why were you never in the same place each year?"

"My parents were Vaudeville performers. Believe it or not, I was a child actor and began performing in minstrels and Vaudeville shows at age three. I can't even tell you how many times I would go to sleep after a show and wake up the next morning in a new location for our next performance. We traveled all over the United States."

"What did you do in the show at three years old?" I had so many more questions but that was the first to roll.

"A three-year-old can do about anything they want on stage and entertain an audience. I pretended to play a toy guitar and piano until I learned to play real instruments. The troop taught me enough dance steps to fit in. And I was written into the acts as often as possible. Being a child, I could get a laugh when the others bombed. After I learned to play and write music and could play a variety of instruments, I was in most every show in one way or another."

"When Theo got old enough, did he act in your show too?"

"Yes, if you were a member of the Dalton family, you performed. Theo's mother was also one of the actors in the troop. We taught him as we were taught. He was only six when she died."

My poor Theo. It must have been horrible to be a six-year-old without a mother. My poor Theodore. How did he manage being an only parent to such a young child?

"What was Theo's mother's name?"

"Her name was Gus."

"Gus. Isn't that an unusual name for a woman?"

"Augusta was her given name. But she preferred to be called Gus."

"How did she die?"

While my questioning saddened him, I could tell he was pleased that I wanted to know about him and his family. After a brief pause, he continued.

"At that time, we were performing on a showboat out on the Black River near Corning, Arkansas. Being a firm believer in the show must go on, she waited until our boat docked to tell anyone she was having an appendicitis attack. Her appendix ruptured and peritonitis had set in before we could get her to the hospital. There was nothing they could do after the infection spread into her bloodstream."

"That was terrible. She was so young. How many years were you a performer and why did you stop?"

"The hand of the great depression had a strong grip around the neck of the economy. Unemployment doubled. If people had money, they used it to put food on their table. Being entertained was not a priority. Times were hard for everyone—even entertainers. Vaudeville didn't last long, at least not for me after that.

"My parents grew older and died a year after we loss

Gus. I did my best to keep the act going, but I was twenty-nine years old with a seven-year-old son and no family left to help me with him. So, I sold the minstrel show; boat and all. A circus tent and my musical instruments were all I kept when Theo and I moved here to Bragg City."

"I can imagine how hard that must have been. So, did you farm? Or what sort of work did you do when you moved back to Missouri?"

"Well, after our conversation about the Farmer's Almanac, you can tell I knew nothing about farming. But I picked up a few mechanical skills just being around when the showboat would break down and by helping the others to raise and lower our tents. So, I bought a tool and machine shop and worked at it during the week when Theo was in school. On the weekends I showed movies in the tent and hired a few local performers to do live shows during intermission and after the movies."

"I'm confused. As far as I can see, you don't go to work anywhere now. If I gave it any thought at all, I guess I supposed you were retired. Although, come to think of it, you are still too young to be retired."

"I eventually sold the shop and the tent and bought a movie theater in Bragg City. A few years later, I sold the theater too. Those deals were very profitable. Also, I was most fortunate to have had a very thoughtful, and resourceful mother. Unbeknown to me, she had withheld a portion of my earnings from the minstrel shows and put it along with some additional family money into a savings for me to be collected at her death. I held on to as much of that money as possible and lived on what I could make at the machine shop.

As soon as the economy caught its breath again, I could breathe a little easier too. I invested most of my savings into an ammunition factory in St. Louis. That investment has paid well."

"I don't know if I am more shocked at you being wealthy or that you were a child Vaudeville actor."

"I am just a blessed man. Blessed to have such an insightful mother. Blessed to have a son like Theo. Blessed to have such a rich, full, interesting life. And now, blessed to have you and the opportunity to have a part in the life of this new, sweet, child we will welcome soon. If I am rich in anything, it is in blessings."

"We are blessed to have you too."

My mind was swirling. I knew I would probably have more questions later about Theodore and his interesting life. But I needed to process the ones he had already answered for me today. As for me, I was only sixteen. There wasn't a whole lot to know about me. And what there was, he mostly already knew. Anyway, to learn that his son and I conceived a child and he saw the need to rescue us from a life of shame and ridicule would have been hard to top.

"So, do you put these strands of tinsel on one at a

time or just haphazardly throw them on the branches?" He asked, pulling me from the swirl and back to the present.

"Oh no. Mama could tell right away if we didn't put them on one strand at a time. And we did plan to have them over before Christmas, right?"

"Yes, we did.

"You start on that side, and I'll start over here and we will meet in the middle. Do it like this, see?' I shared my tinsel-hanging expertise, as Mama had shown me so many times.

"Just reach up as high as you can and I'll get the top branches by the star," he suggested.

"Sounds good to me. You know, I think that is the most brilliant tree topper I have ever seen."

"It's a gold-plated replica of the star of Bethlehem. My mother told me they bought it after one of their shows in New Orleans the Christmas before I was born. I don't think I have ever seen another one like it either. Hey, do you think I need more tinsel?"

"Yes, I do," I said, handing him another open box.

"We wouldn't want your Mama seeing any sparsely covered branches when they come. I think your Mama and my mother would be a pair to be reckoned with. Yours would be checking the tinsel and mine would be making sure the star was straight." We laughed.

"Want me to make us a bite to eat while you finish adding tinsel to the top?"

"Yes, I think I've worked up an appetite with all this wreath hanging, tree decorating and life sharing." He began humming *Santa Claus is coming to Town* under his breath. I had never heard him hum or sing before. I could not help but wonder what other surprises lay in store where he was concerned.

As I LAY in bed that night, I was still amazed at all Theodore had shared with me earlier. It was hard to picture such a quiet, distinguished, so reserved man as a vaudeville performer. He must have been very talented. He probably still is. Obviously, some of those talents were passed down to Theo. Would those same talents be passed on to my—our baby?

And was I still such a child that I had not questioned how effortlessly he seemed to show up with things of value? He said that kitchen stove was the best you could buy. He never flinched once at the cost of the finest quality of furniture we bought for the nursery. Even if I hadn't, I'm sure the salesman figured out right away that money wasn't an issue with Theodore that day.

He could have chosen a less expensive Christmas tree, one that required less ornaments and other decorations. I suppose I am still childlike. Few children wonder how their parents provide for them, as long as they provide. Hopefully, that was one worry our child would not have.

Chapter Ten

I FELT IT eventful for my parents to be coming to our home on Christmas Eve. It was one more sign they had accepted mine and Theodore's marriage. I wanted everything to be as near perfect as possible. With the exception of Theodore's bedroom of course, I had spit-shined the entire place. Mama wouldn't need a white glove to inspect for cleanliness, her keen eyes were enough. Their visit was still three days away but if I did a little every day and then another once over right before they were to arrive, hopefully there would not be one speck of dust left for her to find.

It was not as though she could scold or punish me if things didn't meet her approval. That was my fear as a child. Now, personal pride overshadowed fear. For the first time, I genuinely wanted to please and impress my mother—to make her proud. I wouldn't hold my breath for praise to cross her lips, but after years of practice, I could read her expressions. Also, with Mama, it might be as much about what she didn't say as what she did.

Just as I made my last daily swipe with the dust cloth, I heard Theodore's voice. "Lucretia, open the door. Our hands are full."

Deke McCrady, backed awkwardly into the living room, bearing the heavy end of yet another piece of furniture.

"Wait until you see what I have." Theodore was beaming.

"What is it?" I asked.

"It's a Victor Victoria Console Tube Radio-Record Player. The man at the store said it is the newest thing on the market right now. We can either listen to the radio or we can play records. I picked up some popular Christmas albums along with a few of my other favorites. But we can go back together, and you can get some of your favorites too."

"I have never seen anything like that before. It is amazing. Wait, let me move this table out of the way." I said, reaching forward.

"Oh no, you don't need to be movin' that. It's too heavy for you." Before I knew it Deke had grabbed the table and was asking where I wanted it.

As soon as he had it in place and almost before I could turn to thank him, he was by the door, his hand on the knob.

"Thanks again, Deke. I really appreciate your help," Theodore said slipping some bills into his hand.

"He sure is a nice man. Deke seems to be available every time he is needed. What would you do without him?" I asked once he was gone.

"Yes, Deke's a good guy to know." He agreed.

"You are full of surprises. I never know what you will show up with next," I said while thumbing through the records he had chosen.

"Our conversation a few weeks ago about my vaudeville days made me remember what an important part music played in my young life. I think it would be nice for our child to grow up being exposed to as much music as possible. It runs deep in the blood of all of us Daltons."

"I would like for the baby to inherit the Dalton talents, now that I know you all have so many."

"I'd like that too. We can consider this radio-record player an early Christmas present to our family. And on Christmas Eve, while your parents are here, if we can't find any Christmas music on the radio, we can play a record."

"It seems you have thought of almost everything." I marveled.

Ever since he shared about his family and past with me that evening we decorated for Christmas together, Theodore had appeared happier. The gleam on his face nearly matched the glow of the golden star that topped our tree. Christmas seemed to bring out a free, youthful, side of him—and I liked it.

"What about you? Have you been thinking about what you want to get your parents for Christmas?" His question sounded leading, as though he had also been giving it some thought.

"They are a difficult pair to buy for. My dad is nearly impossible. And with the war rationing going on, it is even harder to get for them."

"What would you want to give them if rationing wasn't a problem?" he asked.

"This may surprise you, but Mama loves frilly things, like silk pillows and lacey scarves and handkerchiefs. On the other hand, my practical dad would probably be happy with a new work shirt or two."

"Doesn't either of them ever do anything for pure enjoyment?"

"There isn't anything Daddy enjoys more than listening to ball games on their radio. He is a serious St. Louis Cardinals fan. Stan Musial is his favorite player."

"And your Mama?"

"Other than having everything in her world spotless and in order, she loves needlework and baking. But because they are rationing things such as flour, sugar, butter, and cooking oil, it has put a damper on her being able to bake as much as I am sure she would like to. Mama is a homemaker before she is anything else, but she does love to crochet and embroidery in the evenings while Daddy listens to the radio."

"Then we need to go Christmas shopping for your parents. Want to do that tomorrow? Do you know your dad's shirt size?"

"I'm pretty sure he wears a large. Yes, tomorrow would be good so we can get our rations too. I have some baking to do myself."

"All right, that's a plan. But for now, I'll find us a Christmas record to listen to while you rustle us up a bite to eat."

"Sounds good. I think the pot of beans I started this morning should be done. I just have to fix some cornbread and fry up a few potatoes and we're set."

Before long, I found myself swaying to the smooth voice of Bing Crosby's White Christmas while Theodore sat cross-legged searching for the next record to play after Bing was finished.

"I hope it snows for Christmas this year. I love to wake up to snow on Christmas morning," I said, still swaying slightly as I placed the cornbread into the oven.

"Lucretia, I will do my best to make all your other wishes come true. But we can only hope for a snowy Christmas morning. That is beyond my control."

Our eyes met and he smiled. I had no doubts this man would do anything to bring happiness to me—if it was within his control.

AFTER BREAKFAST THE next morning, Theodore and I took time to make a list before heading to town. We wanted to make sure we didn't forget anything with

Christmas Eve only being two days away. Embroidery thread and crochet yarn for Mama, shirts for daddy, maybe another record or two to add to our collection, and our rations.

Finding work shirts for my dad was easy. I had to spend a little more time choosing colors of thread and yarn for Mama. *Boogie Woogie Bugle Boy, Chattanooga Choo Choo,* and *Juke Box on a Saturday Night.* Those were songs Billie Kay and I used to dance to when we went to the barn dance, and I met…

I stopped myself. I didn't want to think about things that would make me sad. Maybe I'd think about those things another time. As for now, I only wanted to dwell on happy memories. It was almost Christmas. We were buying gifts for my parents who were going to visit us in two days. Our baby would be arriving in about three more months. And Theodore's star was twinkling on top of the tree we decorated together at home—our home.

I lingered briefly by a display of silk material on our way to the register but quickly dismissed the idea when I saw the price.

"I wasn't sure which threads and yarn Mama already had so I got her a variety of colors. But I know she will love those lacy handkerchiefs for sure." I said in the car on our way home. I almost felt giddy, like I had as a child looking forward to Christmas. Only today was about giving and not receiving. I hadn't realized before, what a pleasure giving could be.

"I'm sure she will be happy with all of your choices. I've noticed you have a great eye for color and style."

"Well, I know my dad will love those shirts and that wide brimmed hat too."

"I've never worked in the fields like your father has but I can only imagine how hot and uncomfortable it must be. Just think. Next year, we will be buying baby dolls or baseball bats to wrap and put under the tree. Won't that be fun?" Now, he was the one sounding almost giddy.

"Theodore, that is the first time I have heard you even hint that the baby could be a boy."

"I still feel like we will have a girl. But we can't predict that any more than we can predict that we will wake up to snow on Christmas morning—right?"

"Right. Well, it did snow on Thanksgiving night. And we do have a Jenny Lind baby bed in the nursery, ready to assemble. That bed is undoubtably a girl's bed. We will keep our fingers crossed about both the baby and the snow," I said holding up both hands with crossed fingers.

"I just remembered. I should check that Farmer's Almanac when we get home. It came pretty close about the first frost of the year, maybe it will have information about snowfalls too." He smiled.

"Surely it will. It has something about everything else. I'm glad we picked up our rations today. I need to plan what I am going to bake to be able to stretch that pound of sugar and make it last for the next two weeks. Funny, how I never gave things like that a thought before. It never occurred to me how Mama managed. I will have to ask her about that."

"I'll bet she will be surprised when I can talk Almanac with her. I'll do a little more studying on it while you're stretching sugar."

We laughed.

We laughed often lately…

Chapter Eleven

BECAUSE IT WAS Christmas Eve morning, and I was anxious about the meal and desserts I planned to serve my parents that evening, my eyes sprang open much earlier than usual. It was a challenge for me to find dishes Mama had not already perfected. Recreating one of her signature dishes would look more like a competition than a simple holiday meal. Although Theodore was quick to boast about my newly acquired cooking skills, I knew they paled pitifully compared to Mama's. After going through my cookbook several times, I settled on a jelly cake and wedding cookies. If she had ever made either, I could not remember. After tossing and turning until my covers were in a rumpled mess, I knew there would be no more sleep for me. So, I got up.

I saw a note from Theodore on the kitchen table as soon as I turned on the light. Where could he have gone? He must have left before sunrise.

Dear Lucretia,

I had a couple of errands to run. Will explain when I return.

I am sure I will be back by the time the biscuits are out of the oven, if not before.

See you soon,
Theodore

Since I had no way of knowing when he left, I didn't get in a rush to start breakfast. Instead, I got my cookbook out and began mixing cookie dough. I tripled the recipe to make three batches—one for the evening, one for our own cookie jar and one to send home with my parents. A nice batch of wedding cookies could be one more gift for them. Suddenly, it seemed I couldn't give them enough.

The directions said the cookies rolled better if the dough was refrigerated before baking. Following directions was at the top of a long list of things I had tried to learn lately. It was also one of the less challenging tasks to master. Someone else had done the thinking for you. All you had to do was—follow directions.

The wall clock chimed seven times. Surely, Theodore would be home soon. I needed to start thinking about breakfast. I had just placed the last biscuit in the pan so I could slip it into the oven as soon as he arrived when I heard a loud knock.

I expected to see a grinning Theodore with his hands too full to open the door again, but instead, I was met with a partially toothless smirk and an offending stench of two very unsightly strangers.

"Mornin' mam.' I'm Wiley Bunkus and this here is Clave Tay…"

Theodore's truck pulled into the yard before the man could finish with the introductions. He hadn't arrived any too soon. My hand was already on the knob to close the door. The appearance and stench of them had me unnerved.

"Wiley, Clave, you fellows beat me here," Theodore greeted the pair as he grabbed a small bag on his way out of the truck.

"Well, it sounded like you was in a rush for this stuff. So, we got right on it, Mr. Dalton."

"I'm glad you did. Lucretia, these are um…friends…of mine. This is Wiley Bunkus and Clave Taylor. They live over around Five Points. You know, on the other side of Muddy Ox? This is my wife, Lucretia. Just put that crate there inside the door, Clave," Theodore said as he slipped some money into the man's hand.

"Wife?" Wiley remarked, his eyes moved from my face and centered on my expanded belly.

"Pleased to meet you," I managed. Those two didn't look like any friends of Theodore's that I had ever met before. It was obvious they were equally surprised to see me.

"Scuze me, Miss Lucretia," he grunted.

I stepped back as he stumbled on the threshold and nearly dropped his burdensome load.

"Nice to meet you too, Ma'am. Mr. Dalton, you know we are always ready to oblige you. Just call on us any time," Wiley said.

"You all have a good Christmas now, okay?" Theodore said as they were leaving.

"Fer sure," They responded, almost in unison.

"Some of your surprises here lately have shocked me. But those two? They don't look like anyone you would be especially friendly with," I whispered, hoping they were out of earshot.

"Aw, Wiley and Clave are okay. They are known to lean a little light on soap and water and heavy on the moonshine from time to time. And the law has had to settle a few squabbles between them because when they get drunk they forget where their property lines are and get into a ruckus about it. But they would do anything to help someone who needed them though."

"And you needed their help this morning?" I quizzed.

"We needed their help—you and I."

"Well, I'm confused," I admitted.

"We—needed them for the contents of this crate."

"I don't' know what is in it, but it took everything that poor man had, to get it inside the door," I said.

"It's extra rations. I don't question where or how they get them. I just know they can. They needed the money, especially here at Christmas. They both have kids. I thought we could make up a nice basket of food rations for your parents as another Christmas gift and have some extra for our own pantry too. That way, your Mama can bake as much as she wants for the holidays. And your dad can eat until his heart's content. And you won't have to fret about how to stretch that sugar we got the other day until we can make another run to town."

"I didn't know there were extra rations out there to be had."

"There is almost extra anything a body wants if money isn't an issue and you know the right people who seem to always—know the right people,"

"But…"

"Shh…Money can talk, but it can also keep a secret. Hey, I'm hungry. How long before breakfast?" He changed the subject and started down the hall to his room with the small bag tucked under his arm.

"The oven is hot, and the biscuits are ready to go in. The rest will be ready when they are."

On his way back to the kitchen, he slipped a tiny package under the tree. "What time are your parents arriving?" He asked casually, as if it had been our first exchange of the day and as though he hadn't been on his secret, early morning, mission.

"I told them to be here around five. That way we would have time to visit after dessert."

"Want to give them the ration basket tonight as a Christmas Eve present? We can save the other things we got them for tomorrow." I loved how he was so excited about Christmas.

After breakfast, he began sorting the contents of the crate while I did dishes. When I joined him, the food products were evenly divided into two piles, one for my parents and one for us. A good-sized smoked ham topped each pile.

"My parents will be surprised to get these extra rations. I am sure glad you know the right people—who know the right people."

"And that's not all. Wait until you see the rest," he was grinning from ear to ear as he pulled the crate closer.

"Oh Theodore, Mama will love this," I said pulling a bundle of silk material from the crate. "This ivory color is beautiful."

"And I think your dad will find these boots and thick wool socks useful. The boots will not only come in handy this winter but the rest of the year too. I'm not sure how many more snows are coming, but it rains more in the spring here in the Bootheel of Missouri than anywhere I have ever been. And I've been a lot of places. Every man needs a good pair of rubber boots in this place."

"I hope they fit. I'm sure the large shirts we got him will do, but I've never paid much attention to the size of Daddy's feet."

"If they're too big, he can wear them over his shoes

or double up on the socks."

"I'm positive he will make them work, one way or another," I said.

"Um…Well…um…I told the guys to get as many rationed items as they could find. I guess they took it upon themselves to get these," Theodore blushed as he pulled up a couple pairs of nylon stockings.

"Mama wears cloth stockings year around," I said, quickly grabbing the nylons and stuffing them inside my apron pocket.

"I think I have a bushel basket out in the shed just the right size for packing their things. Suppose you can find some ribbon to make one of those pretty bows of yours to go on top?"

He was still slightly blushing as he stood to go outside for the basket. I couldn't keep from smiling once he had gone. Mama would never wear those stockings, not even to church. But I just might, after the baby is born. I found it unusual, but also refreshing for a man his age to blush like a schoolboy during our awkward moment. He also had never looked more handsome.

"What are you smiling about," he asked. I wasn't aware I was still smiling as I returned to the living room with my bow and met him returning with the basket.

"I guess because I know how pleased our gifts will make Mama and Daddy." I didn't totally lie. I was certain my parents would be pleased and appreciative. But I didn't want to tell him I was also smiling because of his schoolboy-like blush.

"Having you and the baby and your parents has made Christmas more enjoyable for me than it has been in a very long time."

"Well, I am sure when Theo was around you enjoyed Christmas."

"We always made Christmas special for Theo when Gus and my mom and dad were still alive. I even tried to keep up the tradition for a while after they were all gone. But after Theo turned fourteen, mostly all he really wanted for any holiday, or his birthday was money. I was glad to have it to give him, but the gift becomes less special for the giver when it's only money."

After wrapping my parent's other presents, I started baking. Theodore pulled out the Almanac, I supposed to cram a few more facts in his head so he could, as he called it, *talk Almanac*, with Mama. The next time I glanced in his direction, the book was lying in his lap, and he was snoring softly. I wasn't surprised since he started his day while the chickens were still snoozing on their roosts.

I planned to make a meatloaf for our meal but the ham that came with the rations would be much more festive. An hour or two in the oven for the ham and another hour for the sweet potatoes would do fine. The remaining side dishes wouldn't take long at all. I followed the recipe line for line for making the jelly cake. If I said so, myself—it was a masterpiece. Next came the cookies.

The house was already near spotless but since dust happens every day, I ran a cloth over every visible surface one more time. On my last pass by the Christmas tree, curiosity got the best of me. I picked up Theodore's mysterious package for a closer look. It was small, made no sound when I shook it, and strangely enough, was unmarked. Maybe it wasn't even for me. Until this package, every gift that wasn't for my parents he said was for us—our family. I assumed we weren't getting for each other. I was glad we weren't. I didn't have money of my own. We planned on getting for the baby after it came; after we knew if it was a prince or a princess. Maybe he got a surprise gift from both of us for the baby that would do for either one. That was probably it—a baby gift.

I dropped the package and pretended to readjust the tinsel when a snort came from the couch. Theodore was only switching positions. My snooping could go undiscovered.

Changing and freshening up these days didn't take long. My clothing selection was reduced to anything that would accommodate a swollen belly. The image in the painfully honest mirror was not kind. I could only hope my hips would narrow down and my waist could be cinched back to near normal once the baby came. After tying my hair back with a red ribbon, I positioned the bow slightly to the side, like the film stars in their movie posters. One thing hadn't changed—my face. The bright ribbon highlighted the youthful glow in my cheeks. Even if my body didn't, my face remained that of a sixteen-year-old.

The sounds of placing plates and silverware on the table and opening and shutting the oven numerous times woke Theodore.

"Umm something sure smells good."

"Sorry if I woke you. But it might be a good thing in case you have any freshening up to do. My parents will be here soon."

"I can't think of a better way to be woke up than with heavenly smells from a kitchen and by a beautiful woman with a red bow in her hair.

You look like Christmas." He smiled.

Chapter Twelve

"**O**H, MY GOODNESS," Mama exclaimed when we gave them their basket of rations.

"We wanted to give it to you tonight in case you had any last-minute baking to do before tomorrow's meal. Uh…I mean… not that you probably don't already have everything done. I mean…you don't have to do anymore baking…" I think Theodore realized it sounded as though he was asking her to do even more cooking for us. He struggled for the right words to smooth over what actually sounded like a hint or a request.

"Oh…my…" Mama dismissed Theodore's blunder as she stroked the silk as though it were a soft kitten.

"Isn't it beautiful, Mama?"

"Lucretia, where did y'all get this? This is no ordinary silk."

"Theodore's friends Wi…"

"I don't know a lot about silk. But Lucretia said you were especially fond of it." Theodore interrupted me before I could disclose his source.

"But…" Mama continued.

"Now, would you ask Santa Claus where he got the

stuff in his sleigh?" Theodore teased.

"No, we wouldn't," Daddy butted it, obviously seeing Theodore's need for discretion.

"This is a Christmas Eve present. We will bring your real gifts tomorrow," I added.

"We appreciate it, but y'all didn't have to go all out like this. We don't have store bought gifts for you. We only have handmade things. And I didn't think to bring anythin' to you tonight. To tell you the truth, I never heard of givin' presents on Christmas Eve. We always did good just to come up with anythin' for Christmas mornin'." She was visibly humbled.

"Mama, anything you would make by hand would be so much more special than store-bought gifts. Besides, you and Daddy have given to me my whole life. If we have it to share, what better time to do it than Christmas."

"But where did y'all get…?"

"Remember," Theodore interrupted by raising a finger as if to caution. "Don't look a Santa Claus in the mouth."

We all laughed.

In the background, the smooth voice of Bing Crosby sang, *White Christmas*. Daddy and Mama inventoried their rations again, while commenting about how one item or another would come in handy. Theodore sat on the couch watching them. My eyes were centered solely on him as I sat across the room. His countenance was glowing. He really couldn't have come up with a more thoughtful or useful gift for my parents. This man I married was a genuinely nice person.

"I'm going to make a pot of coffee. Anyone ready for dessert?" I asked.

"Me. I am ready for that jelly cake. I better eat some soon before I fill up on any more of these delicious cookies," Theodore said, reaching for one last cookie from the plate I had placed on the coffee table.

"Sounds good to me. Yes, siree. These cookies are real tasty. Jelly cake? Emmy, you haven't made a jelly cake in years," Daddy said between bites of his third or fourth cookie. I had lost count.

"I used to make them all the time when we first got married. I guess I just moved on to other kinds of cakes. Yes…Lucretia, your cookies are good."

Mama had only said my cookies were good—not delicious or tasty. But again, with Mama, that was better than had she not said anything. I was glad to have already set the cake down on the table. I might have dropped it when Daddy made that comment about her having made jelly cakes before. Oh well, I guess I was silly to think I could come up with any dessert recipe that was new to her.

"How do you all like this radio-record player? I bought it in Blytheville the other day. If the radio isn't playing what we want to hear, we can find a good record. Also, after the baby comes we can play lullabies anytime it is fretful." Theodore winked. I think he swayed the conversation because he saw my panicked face after Daddy made the cake comment.

"I've been lookin' at that thing. Emmy, we need one of these. I could hear the ballgames real good on a contraption like this."

"The way things are right now. I don't know what we'll look like when we get to where we can afford somethin' like that," Mama scoffed.

"Yer right, Emmy. Guess my radio will have to do. It usually don't take too long for the static to work out of it. That sure looks good, Lucretia," Daddy said as I served him his coffee and cake.

"I know you all wouldn't have any way to know it, but Theodore could sing lullabies to the baby himself. This will shock you. But he was a vaudeville performer along with his family."

"You mean yer one of THEM Daltons? The Dalton Bunch I heard 'em talkin' about down at the Big Store?" Daddy was surprised.

"Yer the Dalton with the tent show? The one who puts on all 'em movies?" Mama was amazed.

"Yes, that is Theodore," I was pleased to say.

"Will wonders never cease?" Mama remarked.

"If that don't beat all," Daddy exclaimed while slapping his knee.

"Theodore told me all about it the evening we were decorating for Christmas. He's traveled everywhere, it seems. See that gold star on top of the tree? His mother bought that in New Orleans when he was just a child. Isn't it beautiful?" I was so glad to share Theodore's story with them.

"It shines like real gold," Daddy observed.

"It is genuine gold. My father used to lift me to place it on our tree every year. I lifted my son, Theo, so he could do the same. And I will see that our child will carry on the tradition," Theodore said.

"Isn't that sweet?" I smiled.

"Now, the star can have two meanings. Because it is gold, it can also signify Theo's sacrifice in service. People usually hang a gold star in the window to honor a son who died in combat. I just haven't gotten a star to hang there yet," Theodore glanced over at me, I suppose to get my reaction.

"We're sorry you lost your son. The death of a child is probably the deepest stab in the heart that a parent can suffer," Daddy said.

"I heard Gracie Thurman tellin' the ladies at church last Sunday that she was going home to put a gold star over the blue one she had in her window. Her son got killed in combat too. Did you get a blue star when yer son went to war?" Mama asked.

"Yes, his blue star is in my bedroom window."

Daddy looked at Theodore, then Mama, then me, but didn't speak. I was sure he had questions about Theodore having his own bedroom. I was also sure she would fill him in later.

"Why aint it hangin' here in yer front room?" Mama asked.

"I don't know. I guess I just wanted his star close to me."

"You can keep it in your bedroom if you want, Theodore. But if you didn't put it in the front window because you thought it would make me sad, then don't worry about that. It won't bother me to have Theo's star there. If it is in the front window, we can both feel close to him."

"I didn't want to bring anymore sadness on you than you already have," he said softly.

Mama broke the silence of our solemn moment. "We better get on home, Asa. I want to get an early start in the morning."

"It's not late yet. You all don't have to rush off. We have several more records to listen to."

"Lucretia, your Mama's right. Besides, I was listenin' to our radio before we came. They're callin' for some weather to hit us later on tonight."

"The Farmer's Almanac also gives it a slight chance," Theodore happily announced.

"So, you follow the Almanac too? So do we. There is very little I decide on without checking it first. Do you know if you get your hair cut in the dark of the moon it won't grow back as fast?" Mama added.

"Yes, I do. As a matter of fact, I remember just

reading that today." Theodore was clearly proud of himself.

"Okay, Daddy. If you must go. But let me give you these cookies I made for you all to take home."

"Thank you, Theodore for our basket of rations. That was mighty thoughtful of you," Mama said. I thought for a moment she was actually going to hug him but patted his shoulder instead.

"You are welcome. May this be the first of many Christmas Eve's we share as a family." Theodore reciprocated the pat on her shoulder before reaching to shake Daddy's hand.

"We'll see y'all tomorrow around four o'clock?"

"We will be there for sure, Miss Emmy," Theodore replied.

I was stunned when Mama pulled me close for what was almost an embrace. "Next time, try grape jelly and sprinkle a few crushed pecans on top. Your jelly cake will be even better. But…but your strawberry jelly cake was delicious too," she whispered in my ear.

"Thank you, Mama. I will try that next time." I whispered back.

"Wait. Let me get the broom to sweep the steps. It is starting to snow," Theodore cautioned.

"Guess you're not leaving too soon after all. It's not bad yet but be extra careful going home. See you tomorrow. Merry Christmas." I hated for them to have to drive in it, but I couldn't be happier that it was snowing, and Mama had said my cake was delicious. She complimented my cooking, and we would have a White Christmas like the one Bing Crosby sang about. I almost couldn't believe my ears or my eyes.

While Theodore walked my parents to their car, I gathered the dishes and put them in a pan to wash them with the breakfast dishes in the morning.

"You got your wish," he remarked while stomping the snow off his feet before coming back inside.

"It has made this Christmas absolutely perfect," I exclaimed.

He picked up the small box he had placed under the tree earlier and asked me to join him on the couch. "I have a Christmas Eve gift for you too."

"I didn't think we were going to get gifts for one another. You know I don't have any money of my…"

"Okay, we won't call this a gift just for you. It is for me too."

I was stunned for the second time that night when I opened the box. I had never seen such a brilliant ring in my life. He smiled before gently sliding the ring next to the gold band he had placed on my finger on our wedding day.

"I didn't have time to buy you an engagement ring before we were married so I'm giving you one now. You don't have to think of this as a gift but as what you should have had all along. A plain band is not right for you. Lucretia, there is nothing plain about you. You're beautiful and you deserve a ring that is beautiful too."

"I don't know what to say. I have never seen anything so grand. Thank you…thank you."

I raised my hand to eye level for a closer view of its brilliance. The Christmas tree lights reflecting in each diamond made it even more radiant. Theodore stared at me as I watched it sparkle as a child would if playing with a snow globe. Without saying a word, he took my hand in his and kissed the ring. Then kissed my forehead. Unlike the kiss on my forehead the day we were married, his lips lingered for a time.

"Merry Christmas, Lucretia…I…um…goodnight." He swallowed hard. His voice was raspy.

"Merry Christmas, Theodore. Goodnight to you too," I whispered softly. He squeezed my hand gently before releasing it.

I COULD STILL feel Theodore's lips touching my forehead and the squeeze to my hand as I lay wrapped tightly inside my warm quilt. The only other man that had kissed me so tenderly was Theo. I tried hard to remember what Theo's lips touching mine felt like, but I couldn't.

Why?

Chapter Thirteen

"**Y**'ALL GOT HERE just in time. The chicken n dumplins' are done and the dressin' is 'bout ready to take out of the oven. Lucretia, you want to set the table?" Mama said as soon as we arrived.

"Your kitchen smells heavenly as usual, Mama."

"Yes, it does. We come bearing gifts. Where would you like them?" Theodore asked.

"Go on and put 'em in there under the tree. Asa, you, and Theodore can sit in the living room 'til me and Lucretia get the table ready, if you want to."

Daddy looked a bit shocked to be invited to sit in the living room but happily obliged. He and Theodore arranged the presents under the tiny, artificial tree, decorated with the same lights and ornaments, which sat in the exact corner of the room for every Christmas I could remember. However, it looked and felt different to me now that I was no longer a child and had a house and tree of my own.

"I'm gonna save that ham y'all got us for another meal since I'd already been fattin' up this hen for a good long while now. Can you make a place for this pan of dressin' real quick, Lucretia?"

"You won't hear us complaining, Mama. I don't know anyone who can make better chicken and dumplings than you. You'll need to tell me your secret someday."

"I will. But you have turned into a pretty good cook these days, yourself." I was glad to have been already sitting down, upon hearing her compliment my cooking like that.

"I still have a long way to go to match you, Mama. I will always need your help."

She stood still for a second. Her smile was all I needed.

"You men hungry in there?" she asked redirecting the focus.

This time, in addition to asking God to bless the hands that prepared our meal, Daddy asked for a special blessing on Theodore, me, and our baby. It was such a sweet prayer.

My heart swelled.

"I think I'm going to have to let this wonderful meal settle a while before I can tackle any of your delicious desserts." Theodore patted his stomach and pushed back a bit from the table.

"Me too. Emmy, you outdid yerself," Daddy said giving his belly a similar pat.

"Guess we can open our presents now," Mama suggested.

"Sounds good to me," Daddy agreed.

"Lucretia, you want to give out the gifts like you have always done?" Mama asked.

Before I could oblige her, Theodore sprang into action. "Why don't I do the honors this year since you may have a little trouble bending down these days."

"That would be nice." I was glad to break tradition. My bulging belly had become more of a problem now that I was a full seven months.

"Daddy, you start. Go on, open your gifts first."

"Y'all didn't have to get me anything else. The boots was …look here Emmy, they got me a couple of nice work shirts and some good warm socks. Y'all knew just what I needed."

"There's another one there to open, Daddy."

"My, my," he exclaimed as he unwrapped a new pipe and pack of Captain Black Original pipe tobacco.

"I told Theodore that was your favorite brand of tobacco."

"That kind don't smell up the porch as bad as some of 'em other brands he smokes sometimes. 'Course, tobacca is tobacca. Aint much you can do to flower it up. But if he's gotta do it. That's the one to have," Mama spouted.

Daddy quietly examined each of his gifts for a second time before stacking them neatly beside him, never responding, but ignoring her comments completely.

"Okay, Miss Emmy. It's your turn," Theodore directed.

"I love these sweet, lacey, handkerchiefs. Lucretia, I know you had a hand in picking these out for me. And I'm so glad to get all this yarn. I have in mind to make a lot of things for the baby."

"I didn't wrap this one, Miss Emmy. I got both of us one for next year," Theodore said, handing her a new 1944 Farmer's Almanac.

"Oh, good. I was sure going to be gettin' one on my next run to town."

"Well, I just saved you a trip." Theodore smiled.

"Mama, here's one more present," I said handing her a small package.

"What could this be? I can't think of another thing I could need."

Her expression was one of surprise mixed with pleasure as she unwrapped two new combs for her hair. "I've never seen you wear decorative combs like these. I think they would look so nice on you."

"Now Lucretia, you know I've never been one to wear fancy things."

"They are not fancy, Mama. They are elegant. There is nothing wrong with elegant," I argued while removing the plain brown combs and replacing them with the new, carved, sparkled, ivory ones.

"You look like a young girl, Emmy. Like you did on our weddin' day," Daddy said.

"I wouldn't go that far. But they're real pretty. And they sure do sparkle."

"They are beautiful. Mama, you are beautiful."

"Okay, enough about me. Let's do your gifts now." Having never been comfortable under a spotlight, she was anxious to move swiftly on.

"Lucretia, go on and open yours."

I wasn't sure I ever wanted Mama to see the patchwork baby quilt I made, after seeing the delicate stitching on the creation before me. Of all the quilts I had seen her make, to say the others paled in comparison was a vast understatement. I was confident my baby would feel the love woven into each stitch with its first swaddling. An overwhelming warmth of renewed unity swept over me, confirmed as the tiny life within me leaped. I knew Mama felt the unity too, by her lack of resistance to my impromptu embrace. Her eyes welled with tears, though she tried to will them away.

"I crocheted it a hat and booties to match too. I made 'em white for now. I plan to make a lot more things after it comes and we know if it is a boy or girl."

"We feel like we're having a girl. But time will tell," Theodore added cautiously.

"Now, it's your turn. We didn't know what to get you since we didn't know what you like or needed. But Emmy started on this as soon as we got home last night. Hope you like it."

"It's a gold star to put over the blue one you already have for your son." Mama blurted before Theodore got her gift completely unwrapped.

"Miss Emmy, you couldn't have made me a better gift. Thank you. I will be sure to put it in its place of honor as soon as possible."

"I didn't try to wrap this gift I have for you. It just didn't seem to be the kind a thing you wrap. But I noticed the last time we were at yer house that you were a little light on tools. I've collected enough over the years that I can share mine with you and never miss a wrench. To my way of thinkin' a man needs his tools." Daddy pulled a worn box from behind the tree and opened it proudly to display a generous collection of used tools. "Aint none of 'em new but sometimes tools just work better after they been broke in a bit anyways," he added.

"Your right, Asa. Now, I may have to get you to show me what some of these are for and how they work." Theodore held up an unusual looking wrench. He was visibly touched by my dad's willingness to share his prize tool collection with him.

"Be glad to—anytime." Daddy smiled.

"Okay. Anybody ready for some coconut cake or pecan pie?" Mama offered.

"I'll have a smidgen of both if that's alright with you," Daddy stood to follow Mama and me into the kitchen.

"Me too," Theodore echoed, trailing close behind.

"I don't think anyone in Muddy Ox or for that matter, any of the surrounding towns can make a pecan pie like Mama's," I bragged.

"Well, pile it on and I'll be the judge of that," Theodore said.

I couldn't believe how quickly things had changed in just seven months. Sitting around the table with my parents, enjoying Mama's extraordinary desserts, and having adult conversation was exhilarating.

"Theodore, want to step outside with me while I have a draw or two on my new pipe and try out that tobacca?"

"Sure. Okay." I knew standing outside in the cold and smelling pipe tobacco, was the last thing Theodore would have wanted to do. But I also figured he was not about to pass up some male bonding with my father.

"Now, Asa, I know that's some good tobacca, but you make sure you get far enough away from the door that none of it don't drift back in here. You don't want to be spending next Monday helpin' me wash and rehang all these curtains."

Mama was serious and Daddy knew it.

"We'll go out under the willow tree. Is that far enough?"

"That'll do," Mama conceded.

"I remember the times Billie Kay and I spent out under that old tree studying for tests and talking girl talk," I said.

"She was another one I wanted far away from the house. That girl's shoes were most always muddy. If they weren't muddy, they were just plain dirty."

There was the Mama I remembered.

But I knew now that all I had to do was ask for her advice or help, and the Mama I had grown to like better reappeared.

Instead, I took a chance on bringing up Daddy's reaction to her new combs. "Mama, I can't recall ever hearing Daddy use such words of endearment to you. That was so sweet."

"I know it's hard to imagine, but your daddy and me was young once. Believe it or not, he used to be a real sweet talker."

"Really. Tell me about your wedding day. I don't remember ever hearing about it before."

"Me and your Daddy was just kids when we got married. I was sixteen and he was only seventeen. My daddy never liked Asa. Said he was too green around the gills to be a husband to anybody, much less me. He never said it in so many words, but I was his favorite, bein' the baby girl and all."

"Did Grandma like him?"

"I'm not sure if it was a matter of like or dislike but she knew I was smitten head over heels with Asa. She convinced my daddy to give in for us to be married if he liked him or not.

"Mommy made me a long, white, taffeta dress with a big skirt. It was purdy fancy for back in those days. But again, I was their baby girl."

"I bet it was beautiful. I love taffeta."

"Daddy walked me up to where Asa and the preacher was standin' and then went and sit down next to Mommy. I was so nervous the whole time the preacher was talkin' that I wadded my dress up in my hands and didn't even know it. There I was, in front of everybody, with my petticoat a showin' clear up to my waist. Mommy finally caught my eye and motioned to let me know what I was doin.' When I dropped my dress, Asa grabbed my hand and slapped a ring on it. The preacher pronounced us husband and wife. When I walked back down the aisle, the whole front of my skirt was a wrinkled mess. You can be sure, people talked about that weddin' for many years after."

Mama threw her head back and laughed like I had never seen her laugh before. I couldn't help but wonder why this was the first time she had ever shared that story with me.

"YOU WEREN'T EXAGGERATING. I've had a lot of pecan pies. But your mother's is the best I've ever had," Theodore said once we were in the car and on our way home.

"She made sure I had her recipe before we left. I'll

try my hand at making one soon."

"Between you and your Mama, you two are going to fatten me up."

"I've always heard that the way to a man's heart is through his stomach."

"I think you know you've already found your way to my heart, Lucretia."

If I wasn't completely certain, after glancing down at the ring on my finger, I knew I was well on my way.

Chapter Fourteen

THEODORE ARRANGED HIS box of tools under our tree when we got home, which I imagined was an attempt to extend the Christmas magic a little longer.

"I was reminded about the Bible story of the widow's mite my mother read to me as a child. Those two small coins were all that poor woman had. But she gave them anyway. And those tools were all your father had to give. But he was willing to share a portion of his all with me as a Christmas gift. I can't think of any costly, brand new, tool I could buy that would mean more to me than the rustiest old wrench in that box Asa gave me today."

"He never had a son to pass anything like that on to. It's clear he thinks a lot of you."

"I'm a little old to be his son."

"I think it doesn't have anything to do with age. It's about your being my husband and a father to our baby."

"Well, I've grown pretty fond of him too."

After fitting the pie and cake Mama sent home with us into our already packed refrigerator, I laid the blanket and other things in the nursery on my way to bed.

It had been a good last two days, I thought while

snuggling inside my covers. I almost felt a childlike giddiness about the holidays. I had always loved Christmas and everything about it. At the same time, I felt a little deflated that now the only thing left to celebrate before the harsh cold of January and February arrived, was New Year's Eve. I would have to ask Theodore how his family usually saw the old year out and welcomed the new year in.

We always stayed up until midnight and went out on the porch to bang pots and pans after Daddy shot the gun in the air a few times. Then, we yelled Happy New Year to our neighbors and waited for them to yell back.

A thrill of excitement mixed with fear hit me. The baby was due to arrive the last part of February. A part of me couldn't wait to meet the little life I had come to know as a kick and a wiggle—sometimes a pain. The fear was because of my lack of confidence at being a mother. Suddenly, Mama's words came into my head, *"Don't worry about how yer gonna' take care of that baby. It just comes natural to us women. The good Lord took care of that too. It's called mother's instinct."*

"I'm counting on that promise, Mama," I whispered to myself before drifting off to sleep.

WHILE I CLEARED the breakfast dishes the next morning, Theodore moved Theo's star to the living room window. Then he carefully covered it with the gold one Mama had made for him.

"I'm glad you put that in here for both of us to see. Also, no one else was going to see it in your bedroom. People need to know the sacrifice he made for us and our country."

We were still standing quietly gazing at Theo's stars when there was a knock on the door.

"Miss Emmy, Asa, you all come in out of the cold. What brings you out so early this morning?"

"I wanted to bring y'all some of this chickin' n dumplins' so you don't have to cook for supper tonight. Lord knows we had plenty of it left over. I don't know why I didn't think of it last night. Guess I was just makin' sure you left with those desserts. It was clear to see how much you loved 'em."

Neither needed a second invitation to come inside. The temperature had dropped considerably over night. The brutal Bootheel winter was once again living up to its reputation.

"You and Daddy came all the way over here in this cold weather, just to bring us tonight's supper? That was sweet. But you really didn't have to do that."

"I made an extra pie for the Widow Halls. Brought some leftovers for her supper too. Her children have all but forgotten her. It's so sad, especially at the age she is now. And it's even worse, bein' alone and forgotten during the holidays. I thought some good food and a little company might cheer her up a bit."

"Y'all had a hand in helpin' us to cheer her up too. We wouldn't have had the stuff to make her this pie if you hadn't give us them extra rations," Daddy added.

"We're proud that we could help. I'll also pass it on to the guys that got the rations for me. Isn't that what Christmas is about? Neighbors helping neighbors?"

"Theodore knows a lot of people who know a…"

"Ah…let's just say my line of business being in the entertainment world has allowed me to cross paths with a lot of good people," Theodore waded in before I went too deep.

"Well, we can't stay. We want to get back before any more bad weather hits later on, like the Almanac says it's supposed to do."

"Mama you are so thoughtful to do this. And yes, get back home as soon as you can."

Theodore walked them to the car as he had at the end of each of their visits. I thought about how many people at my parents' age would have said their good-deed-doing-days were past. But not them. They found joy in bringing a little happiness to those who had very little to none. I was proud of my Mama and Daddy.

THE BAD WEATHER came just as Mama and her Almanac predicted. We didn't see them again for the rest of the week. We wouldn't have celebrated New Year's Eve with them anyway, the celebrating being at midnight. We might have had dinner with them on New Year's Day had an ice storm not hit. Daddy always said a body might can drive on snow, but no one can drive on ice. Theodore echoed him.

Mama always made us cinnamon rolls to eat at midnight and we had grape juice for toasting the New Year in. I followed tradition. Theodore had a stack of records lined up. But of course, *Auld Lang Syne* was saved for the stroke of midnight.

He said his family shot guns and banged pans too but not until after their midnight dance.

We agreed to mix our traditions and do a little of both.

I had the pans and spoons ready. The grape juice was poured. And his shot gun was loaded. He took me in his arms for our midnight dance as soon as the record began. I was amazed how easy it was to follow his lead. He was an excellent dancer.

We stopped dancing at the stroke of midnight but remained embraced. "I guess I left out the most important part of the tradition," he whispered softly.

"What part was that?" I whispered back.

"The dance partners are supposed to kiss when the clock strikes twelve."

Our stare was never broken.

"Well, if it's tradi…"

He kissed me tenderly before I finished my sentence. We forgot to bang pans, shoot his gun, or yell to the neighbors. I was lost in the music, in his arms and in his kiss. I wanted him to kiss me. I even wanted him to kiss me again.

After that first one, I knew I wanted him to kiss me every night for the rest of my—our lives.

Chapter Fifteen

I SNUGGLED INTO bed and pulled the covers to my chin. As I closed my eyes, I could still feel Theodore's strong embrace, and his warm lips tenderly pressed against mine. If I was to be honest, I knew he was going to kiss me a few seconds into the song. To be more honest, I wanted him to kiss me again after the song was over. Instead, he released me and took a half-step back. His voice was soft and broken as he gently stroked my hair and wished me Happy New Year 1944.

Then he slipped the record into its sleeve, turned off the player, and headed to his room. His respectful restraint proved much about his character, despite my moment of weakness.

Ironically, my thoughts went to Theo. If he could have seen our kiss from somewhere beyond, would it have bothered me if he had?

It did not. Instead of feeling bothered, I finally felt at peace about his passing. Having his star in the window where all could see helped me accept that he was gone and would never return. I imagined it did the same for his father. Theo was no longer hidden away but was now honored openly and honestly. I felt his sanction over mine and Theodore's decision to make a life for our baby—and us too more solid now than ever.

I rolled to my side and struggled to find a comfortable sleep position. As difficult as it was now, what would the next two months be like? Before drifting off, I resolved that not only I could, but I wanted to be a wife to Theodore in every way he needed me to be—when the time was right.

"YOU KNOW WHAT I would like to do?" Theodore asked as he took his place at the kitchen table the next morning.

"No, what?"

"I want to get one more thing for your parents today. I know the holidays are over but as far as I know, there isn't a rule somewhere that gifts can only be given on holidays."

"Theodore, you were more than generous already. They aren't expecting…"

"I know. But didn't you see how Asa's eyes lit up when he saw our radio? If anyone ever needed one of those, he does."

"Wasn't that pretty expen…?"

"No matter. He should have one. The roads will be

clear soon. Want to take a ride with me to Blytheville and see if they have any more like ours? I would really like to do this for them."

"Well, if you insist, but they aren't expecting anything else from us. I'm certain of that."

"I know. But I think it would make us enjoy ours more to know they had one too."

"Okay, if you put it that way. Let me clear the dishes and get ready."

"No rush. I want to do a little organizing in the tool shed. There's a perfect spot out there to put that box of tools Asa gave me. I just have to move some things around. The shed can finally earn its name. It won't just have shovels, leaf rakes and garden hoes in it. It will actually house tools too."

"Daddy was so proud to give those to you."

"No prouder than I was to get them. Happy New Year again," he said, pecking me on the cheek before grabbing his coat and gloves and heading out the door with his box of tools.

The peck on my cheek surprised me. Guess he felt more comfortable taking liberties now. I was glad to see his light mood. I was also thankful not to discuss our kiss from the night before. Maybe his going on so about the tools was his way of avoiding it as well.

It was a good thing we went after the radio when we did. We were able to get the last one in the store. Theodore stopped by Deke McCrady's to ask for his help, since it was so heavy. He wasn't home. But luckily, Larson Strom was pulling into his yard when we passed by his place. He automatically got back into his car and followed us after Theodore explained our situation.

My parents were surprised to see us, more especially when they saw Larson helping Theodore carry in such a large box. Theodore had informed him about the no-shoes-rule of Mama's before we went inside. He didn't look thrilled but obliged. I wasn't sure Mama felt like her demands were met after seeing the crust on his ankles and sockless feet after he slipped out of his shoes. She didn't comment. But from the look on her face, I knew she would be reaching for her mop once we were gone.

"What on earth do you have there?" Daddy asked as he stepped aside to give them access to the living room. Mama's face was now a bright crimson. But she somehow managed to hold her tongue about our helper's appearance.

"Another gift, Lucretia? Why Christmas was last week," Mama's voice was slightly faint as her eyes shifted from Larson's feet to the box and back to his feet.

"Yes, but today is New Year's Day," Theodore said happily.

"So, you give us a Christmas Eve gift, then shower us with more things for Christmas morning, and now you're givin' us a New Year's Eve present too? Well, I never." Daddy chuckled.

"We don't have to consider it a gift. Let's say we wanted you to have it—just because," Theodore said.

"Oh my, Asa. It's one of them fancy radios like they got for themselves," Mama gasped.

"Y'all didn't hafta do this." Daddy sounded shocked but he couldn't hide the broad smile on his face.

"Now, let's not go down that road again. We didn't do it because we have to. We did it because we wanted to. Besides, we can enjoy ours better if we know you're over here cheering on the St. Louis Cardinals at the same time."

"Well, one thing for sure. He's got a smile on his face as big as a wave on a slop bucket." I had heard Mama use that reference before. This time Daddy's smile put perspective to it.

Larson grabbed the empty box and made his way to the door. "You can pitch that in the back of my truck Larson, if you like," Theodore said, handing him some bills while following him out.

"If it's okay with you, I'd like to have it. My mom has more uses for cardboard than you can imagine. She'd be tickled to death to get this big ole' box," Larson grinned.

"Absolutely, you are more than welcome to it," Theodore said.

"Hey, Larson. Do y'all have a radio?" Daddy asked.

"If you can call it that. It's about the size of a shoebox and you caint hear nothin' much on it sometimes for the sound going in and out. Aint nothin' like that thing Mr. Dalton just got y'all."

"If you want it, you can have this one. We won't be needin' it no longer now." Daddy offered him the radio we had listened to since I was a child.

"That'd be nice. Thank you. Mama will never miss The Grand Ole Opry now." He effortlessly picked up the radio, grabbed the box and continued to the door.

"Say hello to Mrs. Strom and tell her Happy New Year for us," Mama yelled to Larson.

"I'll do it Mrs. Bertram. Same to y'all. And thank you again. As for you, Mr. Dalton, you can call on me anytime." Then he was gone.

"That man has one of the sweetest, kindest, most Christian mothers in this whole town. *And the crustiest feet and ankles I ever seen!*" Mama whispered the part about his feet for my ears only. Immediately, her face went back to normal as if saying it to me released a valve of pressure.

She put on a pot of coffee and set some leftover desserts on the table while Theodore set the radio-record player up for Daddy.

Neither of us spoke for a while on our way home. However, Theodore's smile spoke volumes.

"You get more pleasure out of giving things to others than anyone I have ever seen," I broke our silence.

"I loved that smile on Asa's face when he saw that radio. And look what happened. Our gift to your parents went way beyond what we had intended. It provided them the opportunity to also give to Larson and his mother. So, not only did the Strom's get a better radio than they had before; your parents got the pleasure of giving it to them. Our morning trip to Blytheville turned into a trickled-down blessing for all of us. Yes, that makes me feel good."

"Me too."

We rode in silence again for the rest of the way home. I was thankful because of the generosity of this man and the opportunity to be a part of it.

I couldn't think of a better way to start out a new year.

Chapter Sixteen

M AYBE IT WAS because it was such an exceptionally cold winter, but the next two months seemed to drag by. Mama and Daddy braved the elements at least once a week to visit and check on me. To Mama's knowledge, she promised that my pregnancy was normal. But nothing felt normal to me. When I thought surely I was as big as I was going to get, the next time I put on a maternity dress or a pair of shoes, it was all I could do to make them fit. It was especially a struggle to get all of my undergarments on. Mama half-joked one day about bringing me a few pairs of her bloomers and a couple of her brassieres to wear until after the baby came. When she saw I didn't laugh about it, she let it drop.

My usual gait was now a waddle. I had to remove the beautiful rings Theodore got for me because my hands were so swollen. Using her almanac and what she called her 'woman sense,' Mama figured to the day when my baby should be born. By her calculations, I had two weeks and one day to go. Her almanac had never failed her before as far as I knew, so I felt that I somewhat had a sense of knowing. At least that was how I felt in the beginning.

However, during her most recent visit, Mama admitted that truthfully, first time babies were prone to choose their own time of arrival. And sometimes a woman's water broke on its own. And sometimes, it had to be broken. Also, some labor pains started in a woman's back, but others began in their stomachs.

In other words, the only thing I knew for sure was—I didn't know anything for sure.

Theodore left for Kennett soon after breakfast to pick up our rations and a few other things on our list. I was still trying to get comfortable on the couch when there was a knock on the door. Assuming it was Mama, I yelled for her to come on in.

"Hey girl. Do you always tell whoever is at the door to come on in now?" Billie Kay quickly closed the door against the cold February wind.

"Billie Kay. I thought you were Mama. She is supposed to come today."

"I hadn't seen you in months. I lost track as to when the baby was due. But I see you are still hatchin'." If she had known how miserable I felt, she would not have been so free with her jokes.

"According to Mama, I have two more weeks and a day to go."

"Cretia, you are huge! And you look tired and absolutely miserable."

Her honest assessment of my appearance was more

than I could handle. I knew she hadn't intended her words to sound unkind and insensitive but that was exactly what they were.

Had I not already been so emotional and also not been dealing with my unquenchable pains all day, I might could have handled her comments a little better. But instead, my response was an uncontrollable flood of tears and wailing sobs.

"Oh Cretia, I am sorry. I wouldn't hurt you on purpose for anything in this world. I'm just a big mouth."

"No. You are right. I am huge and miserable. And I'm scared Billie Kay. I'm scared. I was counting on everything Mama told me about pregnancy to be the way it was supposed to be. But now, she doesn't sound sure of herself at all. And if Mama isn't sure, how can I be?"

"Cretia, there aint nothin' that can mess you up. You are beautiful and always will be. I don't know much about having babies but I aint never seen a woman that didn't get big during her time. Why, you are the most gorgeous pregnant person I have ever seen. And after that baby comes, you'll be thin again. Really, I am so sorry. Please forgive me. I didn't come here to upset you. I just missed my friend and was hoping to meet that sweet baby of yours."

"I forgive you. Guess I'm just overly emotional today. I sure don't feel pretty. This has been the worst day for me. I can't get comfortable any way I try to sit or lay. You will be smart if you wait a long, long time before you get pregnant. Take my word for it."

"I'm in no hurry. And it has nothing to do with what you just said., I haven't found anyone I want to settle down with or who wants to settle down with me." She laughed.

"You have plenty of time, Billie Kay. No need to worry or rush."

"I'm not—and not planning to. Anyway, I was wondering how you were doing is one reason I came by. Another reason is I'm going to be moving away in a few months. I have a cousin on my daddy's side, who lives in Galveston, Texas. We hit it off real good while they were here visiting for Christmas. She is a year older than me. Anyway, she also dropped out of school and was waitressing for a while. But now she has a good factory job and is going to try to get me on too. I can stay with her until I get a place of my own. It's right near the ocean. I've always wanted to see the ocean. Haven't you?"

"Maybe someday. But right now, I'd settle to see a good night's rest. And to see Theodore. He's supposed to bring me back a bottle of Sloan's Liniment for my back."

"I wondered where that handsome man of yours was."

"He went to Kennett for our rations, groceries, and some liniment for my aches and pains. He is really good to take care of me."

"Hmm. Something is going on, Lucretia. I see the light in your eyes when you speak his name. Come on. Fess up. Have you admitted to yourself yet that you love him?"

"I never could hide anything from you, could I? We haven't said love to each other yet but…"

"But what?"

"I think I do love him. And I'm fairly sure he loves me too."

"And how do you know this if he hasn't said so?"

"I just know." Even though she was my best friend, I didn't want to tell Billie Kay about our New Year's Eve kiss. I wasn't sure why. I guess it was too personal to share. Not even with her.

"I feel like you are holding back with something else but it's okay. I need to run now. I still have to keep up with this job until I get that other one. I'll be back in two weeks and two days. That will give you a day to recover. My bet is your Mama knows her stuff."

"I hope so."

"You just stay where you are. I'll let myself out."

"I'll take you up on that. See you soon. Thanks for coming by."

I wasn't sure I was completely truthful when I said I hoped Mama knew when the baby would come. The thought of waiting two more weeks and a day and feeling so miserable was not a pleasant one.

Billie Kay hadn't been gone for much more than a half hour and I had changed positions at least three times. I was trying to shift hips again when another knock came on the door. Guessing it was surely Mama and Daddy this time. I invited them in.

"Lucretia, you alright? You've never not opened the door for me before."

"Yes, I figured it was y'all. Mama, I am so miserable. I can't make this pain go away no matter how I sit or lay. I've wiggled around so much I'm about to wear a hole in this couch."

Daddy didn't say a word but remained standing by the door.

"How long has this pain been going on?"

"It started early this mornin. But it's getting worse. I must have slept wrong last night or something. I'll be glad when Theodore gets back from town. He's bringing some Sloan's Liniment. Maybe that will help. See, I just got comfortable and here comes another one." I grimaced with pain.

"Where is this pain? And how often are they coming around?" Mama eyed me curiously.

"My lower back. At least every fifteen minutes, maybe ten."

"Tell you what, let's get to the bedroom. Might be good for you to lay down."

Mama was helping me stand when Theodore came through the door, carrying several bags.

"I got your liniment," he announced, grinning from ear to ear.

"I'm afraid she doesn't need liniment as much as she needs Dr. McFarnz. And judging from how often her pains are coming, I wouldn't dawdle if I was you." His huge grin was replaced with terror and concern. Theodore looked at me and then to Mama. She shooed him with her hands. He handed the bags to Daddy and was back out the door.

"Mama. You said by the Almanac, I still had two weeks and…"

"Honey, babies don't always go by the Almanac. Let's get you to bed now."

"Oh no," I moaned. A watery gush ran down my legs and puddled at my feet.

"Don't worry about that. Your water just broke. I'll clean it up after I get you into that bed."

Chapter Seventeen

MAMA HAD TWO kinds of herbal teas for me, in addition to several pans of boiling water and a stack of clean towels for the doctor when he arrived.

"Here Lucretia, sip some of this tea. This 'un will help with the pain and the ginger root will aid in healing after this is over."

"Where is Theodore?" I grunted.

"Your daddy is walking with him outside. He'll be okay. Don't know about all the ruts they're makin' in that yard out there though." Mama chuckled before offering me another sip.

"I don't want him to hear me whining like a baby through this," I gritted through another contraction.

"Don't you be worryin' about him. You just worry about gettin' this baby here," Mama said. Her hand shook while wiping my face with a cool cloth.

"Yer right Miss Emerald. Looks like you've got things under control pretty well up 'til now. But let's see how much farther we have to go here." The doctor added as he arrived and entered the room.

"Glad yer here Doctor. Her pains are getting more active now. Said they started sometime before daybreak this mornin.' I got plenty of water boilin' and a stack of towels handy when you need 'em."

"Well, Emerald, don't think there's a need for us to get too impatient right now. This baby doesn't look like it is in a hurry to make an appearance any time soon," the doctor said after his examination.

I, not knowing exactly what to expect, didn't grasp the true meaning of his advising us not to get impatient. If what I was experiencing was called labor, I felt like I had already done a day's work. Surely, I had earned having this baby soon, if not sooner.

However, the discomfort I had complained about before, was mild compared to the *real* pains I bore through the night. My utterings were no longer whines but were full-blown screams before it was over. At that point, I didn't care if Theodore, Daddy or even the neighbors heard my cries. I had lost all track of time and couldn't see any near end to my agony.

Finally, hope arrived from the words of the doctor in the early hours of the next day.

"Okay Lucretia, I know you are worn out, but we are almost there. Just give me one more big push," the doctor directed.

Mama had stopped trying to administer tea, rub me with liniment or do anything else for me by that time. Instead, she gave me a rolled washcloth to bite down on—and prayed.

"It's over, Lucretia. She's here," the doctor exclaimed.

I fell back on the pillow from sheer exhaustion and sobbed as he laid my baby girl across my chest, then wiped his own brow.

"Theodore said the entire time, he felt as though we were having a girl." My words were barely audible.

"I'll go get him now so he can see the baby." Mama was beside herself with joy and undoubtedly relief.

Theodore came and stood by my bed. His hair a tousled mess, shirt untucked, and his face looked drawn from worry and lack of sleep, a stark contrast to his usual neat appearance.

"Thank you, doctor. We have our little princess, Lucretia. You did good," Theodore whispered and kissed my forehead.

"You and Mama said the whole time it was going to be a girl. I was secretly hoping it would be."

"She is everything we hoped for. She has a head full of dark hair and is beautiful just like her mother." Tears were now trailing off Theodore's chin.

"I am so tired," I sighed weakly.

"You get some rest now. I'll be right in the next room if you need me. *I love you*," he whispered in my ear before leaving my side.

I'm not sure how long I slept. But I woke to the sound of muffled voices in the other room. The baby was swaddled and laying in her cradle beside my bed.

"You really are a beautiful baby," I whispered as she

cooed sweetly. The dark hair on her little round head, framed her face perfectly. "Theodore is right. You have my oval face and button nose. But that dimple on your chin is one hundred percent—Theo's."

How sweet.

She whimpered. I touched the cradle lightly to set it in motion. The rocking soothed her, and she was still once more. I marveled how her tiny mouth puckered when she fretted. There was no denying. I was in love. I now knew exactly how love at first sight felt.

"I thought I heard something," Theodore tip-toed back into the room.

"She whimpered but quieted as soon as the cradle began to rock."

"That cradle was a perfect choice. Don't you think?" He smiled.

Remembering the challenge we had given the store clerk while trying to make our selection and how later that night Theodore had painstakingly put it together as I read him the directions, brought a smile to me also.

"Yes I do. And I think she would agree too, by the way she went right to sleep when it rocked her, that is if she could talk."

"What should we name our princess?" Theodore asked brushing his finger across her pudgy cheek.

"I was thinking about that before you came. While cleaning before my parent's first visit, a book caught my eye as I was dusting the bookcase in the living room.

Since that day, I've read it twice, some parts of it three times."

"Which of my books was that compelling?" he questioned.

"*Gone With the Wind*. I got lost in it. The characters came alive to me each time I read it. I would like to name our little girl, Scarlett—Scarlett Estella Dalton. That is, if it is okay with you. Estella is my mother's middle name."

"That is beautiful. And I like that we will be naming her after your mother."

"By the way, what was your mother's name? You have never said." I immediately felt a little selfish not to consider any of his family's names.

"Her name was Annella Coleen. Everyone called her Annie." A softness swept across his face at the mention of his mother.

"Well, I promise. If we have another little girl. We will name her after your mother."

I spoke before I thought. Theodore turned quickly and met my eyes. By his expression, I was sure my face was ghostly white.

"Uh…I mean…uh…" I stammered.

"I think nothing would please my mother more than to have one of our daughters, should we have another one, be named for her," he agreed quickly to mask my awkward moment.

Immediately, little Scarlett didn't just whimper, she

cried. We turned together to attend to her but before either of us could decide what to do, Mama arrived and sprang to action.

"I've just been hopin' that baby would make a noise so I would have an excuse to pick her up," Mama gushed as she scurried to the cradle.

"Did I hear our granddaughter call for her grand-pappy?" Daddy peered around the bedroom door.

"I bet she needs changin.' Asa, I'll bring her in there to do it. After that, you can get a good look at her. Lucretia, you just stay put. I'll clean her up and bring her right back to you. Oh, you sweet little angel. My goodness, Asa, she's the spittin' image of Lucretia when she was born."

Mama swept up the baby before either of us could say a word. I hadn't realized my dad hadn't seen her yet. She was going to be one loved little girl—no doubt.

"What's her name gonna be, Lucretia?" Daddy asked.

Theodore looked at me and said, "Scarlett Estella Dalton."

After hearing she had a namesake, this time, it was Mama who had the slop-bucket-smile.

Chapter Eighteen

"I TALKED IT over with yer Daddy and I am going to stay and help you for a few days."

"That's sweet of you, Mama, but won't Daddy need..."

"Yer Daddy is a grown man. He can fend for himself for a little while anyway. Besides, he'll be back over here every day as soon as he gets his chores done to eat and then gush over that baby."

"I didn't want to ask you, but I will be glad for you to be here until I get used to taking care of her. Neither Theodore nor I knew what to do when she cried earlier."

"Oh, don't you worry 'bout that. Instincts will kick in before you know it. But it's not just my idea to stay and help you for a while. Doc McFarnz suggested it before he left. You had a rough time birthin' that baby. He said he was afraid he was going to have to take her cesarean if she hadn't come when she did. Said if she had been any bigger, he would have had to a done it fer sure. It might take you a little longer than usual to bounce back from this."

"Is that normal? Is having a baby always that bad?"

"You're young for one thing. This was your first baby for another. It's never easy, but some births are just rougher. You'll be okay. And like I told you before, the pain of it all sorta fades away after a while."

Scarlett whimpered.

"I bet that little girl is hungry. You ready to try yer hand at nursin' now?"

Nursing was harder than I had imagined. And it also hurt, at least at first. It was nothing compared to giving birth but was hurtful, nonetheless. When I asked Mama if everything about babies was painful, she just said, "This too shall pass."

And it did.

AFTER EIGHT DAYS of her mentoring, I felt more comfortable with most duties having to do with mothering. As she had promised, everything I had gone through was overshadowed by the joys of our baby.

"Alrighty now. I've got y'all several meals cooked up and ready for you in the refrigerator. All either of you will have to do is warm 'em up."

"Emerald, I don't know what we would have done without you," Theodore patted Mama's shoulder on her way to the door.

"I was glad to do it. And it ain't like Muddy Ox is a long way from Bragg City. I can be here lickety-split again if you need me."

"If little Scarlett gets to frettin' and you can't get her calmed down no other way, you just lay her flat on your lap and bump your knees up and down real easy. She loves that. 'Course, she's a little spoiled to havin' her Grandpappy do it, but you'll get the hang of it after a while," Daddy said smugly as he held the door for Mama.

"I'll do my best to copy your technique if I can, Asa." Theodore laughed.

Mama made sure I was positioned comfortably on the couch and rolled the cradle into the living room for easy access. She and Daddy had kissed the baby's cheeks several times and both looked at her longingly before leaving.

"You think we can do it on our own?" I couldn't hide my uncertainty once they had gone. The lines across my brows said it all.

"We will figure it out. It's been several years since I had to deal with a baby but I'm sure most of it will come back to me."

"But Theo's mother was older than me when he was born." Tears rolled like they had several times already and it was only a little past noon.

"Her age didn't matter. She had never given birth before either. And she didn't have an expert such as your mother to show her how and what to do. We can do this. I have no doubt." Theodore dropped beside me and patted my hand. His voice soothing and assuring.

Mama labeled my frequent burst of tears as '*baby blues*.' Maybe it was. But I was experiencing all sorts of unexplained emotions. Again, Mama said it was all normal. Seemed normal was her answer to all my questions. The prolonged recovery and the pains were normal. The tearful outbursts were normal. My insecurities about being able to take care of my baby were—normal. All I knew was I couldn't control any of it and it appeared without notice. Normal was nowhere near how I felt at the moment.

Scarlett wiggled and stretched her feet out of the blanket. She opened and closed her eyes a couple of times and pouted her lower lip. Her dimpled chin quivered as she formed another pout.

"She has Theo's dimple in her chin," Theodore said softly.

"Yes, she does." Tears brimmed my eyes once more.

"I'm glad. He would be so proud." I could tell he was also fighting tears.

"It's okay. Don't hold back for me. I understand." I laid my hand on his.

"I think I'm feeling sadness and joy at the same time, if that is possible." His voice quivered.

"I noticed the dimple in her chin and felt the same

way right after she was born," I admitted.

"We haven't talked about this before, but I think we must. I will be her father as far as she knows, but when she is old enough to understand, don't you think we should tell her about Theo?"

"Yes, I believe we should—but only when we are certain she is old enough to understand."

"Good. I am glad we have the same idea about that. I think it will only be fair to her and to Theo to know the truth one day."

"So do I." He looked as though there was a great weight lifted from his shoulders. I felt at rest about it too.

No sooner had we come to our meeting of the minds than there was a knock on the door.

I laughed. "I bet Mama forgot to tell us something."

Theodore opened the door expecting to see my parents again but welcomed Billie Kay instead.

"Come in."

"Hello. I wanted to come and see Cretia and the baby. By her Mama's predictions, she should be at least a day old by now," Billie Kay began as soon as she stepped inside the door.

"Mama was a little off on her calculations. She is actually eight days old today," I said.

"Your Mama was off by that much? I am shocked. What did she do, read her almanac wrong?"

"No, our little girl decided for herself when to be

born." I laughed.

"Can I get you a glass of tea or something," Theodore offered.

"Yes, thank you," Billie Kay replied.

"Oh Cretia, this baby is beautiful. I felt like you were going to have a girl."

"So, Billie Kay, have you started predicting too?"

"No, but I could just see you with a little girl for some reason."

Theodore handed her a glass of tea and sat back down.

"Lucretia and I always felt like the baby would be a girl," he said.

"Mama wasn't wrong about that part," I added.

"What did you name her?"

"Scarlett—Scarlett Estella Dalton," I said.

"Scarlett. Like in Scarlett O'Hara in *Gone With The Wind*?" Billie Kay asked.

"You read the book too?" I was a little shocked.

"No, not me. I thought you knew me better than that. I was never much of a book reader. I saw the movie with…can't remember his name now. But he didn't look like Rhett Butler. That's for sure."

I was going to be surprised if she had read a book that long. She had to make herself read the chapter assigned to us in school before we quit. I got lost in that thought for a minute. It seemed like a lifetime ago that we were in school together. Actually, it was in a way.

I'm married with a baby and Billie Kay is moving four states away to Texas.

We may never even see one another again.

"…was it Cretia? Cretia, was it?"

"Was it what?" I asked, after being jolted back to the present.

"Was having a baby just the most awful, hardest thing you ever done in your life? I can't even imagine."

I looked at Scarlett laying so sweetly in her cradle and then to Theodore, who was waiting to hear my response along with Billie Kay.

"Yes, it was hard. At least while she was being born. Doctor McFarnz recorded her weighing 7 lbs. 13oz. and she was eighteen inches long."

"Goood grief, Lucretia. I don't even want to think about that!"

"It's okay. Because seeing her in that cradle is like looking at a miracle. Now, how she got here doesn't matter any longer.

Mama said that would happen."

THEODORE EXCUSED HIMSELF. He said Mama had laid out some kitchen duties for him. I knew he was trying to give Billie Kay and me some time alone.

She finally gathered enough nerve to hold Scarlett. "She looks just like you, except for that dimple in her chin. You have a real-life baby doll. Oh, Cretia, this is awful. I won't be around to watch her grow up."

"Yes, except this doll cries and wets for real. I know. I was thinking about that earlier. I wish you weren't moving so far away."

"Me too. But if you ever done any waitressing yourself, it wouldn't take you long to realize you didn't want to make a career out of it. Remember how we used to say we didn't want to work in the cotton patch all of our lives? Well, I don't want to be a waitress the rest of my life either.

"There aren't any real good jobs around here, unless you become a schoolteacher or something. And you know I'm not smart enough for that."

"You're smart. Remember how well we always did on tests after we studied together?"

"Yes, but I couldn't have done it without you. And look at you. You've married a nice man. You have a beautiful baby. I love this place y'all have here. Our lives are different now, for sure. Besides, it didn't take me long after we quit school to realize how much I hated it. I don't see going back to school, let alone going to college in my future—ever."

"But…"

"Cretia, tell me where there's a factory anywhere around here. It's settled. My mind is made up. I'll miss you something awful, but I'm going."

I recognized the determination in her face after seeing it so many times while we were growing up. There was no talking her out of leaving.

Scarlett let out a squeal and Theodore appeared immediately. He picked her up and laid her on his lap, as my dad had instructed.

"Asa was right. This really works. She doesn't seem to mind at all that it's me instead of him."

"Well, I can't stay, but I wanted to see the baby and bring her a gift. I got stuff for Mama to make her this bonnet and a little blanket to match. And I brought this memory book for you. I pasted some pictures of us inside and wrote a few notes under them, so you won't forget me." Billie Kay frowned.

"Like I ever would. What were you going to give us if we had a boy?"

"Oh, my mother had that covered. She said boy babies wear bonnets too. This bonnet is white. See these little slits here? The blanket has them too. I have a pink ribbon for a girl and blue for a boy. Here's the pink one. All you have to do is weave it in."

"Now that's clever," Theodore said.

"It was my mom's idea. She's made a lot of bonnets and blankets for babies. And no one ever knows if they're having a boy or girl. Little Scarlett is proof that Almanacs and wives' tales can be wrong." Billie Kay smiled.

"I'll make sure Scarlett knows where her bonnet and blanket came from when she is old enough to understand. And I'll show her Aunt BeeKay's picture and tell her all about us."

"Maybe not ALL about us." Her eyebrows raised in question.

Theodore laughed. We all did.

"I really have to go now." Billie Kay hugged me and kissed Scarlett several time before standing to leave. Theodore followed her to the door. She offered her hand to him, but he hugged her instead.

"Lucretia's best friend and Scarlett's aunt should be hugged, don't you think?"

"Yes, I do. I really like him Cretia. And I love our little Scarlett. I got to get out of here before I start blubbering."

I watched her drive out of sight. It was strange that less than a year before, our lives were so similar. Now, she is turning one direction at our crossroads, and I am going in another. I can only wish that after she moves away, our paths will join again one day.

"Where did she say she was going—Texas? Theodore asked as he rejoined me on the couch.

"Yes, she is moving there to live with a cousin. I hope that works out for her too. They only met for the first time over Christmas. I hate to see her working in a factory."

Many do quite well in factories. Higher education

isn't for everyone. But while we are on that subject, after the baby gets older, if you want to go back to school, I am all for that."

"I haven't thought that far ahead. But I don't like saying I dropped out of school. And I sure want more for our children."

Theodore started to speak but was distracted by the sound of footsteps on the porch.

"Are you expecting someone else today?"

Chapter Nineteen

THEODORE STOOD TO go to the door. I scanned the room thinking perhaps Billie Kay might have forgotten something.

"Oh, hello," Theodore said hesitantly.

"I am Thomas Rankin, Sir. Actually, Private First-Class Thomas Rankin of the United States Army, Sir. I am looking for a lady named Lucretia. I went to the address I was given, but her parents said I could find her here."

Theodore opened the door wider to reveal me sitting on the couch.

"I am Lucretia."

"May I come in?" He asked.

Theodore's body language was not welcoming until I nodded in approval. Only then, did he step back and ask the young man to sit.

"You have my address?"

"I was a friend of Theo Dalton, Ma'am. Actually, I was with him the day he…the day…he…died. I have a letter for you. Theo finished it the morning of our attack. He made me promise that if I made it out alive, I would see you got it. I am here today to keep that promise."

I took the letter in my extended hand, unable to speak or move.

Theodore sat beside me and placed his arm around my shoulders.

"Don't mind the smudges, Ma'am. We were in a fox hole when he wrote that last part. I put your hair and picture inside the envelope before I sealed it. But I promise I didn't read one word of that letter out of respect for you and Theo. Actually, this is a private matter. Maybe I should leave now."

"No, stay. Theodore and I don't mind you being here,"

"Yes. Stay. Besides, we'd love to hear more about your time spent with Theo. Lucretia, don't you want to open the letter now?"

After first reading it silently, I handed the letter to Theodore and invited him to read it aloud.

June 15, 1942

My Dearest Lucretia,

I'm sorry this is so short. But I have to grab any chance I can get to write you. Still don't have much time. Sergeant said we're moving out again early in the morning. Says we have a big battle tomorrow. I keep your picture and lock of hair you gave me the day I left inside my coat pocket next to my heart. You are always with me, my love.

June 17, 1942

Miss you, sweet Lucretia. Hope you are okay. I regret we had such a short time together. I'll try to make it up to you when I get back home. Sorry your mom makes you walk such a tightrope. But I'm sure she loves you in her own way. Hey, when I get back, I want you to meet my dad. He's the finest man I've ever known. I know you'll love him, Lucretia. I sure do.

June 18, 1942

I will try and finish this letter now. Things getting worse here. This war sure is ugly. I pray I get to come back to you, but if I don't, I want you to make your life count. Live it to the fullest. Be happy. Remember me. Remember us. But find happiness when and wherever you can find it. Promise me you will.

Okay, got to get some shut eye now. Our work

is cut out for us tomorrow. Said it's the biggest battle yet. Will write more when I can.

I Love you,

Theo

"I know you'll love him…I sure…do," Theodore repeated tearfully.

He folded the letter, handed it back to me and gripped Private Rankin's shoulder.

"Thank you for being such a good friend to my son and for keeping the promise you made to him. It means so much for me…us…to have this letter."

"Your Theo's dad? I didn't know. I'm sorry Sir. Theo talked about you two all the time. Every man in our troop felt as though we knew you and Miss Lucretia personally. Your son was a fine man and a brave and courageous soldier, Sir. It was a privilege to get to serve with him. Asking me to keep this promise were his last words."

"I appreciate you searching for me. And I am so glad you found me." I assured him.

"I am too. For some reason, I just felt like that was Theo's Gold Star hanging in your window. But rest assured, Ma'am. If I hadn't found you today, I would be looking for you for the rest of my life. I thought that much of my friend."

Scarlett whimpered and kicked her covers. Obviously, Private Rankin hadn't noticed her until then. Theodore went into action, doing as my father had instructed. She quieted down almost immediately.

"You have a baby, Ma'am?"

"Meet Scarlett Estella Dalton, eight days old today," Theodore boasted.

Private Rankin looked puzzled as his eyes darted from me, to Theodore, and back to me.

"Theo never knew about the baby. I learned of his death the same day I found out I was pregnant," I clarified.

"Well, how about that? Theo was going to be a dad and didn't know it. He would have been so happy if he had known," the private wiped tears.

"I agree. But I think he'd be even happier, if he knew his little girl will be raised by me and the finest man he ever knew."

My eyes fixed on Theodore as he held Scarlett so lovingly with pride.

"No doubt, Ma'am," the Private agreed.

"Look, she has Theo's dimpled chin." Theodore held the baby upright.

"She sure does. Glad you're stepping in to help, Sir. Theo would love that, I know."

"I'm sure he would too." Theodore smiled.

I made coffee and placed some pastries on the table before taking Scarlett into the bedroom to nurse and change her. After I returned, Theo's comrade was eager to answer our questions and expounded upon some of the good and bad times they had shared. Some stories brought more tears. Others actually made us smile. Theodore even chuckled a couple of times when he heard that a few of his own phrases and terms had been commonly used by his son. More importantly, we found a measure of peace and closure in our time spent with Private Rankin.

We never revealed that we were married. I had removed my wedding rings because my hands were swollen and had yet to replace them. There was no evidence there either. He only needed to know he had kept his promise to his friend. Besides, we weren't the main story that day—Theo was.

Chapter Twenty

MAMA CAME AT least twice during the week. She said it was in case I needed her. But I knew she could hardly keep herself away from Scarlett. It was rare for her to show up emptyhanded. She almost always had a dish of some sort for us or a little something for the baby or both. This morning was no exception.

"Where's Daddy?"

"He'll be back in a jiffy. He dropped me off on his way to the feed mill."

"Okay. What do you have for the baby today?" I laughed.

"Well, today is special for two reasons. Scarlett turns two months old, and it is the first day of May. You know that little beauty needs a flowered headband to wear on May Day." She pulled a pair of crocheted booties and a matching headband, adorned with flowers and ribbons from her bag.

"Oh, Mama. How cute."

"I don't think she has a dress that these won't match," she bragged.

"How could she? You have made her a dress and now booties and a headband with every color of the rainbow."

"She's a lucky little girl to have a grandma that can sew and crochet. Aren't you sweet girl? Let's try this on her head now to see if it fits."

"Mama, you know it will fit. It's crocheted. It stretches."

"I just want to see it on her." She grinned whimsically.

"Yes, sweet Scarlett. You are one lucky baby." I smiled.

"I recall when I was a girl, we celebrated May Day every year. It's sad that people don't carry on traditions like they used to," Mama reminisced.

"I remember you making a May Basket to set on our kitchen table. And in grade school our teacher tied long ribbons to a pole and we each held one and danced around it for fun."

"Back in my day, it seemed to mean a lot more to people. My daddy always planted his turnips on the first day of May. And my mother wouldn't think of lettin' us kids go barefoot in the grass until May first.

"Since May Day is halfway 'tween spring and summer, it was seen as a day to celebrate nature in all its glory. Seeds were sproutin' and most of the flowers and bushes were in full bloom. A lot of courtships were bloomin' out pretty good by then too. Young folks today probably think our old traditions were silly, but a young man who wanted the attention of a certain young lady would make her a basket of pretty, fresh picked, flowers. He'd knock on the door and yell 'May Basket' and run. If she caught him, he was entitled to a kiss. People teased that a courtship in May could lead to a weddin' in June. Courtin' in our days didn't get drug out like it does now."

"Theodore and I sure didn't drag out ours. I only knew him a little over a week."

"Ain't none of my business. But looks to me like yer still draggin' it out. Ain't he still sleepin' in one end of the house and you the other?"

"I meant we got married in less than a week's time."

"You know what I'm sayin." Mama's eyes were wide and set.

"But we…"

"Where is Theodore now anyways?" She interrupted.

"He had to go to Kennett and pick up something. I never asked him what it was. When he gets back, we're going to set up the bed in the nursery. Scarlett is getting too big for her cradle."

"Yer milk must be agreein' with her. That's good."

"It must be. She already sleeps all night."

"Now, that's a good baby. You've turned into a good little mama too."

"You 'bout ready, Emmy? Let me get a peck of sugar from our little beauty here, before we go," Daddy said as he arrived.

"She's a beauty alright. How do you like this May Day headband I made her?"

"Now, aint she just the kitten's foot?" Daddy gushed, kissing Scarlett's forehead.

"Yes, she is. Well, we got to be goin.' Just wanted to drop off that bowl of chicken and dumplins' and those things for Scarlett. Y'all still comin' over tomorrow for Sunday dinner?"

"Yes, would you like for me to bring a dish or something?" I offered.

"You just bring that baby girl. That's enough for yer Daddy and me."

"Okay, see you about four-thirty."

SHE HAD BEEN gone for hours but the sting of Mama's pointed words remained. Even making myself busy with hanging and organizing Scarlett's vast wardrobe didn't help me put them completely aside. I was pleased with our relationship since she had mellowed, and I had become more respectful and appreciative of her. But she was right. Where Theodore and I chose to sleep was not her decision or business.

With that thought, I realized Mama's and my ice-water-and-lard scenario wasn't completely dissolved. My obstinate will refused to budge especially when she pushed too hard. A chill ran down my spine. Deliver me if Scarlett inherited that side of me.

I had just replaced the lid on the beans after giving them another stir when I heard a muffled voice and rap on the door. I slightly cracked the door, not being comfortable with answering it since Scarlett and I were alone.

To my surprise, there was a grinning Theodore with a small basket of flowers swaying on the index finger of his right hand.

"May Basket."

"Aren't you supposed to knock and run? And aren't I supposed to try to catch you?" I teased.

"That's how the legend goes but we haven't followed any other rules so far. Why start now? I figured I would skip all that running and chasing stuff and just stand here and wait for my kiss."

"Oh, you did, did you?"

"Yes, after all, you already caught me."

I smiled, took the basket and he followed me inside. When I turned around, he was poised in front of the closed door. We stood silently face to face for a few seconds, eyes locked. I trembled as his arms tightened around me. His warm and welcoming lips left me weak and tingling. Our second, ever, kiss was slow, tender— and passionate.

"Legend says a May Day kiss can lead to a June

wedding," he said softly while holding his embrace.

"We already had a June wedding," I whispered.

"I know. We seem to never follow the order of things."

We laughed.

Scarlett cried.

"What was I saying about the order of things?" He laughed again and lessened his hold.

"She's either hungry, wet, or both." I said on my way to the cradle.

"I understand. I'm hungry too. Hey, I got something to attach to the side of her crib that she is going to love. I saw it today after I left the flower shop. It's a carrousel with little pink rattles hanging from it. We are still putting her crib together tonight, aren't we?"

"Yes. Actually, Mama brought over a bowl of her chicken and dumplings. Supper shouldn't take long. So, we can get started on the crib sooner."

We engaged in a bit of small talk to break the awkward silence. But I'd wager that neither of us could have remembered any part of our rambling conversation. Our kiss had obviously left us shaken. After supper, Theodore went to the nursery to unbox the crib and lay the parts in order. I joined him once the kitchen was done.

"Want me to read the directions again?"

"Yes. It sure made assembling the cradle go a lot smoother. If it worked the first time, it should work again. I've taken inventory and all the parts are here."

"Okay, step one…"

What should have only taken us a little more than an hour, stretched into over two. Neither of us could stay focused. I'd look up from reading and find him staring at me. After losing my place repeatedly, I had to reread several of the steps. We spent a lot of our time chasing nuts and bolts because he kept dropping them.

"Finally, I got it. Now hand me the rollers for the legs and we'll be done," Theodore announced.

My hand brushed his as I passed him the rollers. He nervously dropped two. We both reached for them and touched again. The tension in the room was heavy—like a thick fog.

"Well, it's finished, but it took longer than I thought. Maybe I should just wait until morning, you know, to attach the carrousel. She can sleep now and play tomorrow."

"It really is getting close to her bedtime. So, maybe you should, you know, just wait until tomorrow," I agreed.

The sheets were on the crib and Scarlett was fed, changed, and ready for bed, by the time Theodore had our work area cleared. We stood back to admire our handiwork while she cooed in her crib.

I smiled to see how content Scarlett was in her spacious new bed. I couldn't get Theodore's mischievous grin out 'of my head as he stood at the door with the

May Basket dangling from his finger. Theo requesting in his last letter for me to find happiness when and where it could be found and how he was sure I would love his father as much as he did, burned in my memory. I was still tingling from our kiss and reeling from the passion we generated earlier in the nursery every time our hands touched. Mama's pointed words continued to ring in my ears.

"You know what? You were right. That carrousel can wait until morning," I said softly, while slowly turning to meet the eyes of the man I married. The man who had been there for me in every way I needed someone to be. I was now ready to be there for him in every way he needed his wife to be too.

"Sorry it took so long, but…"

"Don't you think we should call it a night?" I asked, slipping my hand into his before he could finish his sentence.

"Do you think Scarlett will be okay alone all night in the nursery?" he asked, gently tightening his grip, showing he understood.

"Yes, I do. She sleeps all night long now," I said confidently.

THE NEXT MORNING, I lay quietly and stared at the ceiling tiles in my bedroom as though I was seeing them for the first time. Every tile was uniform in size and aligned. Had one tile been out of sync, the rest wouldn't have fit so perfectly. The longer I studied them, I realized I wasn't seeing just tiles, but how my out-of-sync-life was also becoming aligned as it should.

Theodore's comments the day before about us not following rules or the order of things rang true. We hadn't. But it was the order we chose—not one others chose for us.

Waking to the sound of his slow, quiet breathing as he slept peacefully beside me was a beginning, a new order of things for us. All I knew was it felt right.

Theo had wished for me to find happiness. But instead, happiness found me in the person of the finest man he had ever known—and we both loved.

Chapter Twenty-One

"LORD-A-MERCY IT'S HOT today. A firecracker don't get much hotter than the Bootheel does durin' July and August. I aint doin' nothin' but fannin' hot air around here in this kitchen," Mama grumped while fanning a restless Scarlett, squirming on her lap.

"But it's still June. It won't be July for another four days."

"Well, somebody needs to remind Mother Nature of that so she can turn down the heat a little bit."

"And for some reason, the heat is getting to me worse than usual here lately. It can't be my age. I'm only seventeen," I whined.

Mama laughed as she wiped Scarlett's face and neck with a cool cloth.

"No," she replied. "It's gettin' to everybody. Why, this baby's face is as red as my old rooster's comb. Don't think it's got nothin' to do with age. Anyways, I…"

A wave a sickness sent me bolting out the door and into the corner of the yard. It was either bolt or throw up in Mama's kitchen. She eyed me intently as I held to the door frame to steady myself upon returning. She quickly applied a cool cloth to my forehead and eased me into a chair.

"I hope I'm not coming down with something. I wouldn't want to get anything to make y'all or the baby sick," I moaned, holding my head in my hands.

"You are mighty pale. Sometimes watermelons will make you sick if you eat 'em hot. Y'all haven't been eatin' any hot watermelons lately have you?"

"No. Theodore mentioned getting one to ice down for the 4th of July, but he hasn't gotten it yet."

"What did you fix last night for supper? How is he? Is he sick too?"

"We had boiled cabbage, cornbread and I fried a few green tomatoes. Theodore's fine. Matter of fact, he couldn't wait to get with Daddy once we arrived to show him the newest thing he made with his tools."

"Never heard of cabbage and cornbread makin' a body sick. Maybe your fried tomatoes were a little too greasy and they didn't set well with you. I ain't heard of any new sickness goin' around here lately. If you ain't sick from somethin' you ate, I don't have any idea what's wrong with you. If I didn't know better, I'd think you were pregnant. But guess that..."

I raised my head and met Mama's eyes. Her expression changed from puzzled to a full-fledged laugh.

"I...suspected things had changed 'tween you two when you came over for Sunday dinner right after May Day. His grin was wider than the Mississippi River. Y'all kept lookin' at each other like you was hidin' a secret or somethin.' I just figured he was about to spring another surprise gift on us. Guess I wasn't too far off. I'm surprised alright." Mama threw her head back for another big laugh.

"How can I be pregnant? Scarlett will only be four months old in a few days."

"Lucretia, I didn't see a need to bring that up to you considerin' y'all's sleepin' arrangements. But one of the easiest times for a woman to get pregnant is shortly after she's had a baby. Anyways, just like you've done all yer life, you surprised me again."

"Not now, Mama. I don't feel like…"

"Alright, Lucretia. I'll hush 'bout all that and just be happy about gettin' another grandbaby."

"It's not like I'm not happy too. Or that I didn't ever want to have another baby. I did. Theodore and I even talked about it."

"Well then, what are you worried about? You're a married woman. Babies happen to married women."

"Like I said, we talked about it. We just didn't think about it being so soon."

"Babies are a blessin' from God."

"I know, Mama, I just wish God could have waited on that blessing a little while longer."

"Things come on God's time—not ours. We caint get into His business. He's got a reason for everythin.' Evidently, God reasoned for y'all to have another baby now."

"Without a doubt, Theodore will be happy. He adores Scarlett. Mama, he is so good with her."

"Well, I sure couldn't be more pleased. And your Daddy won't know what to do with hisself." She gave another hearty laugh.

"What's so funny?" Daddy asked as he and Theodore stepped onto the porch.

"Hmmm…well…I'll let Lucretia tell y'all."

"Tell us what? Did Scarlett make another one of her adorable, funny little faces?" Theodore asked.

"The only face she's makin' right now is a red one. Asa, you need to do somethin.' This baby is miserable hot and so are we."

"I'll see if I can block in that window fan a little tighter so it will direct more air through the house. We can't have our baby bein' too hot," he said, reaching for the screen door to go back on the porch for his shoes.

"But you all weren't laughing about Scarlett's red face. There's something else going on here." Daddy stopped and sat back down upon hearing Theodore's assumption.

Mama looked straight at me. Immediately, I was the focus of every eye in the room—even Scarlett's.

"Okay. Theodore, I hope you don't mind this being a family announcement instead of a private one, but it's possible we are having another baby."

I wasn't sure what he and my father thought they

were going to hear, but from their expressions, most definitely that wasn't it.

"Well…I declare. I do declare," Daddy exclaimed, looking directly at Theodore as if he was asking for confirmation.

I couldn't tell if Theodore was going to laugh, cry, or faint. Actually, he did two out of three. Tears streamed from his eyes and down his cheeks, before he dropped back into a chair, laughing deliriously.

He sounded somewhat out of control, which scared and confused me for a moment. Mama and Daddy stared in astonishment, mouths agape, clearly at a loss of how to react. Scarlett broke into a big smile, as babies do when adults try to coax them to perform.

When he gained a bit of composure, Theodore saw our reactions and chuckled some more before catching his breath to speak. "This is the most wonderful news I could hear. I am just so very happy."

"Well, I'm glad. I couldn't tell if you were happy or shocked out of your mind," I replied.

"I am both. And very thankful for my—our life right now. This is far beyond my wildest dream."

"So, you don't think it's too soon for us to be having another baby?"

"Not at all. Matter of fact. It is perfect timing. Today is my birthday. You couldn't have given me a better birthday present."

"Your birthday was the day before we got married?"

I was astounded.

"We never ask you before but how old are you anyways?" Mama pried.

"I'm forty-eight years old today. And Lucretia and I will be married one year tomorrow."

"We never knew the date when y'all got married. We didn't want to know, in case some nosey somebody ask us. But since that cat's been let out of the bag now, I guess I need to whip up a birthday-anniversary cake for after supper."

"Okay, Emmy, but just put one big candle on it. We don't want to set the kitchen on fire," Daddy teased.

"Now, now Asa. I thought we were buddies," Theodore joked.

"We are son. We are. Happy Birthday and congratulations. I'll soon have a grandbaby on both knees." Daddy shook Theodore's hand. He had never called him son before.

THEODORE AND I had driven most of the way home without a word until I finally broke the silence.

"I can't believe it. Pregnant again was the last thing I expected to be so soon."

"I know. But truthfully, I couldn't be happier. Remember, we talked about maybe having more children eventually." His slap-happy grin had never left his face.

"Yes. We talked about it, but I just didn't expect it this soon. Mama keeps saying what a good mother I've become, but I really don't know how I will manage with two babies."

"You won't be alone in this. I will be right there all the way. And you won't have to manage—we will manage. Haven't I been helpful with Scarlett so far?"

"Yes, you've been wonderful."

"Well, I'll just step it up and be twice as wonderful from here on." His smile broadened.

"It is just that…"

"Just what?"

"There were things I wanted to do when Scarlett got a little older. I want to learn to drive. And we talked about me finishing school. And…"

"You can learn to drive and be pregnant too. I can teach you."

"Well, I can't go back to school and be pregnant."

"You can get a G.E.D. You know, like a lot of Veterans that dropped out of school to go to war have done. Deke McCrady was talking about it when I ran into him last Friday at the Big Store in Muddy Ox. He's seriously looking into it. He sounded just like you the other day when we were talking. He doesn't like being called a high school dropout either."

"I'm not sure about doing something like that without a teacher to guide me through it."

"Lucretia darling, you can. I know you can. I've already seen how you will do anything you set your mind to do. The sky is the limit where you're concerned."

"You really think so?"

"I do. In fact, I know so."

"Okay, as soon as this morning sickness is better, will you give me a driving lesson?" I reached for a saltine from the bag Mama had sent home with me and made a mental note to put the rest on my bedside table in case the sickness returned the next morning.

"I'll be glad—no, honored. I'm proud you are so independent. I haven't seen many women driving around here. You'll pave the wave for the rest of them."

"Billie Kay can drive. She had to learn when she moved out on her own. Billie Kay. Oh, my goodness. She won't believe I'm pregnant again."

"You had a bad bout with morning sickness with Scarlett. Maybe you should see Doctor McFarnz sooner into this pregnancy. Not to take away from your mother's saltine cracker solution, but he may want to recommend something else to help with that. Also, you may need to start some vitamins since you are having another baby so soon."

We remained in the car to continue our conversation after pulling into the yard.

"You're right. And maybe I'm not pregnant after all.

Just because Mama thinks it is so, doesn't mean I actually am."

Theodore's face went from slap-happy to solemn.

"Of…of course, Mama is seldom wrong. And we are sharing a bedroom now." I felt bad to have shot him down so.

"All the more reason to go see Doctor McFarnz. If you're not pregnant, then we need to know what else it could be." He looked concerned.

"True. Were those fried green tomatoes too greasy? Mama suggested maybe it was greasy tomatoes causing my sickness."

"No, I didn't think they were too greasy. They didn't make me sick. And I ate twice or maybe three times as many."

"Okay then, will you take me to see the doctor to-morrow?"

"Yes. And I think I'll let him look at me too. He may have a miracle, youth-restoring-elixir that is just what I need. After all, I did just have birthday number forty-eight."

"I feel terrible that I didn't know today was your birthday."

"You couldn't have known. I never mentioned it. On this day a year ago, my birthday was the last thing on my mind. Theo's death, your pregnancy, us getting married, and trying to protect both our families' good names were only a few of the many concerns at the time that took priority over my birthday."

"And today was no exception. I took priority again." I sighed.

"You never took anything—I gave priority to you."

"Well, now, I give it back. Your birthday will never be forgotten again. I promise."

Chapter Twenty-Two

D R. MCFARNZ ASKED that I wait in his office so he could talk to us together after he finished with Theodore. I almost knew I was pregnant. The nausea and other symptoms were identical. Mama's suspicions were rarely wrong. But because Scarlett was only four months old, we wanted to be sure.

"Thank you for waiting, Lucretia," Dr. McFarnz said after he and Theodore arrived.

"Okay, Doc. Let's have it. Are we expanding our nursery?" Theodore joked.

"I'd like to talk about you first if you don't mind. I'm concerned with your elevated blood pressure, irregular heartbeat, frequent exhaustion, and that shortness of breath you told me about. All are symptoms of possible heart problems. Now, some might say you've been eating too many greasy foods too. A few added pounds and indigestion can cause some of the same symptoms."

I had a sick feeling in the pit of my stomach that had nothing to do with pregnancy. Was Mama on the right track again, as usual? Was my cooking making Theodore sick? A flood of uncontrollable tears began to roll.

"Oh, Darling. The doctor isn't saying I am in any immediate danger."

"I'm sorry Theodore. I was just trying to make meals that you would like. I always followed the recipes in the cookbook. It was never my intention to make you unhealthy." My last words came as a high-pitched whine.

"Lucretia, first of all, his symptoms are only possible, not actual indications that something is wrong with his heart. If he does have heart issues, it couldn't be your doing. Why, you've only been cooking for him a year now. This type of health issue stems from years of unhealthy living and eating. Now, now, dear. You're just emotional. Pregnancy does that to a woman."

"So, she really is pregnant?" Theodore blurted, pushing his own health concerns aside.

"Her symptoms say yes, but we will know for sure by the end of the week, after the rabbit test is completed. By my calculations, if she really is pregnant, she's about six or seven weeks along."

"The rabbit test?" I questioned.

"I will inject the urine sample you gave me today into a female rabbit. After about 48 hours, if her ovaries are swollen and have turned yellow, it means you're pregnant."

"How do you check a rabbit's ovaries?" I asked.

"Well…I'll have to cut her open to examine them."

"Oh no. Doctor, does the poor little rabbit really have to die?"

"Unfortunately, Lucretia, it's the only way we can see their ovaries."

I had such a bittersweet moment. I could be having Theodore's child and he might possibly have a serious heart ailment. My tears switched from joy to fear, happiness to remorse, blessed to blame. On top of everything else, a poor, innocent, little rabbit had to die to see if I was going to—give life.

I cried again.

"This baby is just an angel. Y'all need to think up some more places to go so we can keep her more often."

"Yes, we will keep her any time. You don't even need to be goin' nowhere a'tall. We'll keep her for the pure fun of it. And just think, pretty soon we'll have two of 'em to love on." Daddy echoed Mama.

"How far along did Doc think you were?" Mama asked.

"He will know more by the end of the week. But if the test shows I am pregnant, I'm about six or seven weeks."

"Hmmm, you don't say," she gave a know-it-all

laugh.

I shot Mama a look that said she was enjoying being right a little too much. But she wouldn't be silenced. "You mean after *the rabbit dies?*"

Of course, my tears rolled again.

"Don't think you needed that test. That's the second time I've seen you cry in the last two days," Mama continued.

"She cried twice in the doctor's office too," Theodore chimed in.

"See what I'm sayin'? People don't cry that much lessen there's a reason for it. She's pregnant. I'd stake my reputation on it." Mama said exactly what Theodore wanted to hear.

"I just hate that some poor little animal has to die to prove I'm giving life."

"I heard they sometimes use mice and frogs fer them tests. Would that make it easier on you? Do you worry 'bout mice or frogs?" Daddy asked.

"He seemed mostly concerned about Theodore," I said, changing the subject and ignoring Daddy completely.

"Theodore? What's wrong with him?" Mama's brow furrowed.

"Why would Doc McFarnz be concerned about him? Last I knew, a trip to the doctor for findin' out if you was expectin', was all about the woman that was carryin' the baby. Is this somethin' new now? They check out the man too? What kind of animal do they test to see if he's goin' to be a daddy? A crow or a buzzard?" My Daddy was on a roll. But Theodore didn't waver.

"I've been feeling a little off here lately. It's been years since I had been to see a doctor. So, since we were going anyway, I had the doctor look at me too. I need to be in tip-top-shape if I'm going to be helping to keep up with two babies."

"What did he think is wrong with you? Looks like you're doin' okay these days—far as I can see." Mama giggled.

"He said Theodore could have some heart issues," I said.

"…or a bad case of indigestion. Doc said sometimes it was difficult to tell a heart condition and indigestion apart. The symptoms are so similar." Theodore tried to downplay the problem.

"Ah…you need some sassafras tea. Yer blood is probably too thick. Sassafras tea is the best thing you can drink to thin yer blood. We didn't make any this year, but I usually make some for Asa and me every spring."

"Give Mama an ailment. She will immediately find a remedy," I said.

"Sassafras tea, huh?" From hearing about the taste of some of Mama's home remedies, Theodore was obviously concerned.

"It's actually not bad. Quinine is what tastes so awful. Be glad it is just tea. I remember she gave me Quinine and sugar when I was young. It was dreadful tasting. Be happy it's sassafras and not Quinine," I reinforced.

"I didn't give you Quinine but once. Rumors went around it would help ward off blue-steel mosquitoes. But that was just a hoax. Aint much a body can do against them pesky things, but swat em' 'fore they bite you."

"Once was enough. I'll never forget that bitter Quinine."

"Well, you can almost put enough sugar in anythin' to help cut the taste. Quinine and sugar can cure a lot of things, but truthfully, it's mostly for worms. Doc don't think you have worms, does he?" She returned to diagnosing Theodore.

"Emmy, I can happily say that he never even suspected worms to be my problem." Theodore smiled smugly.

"Well, I'll see if Mrs. Grimsley has any sassafras root. She usually keeps a supply of herbs and roots like that on hand all year long. If she does Asa, I'll make sure to get enough to fix us a cup too."

Apprehension replaced Daddy's teasing grin. Any protest he had would be in vain. No doubt, there would be a steeping cup of sassafras tea served to him as soon as Mama made Mrs. Grimsley a visit.

Theodore might as well get ready for one too.

"MAMA CAME UP with a cure right away. What remedies did the doctor offer?" I asked once we were on our way home.

"He prescribed something called, Digitalis. From everything the doctor said, your mother wasn't far off about my blood possibly being too thick. But maybe I need to check with him to see if it is safe to drink her tea and take his prescription at the same time."

I could tell by his expression Theodore wasn't looking forward to Mama's unconfirmed sassafras tea cure. However, I knew his only hope was a loophole from Dr. McFarnz.

"You heard what he said to me. I'm supposed to drink lots of milk. Oh, and he gave me a prescription for A and D vitamins."

"I know, I was really pleased to hear him say how healthy you are. We'll get both our prescriptions tomorrow. It's too late to get them today."

"We should stock up on saltine crackers too. He said if they were working for the morning sickness, I should keep eating them. And, I still have the corks Mama brought me, if I start having leg cramps again."

"Well now, you will have a pair of my shoes under the bed and me in it this time. That's bound to make things better." Theodore teased.

"I know the doctor said my cooking didn't cause your problems, but I don't want to add to them either. I'm going to try to fix less fried foods from now on."

"Let's don't go overboard now. He didn't say I couldn't have any fried foods at all. I love how you've learned to fix fried chicken. Also, you and Scarlett have only made my life happier. And happier makes healthier, in my book."

"Maybe that is one reason I am so healthy these days too."

We smiled together.

"Hey, is that Deke McCrady walking on the edge of the road?"

"It looks like him. Wonder why he's walking?" I questioned.

Theodore slowed the car to a crawl and rolled the window down. "Hey Deke, where you headed?"

"My old car won't start again. I was walking to Larson Strom's place to get him to come back and look at it."

"His place is on our way. Hop in and we will drop you off."

"Hello Miss Lucretia. How are you today?"

"I'm fine. Thank you," I replied.

"Deke, this little lady is more than fine. We just

found out we may be having another baby." Theodore was so bursting with pride he couldn't contain himself.

"Holy mackerel! Didn't y'all just have one?" Deke asked?

"Yes, and now we're having another one," Theodore sounded annoyed.

"What do you think is wrong with your car, Deke?" I didn't know a thing about cars, but that was the first question that popped in my mind to sway the conversation.

"I don't know, Ma'am. But I'm sure Larson can figure it out."

Realizing he had rubbed Theodore the wrong way, Deke tried to make amends. "I'm sorry, Mr. Dalton. That was a crazy thing for me to say about y'all having another baby. Guess it just took me by surprise. I'm happy for y'all. I really am."

"That's okay, Deke. That probably won't be the last time we will get that reaction from people. We might as well be prepared," Theodore replied.

"We really can't blame everyone for being surprised. We were surprised too," I added.

When we drove into his yard, Larson Strom was where he most commonly could be found, under the hood of his car. When he saw us, he closed the hood and walked over to greet us.

"Hey Mr. Dalton. How you do, Ma'am?"

I nodded to him.

"Man, I'm sure glad to see you. My car won't start again," Deke barely waited for our car to stop before bouncing out.

"Okay, come on and we'll go see what's wrong with it."

Deke turned to thank us for dropping him off before falling in step with Larson.

"Didn't they just have a baby?" We heard Larson say under his breath as they walked away from us. Despite Deke's apology, our news was too juicy not to tell.

"I was right. We might as well get used to that response from just about everyone for a while." Theodore said as he backed out of the Strom's yard.

"HERE ARE YOUR vitamins and things." Theodore sat my vitamins, his Digitalis, milk, and a box of saltine crackers on the table after returning from Kennett the next day.

"Did you go by and check with the doctor to see if you could take both his medicine and sassafras tea at the same time?"

"Yes, I did. He said he knows how tricky it is to dispute any of your mother's cures. But both are blood-thinners. It wouldn't be wise to take them together. Also, he said to caution you about drinking any at all."

"We know we'll be seeing Mama before the end of day if Mrs. Grimsley had any of those roots."

"The doctor recommended I take a nap whenever I felt tired. When she knocks on the door, if I suddenly feel the need, I could be taking a nap."

"You just could be." I smiled beguilingly.

Chapter Twenty-Three

I T WASN'T LIKELY Mama had abandoned her mission to bring Theodore some sassafras tea, but it was now Friday, and we hadn't heard a word from her.

> *Ride a little horsey go to town.*
> *Horsey's name is Dandy.*
> *Ride a little horsey go to town.*
> *Bring back Scarlett some candy.*
> *Ride a little horsey go to town*
> *Don't be gone all day,*
> *Ride a little horsey go to town.*
> *My Scarlett wants to play."*

Theodore bounced Scarlett on his knee, while singing a song he had composed especially for her. She usually loved his attention but by the second verse she began to fret.

"Guess I'll have to write her another song. This one isn't working anymore. She must be tired of it."

"It's her nap time and she's probably hungry." I knew it couldn't be the song. Being bounced on his knee and him singing to her was one of the things she loved most.

"Her eyes do look a little sleepy. I guess I can go tinker with my tools while you nurse her and get her to bed."

"Come on sweet Scarlett. Let's go feed you while Daddy goes and plays with his tools," I said, lifting her off his lap and heading for the nursery.

"Tinker…Scarlett…Daddy is going to tinker with his tools," he emphasized, smiling on his way out.

I was slipping out of the nursery about a half hour later when he rushed back into the living room, closing the door quickly behind him.

"A car is coming. It could be your mother. I need to be napping too." I raised a finger to my lips and shushed him as to not wake the baby.

"Go—hurry," I whispered as he left for the bed-room.

Peeking past the curtains, I was relieved to see Doctor McFarnz walking toward the porch. I welcomed him, signaling him to shush also.

"We don't have to whisper if we talk quietly," I said once we were seated.

"I thought I'd come by and check on Theodore and give you the results of the test."

Theodore appeared after recognizing the doctor's voice. "Hello Doctor. I…I was getting ready to…I was lying down."

"It's good to hear you are following my suggestions.

So, were you resting because you were tired or were you having a weak spell?"

"He was hiding from Mama," I said not wanting to mislead the doctor.

"I heard your car and thought it could be Miss Emmy. I—we dreaded trying to explain why I couldn't drink her tea concoction. Guess I was taking the coward's way out by trying to avoid her as long as I could," Theodore confessed.

"Emerald was right on track with her thick blood diagnosis. And yes, sassafras tea will help that, but I wanted you to try the Digitalis first to see if it took care of some of your other complaints. Also, it doesn't have the side-effects we've linked to sassafras."

"Oh, I've learned to take her intuitions very seriously. But we thought we could delay a confrontation with her this time, if she thought I was napping when she arrived. You know, until we could give the Digitalis a chance."

"We are surprised that Mama hasn't been over yet. Maybe she hasn't been able to run down Mrs. Grimsley. Can I offer you some coffee or something, Doctor McFarnz?"

"No thank you, Lucretia. I can't stay long. Gotta' go by and check on Katty Simpson over in Muddy Ox when I leave here. Got word her stomach is acting up again. As for Emerald, we all know she means well, but you have to be firm with her this time. I know you dread crossing her, but it's not in Theodore's or your best interest right now to partake of sassafras root."

"Oh, I was going to be firm with her, if I had to be," I promised.

"I am feeling much better. I haven't had any of the problems we discussed in your office. Not even shortness of breath. That is until I ran in here a few minutes ago when I heard your car. Do you think that medicine is doing its job?" Theodore questioned.

We were so deep in conversation we didn't notice another car pulling into the yard or the footsteps on the porch. Hearing a knock, we had no choice but to open the door to Mama holding a bag of sassafras root. Daddy was on her heels.

"Y'all come in. Doctor McFarnz is here too. He came by to check on Theodore and to talk to us." I mouthed that Scarlett was sleeping, hoping they would keep their voices to a minimum.

"Mrs. Grimsley's been over in Lake City, Arkansas, visitin' with kinfolk. It's took me this whole week to run her down. Anyways, thought I'd fix the tea over here and we can all have a cup together. There'll be plenty enough for you too Doctor if you want a cup. That is if you haven't already had your sassafras this year. Lucretia, can you get me your big pot so I can get this root boilin'?"

I stood boldly, ready to explain why sassafras wasn't a good idea, when the good doctor came to my rescue.

"No, I haven't had any sassafras tea this year. And, Emerald, you need to put a halt to fixing it for them now too." Doctor McFarnz was firm and to the point.

Mama wasn't used to being halted about anything. Her immediate expression was disconcertingly unreadable.

"Why are you comin' by to check on Theodore, Doc? Somethin' happen to him?" Daddy quizzed, ignoring how the doctor had daringly stepped on Mama's toes.

"I really stopped by to give them Lucretia's tests results. But thought I'd ask about him too while I was here."

"And why should I halt, as you put it, making this tea?" Mama continued as if she had been temporarily suspended in time.

"Emerald, come sit down and let's discuss this," the doctor pointed to the couch and motioned for Daddy to join her.

"This sounds serious, Doc." Daddy again overstepped Mama's backlash.

"It could be serious. But I'm keeping an eye on him. Now Emerald, you are one of the wisest women in these parts when it comes to ailments and knowing what to do with them. Especially wise for someone who hasn't been to medical school. But you haven't run up against anyone who has Theodore's condition yet. He has other things going on besides thick blood. The medicine I'm giving him wouldn't work well with your tea. In fact, it could harm him."

"We sure wouldn't want that," Daddy chimed in.

"And Lucretia doesn't need her blood thinned right now either," the doctor continued.

Mama sat still for a second before speaking. "Okay, you're the doctor. I know you know best. I can put this root in the cellar 'til next spring. Think it's better for a body in the springtime anyways."

"That would be a good idea," the doctor agreed.

"Alright, I am glad we have that settled. That's enough about tea or me. Now Doctor, tell us the tests results," Theodore urged.

"Well, I hope you all kept that cradle you were telling me about. You'll be needing it in about seven and a half months."

Mama and Daddy forgot that Scarlett was sleeping. I had to remind them again. Even then they could hardly contain themselves.

"I'll soon be bouncin' a baby on both knees at the same time. I'm goin' to be Grandpappy twice over." Daddy was elated.

"I knew it. Didn't I tell you? I'm hard to fool when it comes to tellin' if a woman's in the family way or not. Especially if that woman's my own daughter."

"Well, you hit it on the nose this time for sure, Emerald. Now Lucretia, you need to take those vitamins I prescribed for you. You seem to be healthy enough, but you did just have a baby four months ago. And…no sassafras or any other root teas until after this baby is born. You got me?" The doctor addressed me but looked directly at Mama.

"We hear you," Mama got the message and agreed.

"Thank you, Doctor for the wonderful news. We are truly blessed," Theodore said, placing his hand on mine.

"We all are," Daddy added.

"It's not always the case. But when it is, delivering good news to my patients is a pleasure. You both should take good care of yourselves. It won't be long until you're going to need all the energy you can muster with havin two babies in the house."

"That's another reason I came in for that check-up when I brought Lucretia the other day. I already knew in my heart we were having another baby."

"I am pleased to hear you are doing better, Theodore. But we still need to keep an eye on you. We don't know for sure what caused your symptoms in the first place. I'd like to see you in my office again in six weeks, sooner if you have any concerns out of the ordinary at all."

"He'll be there, Doctor," I promised.

"Yes, he will. We have grown pretty partial to this son-in-law of ours," Daddy said, patting Theodore on the shoulder.

"Well, glad to hear that." The doctor stood to leave.

"Got any big plans for the 4th?" Daddy asked as he walked with him to the door.

"My wife handles all of that. Last I heard, the family is coming over to eat and celebrate with us."

"Sounds good. We'll be doin' the same. Families ought to eat together ever chance they get. Thank you again for the good news," Daddy said as they stepped on the porch.

"Y'all wanna' show up around six on Sunday? That'll give my hen the whole day to cook," Mama stood to join Daddy outside.

"Wait a minute, Emmy. I have something to give you. I was going to drop it by later but since you all are here, you can take it with you." Theodore headed for the refrigerator.

"What you got for us now?"

"A pork butt and this special Kansas City bar-b-que sauce, made by this fellow named Arthur Bryant. Everyone I talk to raves about how good it is. Thought it would be a nice change for our 4th of July supper."

"That's nice. It's been a while since we had any pork. It's hard to come by these days, you know with the rationing and all. But you have a way of getting hard-to-get things. I'll just say thank you and stop there. Yer right. It will be a nice change and I know my old hen will appreciate you for it." Mama smiled and reminded us about six on Sunday before leaving.

"So, it's official. I am pregnant." I said once we were

alone.

"Like your Mama, I already knew too. Maybe that is why I reacted like I did when you told us at your parent's house last week."

"I felt the same as when I was first pregnant with Scarlett. I was pretty sure but guess I wanted confirmation from the doctor."

"Lucretia, I've been thinking about something. And I hope you will agree with me about it."

"It must be very serious by that wrinkle on your brow."

"I want us to start attending church on a regular basis. You've mentioned about you all going to church. But your parents haven't gone at all since I've been in the family, that I have known of. And neither have we."

"We are members and have been regulars at the Bakertown Church of Christ for years. But I'm guessing Mama has been trying to avoid questions about us."

"I'm sorry for that. Sorry it's because of us, too. Is that the little church on the left of 84 Highway before you get to Kennett?"

"Yes, are you familiar with it?"

"No, but the other day, on my way home from getting our prescriptions filled, I felt an overpowering urge to pull into its parking lot. I thought about Theo while sitting there. We were always on the road, going from show to show. Gus and I told him about God and sang bible songs like Jesus Loves Me to him, but we never took him to church. I'm ashamed and sorry for that."

The anguish on Theodore's face was heart wrenching.

"Don't torture yourself. You couldn't…"

"Maybe I couldn't then. I might have failed Theo, but I've been given another chance. Lucretia, I want our children to know how it is to sit between their mother and father on a church pew. Kids need to see and hear their parents pray. They need to grow up hearing church songs and memorizing Bible verses. Will you help me give our children that opportunity?"

"Maybe after this baby is born, people won't…"

"No, we can't wait that long. I feel an urgency to do this now."

"But Theodore, I don't want to embarrass Mama."

"Your mother is a strong woman. I think she will know how to handle any questions or looks thrown at her. We can talk to them this Sunday while we're there celebrating the 4th. Nothing would make me happier than for you, me, and Scarlett, along with your parents to start attending that little Church this very next Sunday."

"If it will wipe that wrinkle from your brow and the sadness off your face, I will do it. Like Mama said. I'm married. Babies happen to married women. I have nothing to apologize for."

"Yes, *we're* married. And you are right. *We* have absolutely nothing to apologize for," he confirmed.

Chapter Twenty-Four

"I TELL YOU what. Yer daddy can come up with almost anythin' if the notion hits him just right. He started buildin' on that slow smoker, as he calls it, no sooner than we got home with that pork butt. It must be workin.' That meat sure is smellin' mighty good. A few people even drove by real slow with their windows down to see where the good smell was comin' from." Mama took Scarlett from my arms as soon as we walked inside.

"So that is what we smelled as we arrived. I'm going out to see what he's built, Lucretia. We may want one too." Theodore sat my dishes on the table and dashed out the door.

"We put the tub with the watermelon we iced down on the porch, is that alright? The strawberries you asked for are already topped, mashed, and sweetened for the shortcake. Also, I brought something called cornbread salad. I got the recipe out of my cookbook. I made it once before and Theodore loved it. I hope y'all will like it too."

Mama had warmed up to the idea of me using the cookbook from time to time to make a new dish of some kind. On occasion, she even duplicated some of the dishes. However, her version was usually better than the original after adding a thing or two to make it her own.

"The tub is good there on the porch for now. Asa can move it later if he wants to. Cornbread and salad? Those two words just don't go together. Why I never…"

You will put them together from now on. I promise."

"Well, I'll give it a try. But I will tell you the truth if I don't like it."

"I know, Mama. I know."

"Can you take this sauce out there to yer daddy so he can swipe it on the meat when it's done? Also, ask him how much longer does he think it will take? When you come back in, you can go ahead and put the shortcake together and put it in the refrigerator to chill."

"Okay. I want to get a close-up look at that cooker anyway. Especially, since we may be getting one like it."

"Sure, we can make y'all one of these too. All you'll need is a barrel, some hinges, a grid to lay the meat on and a few nuts and bolts to put a handle on it. You have plenty of hickory trees for the wood." Daddy said to Theodore as I arrived.

"Sounds like you two have another project in the works. Here's the sauce for the meat, Daddy. Mama wants to know how much longer until it will be done?"

"Aww 'bout another twenty minutes after I get the sauce on it. This is goin' to be some fine eatin' for sure."

"Hey Cretia," I looked up to see Billie Kay coming from her parent's back yard.

"Billie Kay. Hi. I hoped you'd be celebrating the 4th with your parents too." We shared a hug once she arrived.

"Yes, and I'm glad we ran into each other like this. I'm leaving for Galveston on Wednesday. I was going to come see you to say goodbye, but now, you saved me the trip. Is the baby in the house with your mom?"

"Yes, we'll go see her in a minute. You won't believe how she's grown. But can we sit on our stump under the willow tree and talk a bit first?"

"Sure, like old times…almost."

"I'm glad we ran into one another too. I have some news to tell you," I lowered my voice as we sat down.

"What's going on?" Billie Kay whispered.

"Oh, not much except you are going to be Aunt Beekay again."

She nearly fell off her side of the stump.

"That's some news! How old is Scarlett now? This means you finally…"

"She is four months old. And please don't say anything in front of Theodore about us having another baby so soon. He's kind of touchy about it. And yes, it was time we shared a bed. We've been married a little over a year now."

"Hey, I think it is great. Actually, y'all not sharing a bed all this time was the odd part. You expecting another baby is natural."

"I told you I would have to work through it in my own head and heart. And I did—we did."

"Well, that is obvious. You won't hear anything negative from me about your new arrangement. I think it's wonderful. Cretia, we're best friends. I knew you'd be in love with that handsome man one day."

"Yes, Theodore is handsome. But he's so much more than that. I grew to love who he was on the inside long before I let myself love him—the man. Then after I got Theo's last letter a few months ago, I…"

"Wait. Theo died over a year ago. It took a whole year to get a letter from him. How…?" Billie Kay interrupted.

"Remember when you dropped by when Scarlett was eight days old? Well, shortly after you left, a soldier friend of Theo's came. He said before he died, Theo had made him promise to get his last letter to me.

"The letter was written over a span of several days because their unit was being constantly moved from battle to battle. In the beginning, Theo wrote how he wanted to make a good life for us when he returned. But toward the end, I think he almost knew he wasn't going to survive. He spoke so highly in that letter of his father and said he couldn't wait for me to meet him, that he knew I'd love him as much as he did. He encouraged me to find happiness however I could find it if he didn't make it back.

"After that, every time I read his letter, I became more drawn to Theodore. Theo died before I could tell him we were having a baby. But I feel he would be at peace now to know his father is in her life—and mine too."

"That's so sweet. I agree. I think since he couldn't, his dad would be the next best choice to raise his baby." Billie Kay wiped a tear.

"I knew you would understand and not judge me." I couldn't stop the tears either.

"But I have to ask. Why is Theodore so touchy about you all having another baby?"

"He's thrilled. But you know how people talk some-times. We've heard a couple of negative responses that made him uncomfortable. So, you can be happy and congratulate us as much as you want. He loves to hear that. Matter of fact, he wants us to start going to church. You know a few eyebrows could be raised there. But like Mama said and we agree. We are married now. There is nothing for people to question."

"Well again, you won't hear anything negative from me. I for one, am thrilled. I hope you have another girl. It would be good for sisters to grow up together so close in age. They could not only be sisters but best friends too."

"You mean like you and I are?" I asked before giving her a hug.

"Lucretia, I need your help here in the kitchen," Mama yelled.

"I better go. She's trying to cook and look after the baby too. Walk with me to the porch. I'll bring Scarlett out so you can see how big she is getting."

"Here we are. I'm going away to work, and you are a married woman soon going to have two kids and we are still jumping like frogs when your Mama yells."

We laughed while walking arm in arm to the porch.

"Mama has mellowed a lot. Guess I have too. I don't see it so much now as hopping when she yells, as I see it respectfully honoring her wishes. Things change after you're married and have children. You'll see one of these days."

"You really think so?" Billie Kay asked snidely.

Mama must have anticipated that I was bringing Billie Kay to see Scarlett, so she stepped onto the porch with her.

"Hello, Mrs. Bertram. You have a real sweetheart in your arms right there," Billie Kay said.

"Yes, I do," Mama replied cordially.

"Oh, my goodness. Lucretia, she looks so much like you. She is beautiful. Hey pretty girl. I am your Aunt BeeKay," she said reaching for the baby.

Surprisingly, Mama willingly obliged.

Scarlett giggled and cooed as a baby will do to capture someone's heart. Of course, Billie Kay wasn't hard to win over. Mama's smile broadened as any grand-mother's would when one is making over her pride-and-joy granddaughter.

"What did you say her middle name is?" Billie Kay asked.

"Estella, she is named after me," Mama replied quickly.

"Estella. That's a beautiful name. Mrs. Bertram, I never knew that was your middle name."

"My Mama told me once that she named me Emer-ald Estella because Emerald was a treasured jewel and Estella meant star. She called me her shining star."

I stood amazed. It was the first I'd heard about how Mama got her name and the first time ever that Mama ever said more than a few words to Billie Kay—nice words at that.

"Well, your little Scarlett is going to be a star too. A beautiful little star."

"She already is with us," Mama replied.

"Yes, she is," I agreed.

"You women gonna' yap all day? Food's ready," Daddy said approaching the porch.

"I have to run. I want to spend some time with my parents too before I leave on Wednesday."

Scarlett extended her arms for Theodore as soon as he was within reach.

"I see she's a Daddy's girl. Congratulations on hav-ing another baby, Mr. Dalton," Billie Kay said, handing the baby over to him.

"Thank you. Good luck on your new job. And please call me Theodore."

"Okay, congratulations, Theodore."

I gave Billie Kay one last hug before she left. It felt good for everything and everyone to be on such good terms. Life is so much better that way.

Chapter Twenty-Five

I NURSED SCARLETT and got her to sleep while Mama put dinner on the table.

"Alright, pass that cornbread salad and let's see what it tastes like," Mama said, once we were all seated.

"I have a request before we begin eating," Theodore proposed.

"What's that?" daddy asked.

"Will someone please say Grace?"

"Go ahead, Asa."

Mama and Daddy shared a glance after she put him on the spot.

"Um…well…okay. It's been a while, but I'll do it."

Daddy gave a brief but touching blessing on our food, adding how thankful he was for our family, our health, and his and Mama's grandchildren. We all ended with amen.

"Now…go on and pass that cornbread salad," Mama asked.

"Where is it? I don't see no cornbread or salad neither one."

I explained my new dish to Daddy while handing Mama the bowl. "It may not sound like it would be good but, I promise you both will love it."

All eyes were on Mama as she lifted the spoon to her mouth. She never had to say anything. Her reaching for another bite said it all.

"I told you it was delicious," I boasted.

"I had the same reservations, Miss Emmy, until I tasted it. Isn't it good? Lucretia can make cornbread salad for me anytime she wants to. We love it." Theodore declared.

"Okay, spoon me out some. I gotta give it a whirl now too," Daddy extended his hand.

"I'll say one thing for it. They shoulda' give it a different name. It's deceivin' what it's called," Mama grumbled.

"Get that recipe, Emerald. And make us some now and then. You can give it whatever name that strikes yer notion. That stuff is mighty tasty."

"So is your bar-b-que, Asa. Yes, we definitely want one of your slow smokers," Theodore said.

"We can sure make you one for a lot less money than a store-bought one would cost." Daddy was eager to share. He didn't invent the slow smoker but as with Mama, he always put his spin on things he tried to replicate.

"I have something to talk to you about," Theodore began.

Mama and Daddy stopped and gave him their undivided attention. I imagined they braced to hear what else he had to talk with them about. After all, they were still reeling from learning about his health issues and that they were going to be grandparents again so soon.

"Oh, it isn't a bad thing," I added, sensing their concern.

"I'd like for us to go together to your church next Sunday, if you're up for it," Theodore continued.

Daddy's spoon full of food remained suspended inches from his mouth. Mama rested her fork, folded her hands in her lap, and chose her words carefully.

"We haven't been there in over a year now. You know, as to not raise any questions among the congregation. They're a nice bunch of people. But people caint help but wonder 'bout things."

"Let them wonder. Like you said, an entire year has passed. No one knows when Lucretia and I got married. Even you didn't know the actual date, until I told you last week."

"Theodore's right, Mama. Don't you think they'd be more interested in seeing us back at church, than worrying about any year-old gossip?"

"Besides when they're met with Scarlett's sweet face, that'll be all they can think about." Daddy spoke like the proud grandparent he was.

"She's a little charmer. That's fer sure," Mama agreed.

"Theo's mother and I were on the road all the time with the Vaudeville shows. We never took him to church. We told him about God, and he knew the words to *Jesus Loves Me*, but that was about the extent of it. I feel like God has given me a chance to do better by our—your grandchildren."

"So, what do you say, Mama?"

"Lucretia and I could go without you all, but we would love to have you go with us," Theodore added.

"I've been aching to show off our little Scarlett to Sister Wilkes. I don't want to miss her reaction when she first sees her."

"Then it sounds like we're goin' to church next Sunday," Daddy concluded.

"Guess so," Mama consented.

It was as though a cloud had been lifted by Theodore's proposal for us to go to church and my parent's decision to go with us. The burden of trying to hide our secretive marriage had been lifted from each of us as well.

Between Daddy's bar-b-que, my cornbread salad, and all the other delicious trimmings Mama had prepared, we were stuffed. Shortcake and watermelon could wait for later. Anyway, because of Theodore's intervention, the day had already been sweetened by our joint decision to return to church.

Because Mama had never complained about having to finish the meal while Billie Kay and I were catching up, was another sure sign of her mellowing. I liked that every exchange with her wasn't a sparring match with someone any longer.

We all did.

Chapter Twenty-Six

MAMA AND DADDY were waiting for us to arrive so we could walk into church together. Of course, heads turned, and we were greeted with warm smiles and nods when we came through the door.

We filed behind her as Mama led the way. Seeing that a new family occupied the pew she had sat in for years, she had to take the one behind them.

Daddy looked a bit ill at ease. Mama sat staunchly in her seat, defying the obvious gap in her attendance. I nestled Scarlett in my lap while she chewed on her fist. Theodore was surprisingly calm and seemingly relaxed.

After a few preliminaries, the song leader asked us to stand as he led us in, *Standing on the Promises,* followed by *Nearer My God to Thee.* Impressively, Theodore knew the words and blended beautifully with the voices of the congregation.

The sermon was on the parable of the lost sheep. Theodore listened intently, as the minister stressed how the Kingdom of God was accessible to all. That no matter how far a person strayed from God's path, Jesus searched for those who were lost and rejoiced when they were found. That His arms were always outstretched to welcome lost souls to the flock.

When they began singing Just As I Am, Theodore squeezed my hand before walking forward to join the Pastor Abrams at the altar. After they shared an earnest conversation, the minister gladly proclaimed that Theodore had confessed of his sins, welcomed Jesus into his heart, and desired to be baptized.

The song leader led us in *All is Well With My Soul* while Theodore prepared for baptism. Afterwards, *Victory In Jesus* was triumphantly sang by all before we were dismissed.

"It was a beautiful service this morning, Emerald," Sister Wilkes said, giving Mama a bear hug.

"Yes, it was." Mama, contrite and humbled, brushed a tear.

"We've certainly missed you. But we're so glad you are back," Sister Wilkes continued.

"Thank you. We missed you too and we're glad to be here." I heard complete honesty in Mama's reply.

"Lucretia, that baby girl looks just like a doll. I think she's even cuter than some dolls I've seen," Sister Baylor, another of Mama's friends said as she joined our circle.

"You got that right. Our grandbaby is a real beauty," Daddy boasted from the sidelines.

"And you have such a sweet son-in-law. We're so glad you brought him this morning, Emerald," Sister Baylor added.

"Yes, we're mighty proud of him too," Daddy spoke boldly.

Theodore was surrounded by a group of the brethren and didn't hear the ladies crediting Mama with bringing him to church. Honestly, He was in such a happy state of mind at the time, I don't think he would have cared who got the credit. He was just glad he was there. I didn't say anything to steal Mama's thunder either. There was no need to put a damper on such a precious moment.

"Y'all can come by and eat dinner if you like. We got plenty of leftovers from yesterday's supper. I made chicken and dumplins' again from that hen we didn't eat for the 4$^{\text{th of}}$ July," Mama said as we walked to our cars.

"Sounds like a good idea to me. This mornin' calls for a celebration of some kind, I think," Daddy agreed.

"You want to go there for dinner? If they have leftovers, you wouldn't have to cook?" Theodore suggested.

"I really didn't know what I was going to fix us when we got home anyway. And Daddy is right. Let's celebrate."

"Then chicken and dumplings it is." Theodore smiled, opening the car door, and placing Scarlett on my lap once I was seated.

"I am so proud of you," I said.

"I will have to say, I feel a lot lighter. It's been weighing on my mind for a while now. But I never brought it up," he confessed.

"Some people would call that conviction."

I had been to church and had heard enough sermons about sin being called a heavy load that I knew all the terms.

"Have you ever felt the weight of sin in your heart?" he asked.

"Oh yes. Mama has put guilt on me many times."

"What I was feeling wasn't what anyone else put on me. It was me realizing for myself I was disconnected from God. It wasn't how other people made me feel. It was realizing God's absence in my life that made me know something was missing."

As we rode the rest of the way in silence, my mind swirled. Theodore's question about the weight of sin made me realize the conviction I felt was by Mama—not God. Suddenly, I felt weighted down like Theodore had described.

I needed to do something about that.

"I'LL GET DINNER on the table, Lucretia. You can go on and tend to the baby," Mama offered.

By the time I got Scarlett fed and down for her nap, the table was spread.

"Can you yell for yer daddy and Theodore and tell 'em dinner's ready?" Mama asked as I entered the kitchen.

They were perched on Billie Kay's and my stumps under the willow tree. I gained their attention as soon as I stepped onto the porch. But instead of yelling, I motioned to them as not to risk waking the baby. A second invitation was not needed.

"Smells good, Emmy. And I'm hungry. It was a lengthy service this morning—but it was sure worth it. Theodore, would you like to offer the blessing this time?" Daddy asked.

"I will. But you all remember, this is new to me."

"God don't care nothin' about how pretty you pray. He cares about how honest yer prayer is. Yer among friends here," Mama encouraged.

"Okay, here goes. *God, thank you for looking past the man I was and help me to be the man, husband, father, and son-in-law you would want me to be. I hope you can see inside my heart to know how grateful I am that you blessed me with Lucretia, Scarlett, and our baby on the way, because words alone are not enough. Bless this food and the precious mother and father-in-law who so graciously have welcomed me to their family. Amen.*"

Daddy cleared his throat and averted his eyes. Although not a common occurrence for Mama, she teared up a second time in one day. We were the blessed ones. My parents, Scarlett, my unborn baby, and I were better people because God had put this precious man in our lives. It wasn't youthful impulsiveness, infatuation, or lust—it was genuine love. At that moment, the love I felt for Theodore was more overwhelming than I could have ever imagined.

"Okay. Let's eat. Emmy, pass me some of yer cornbread salad," Daddy said, breaking the silence after Theodore's prayer.

"You made cornbread salad, Mama?"

"Thought I'd give it a try. Yer daddy took quite a liken' to it."

"So, what did you add to the recipe?"

"Nothin.' I usually add a tat of somethin.' But I honestly couldn't think of a thing I could add to make it any better than what you brought last Sunday."

I was shocked. I had never known Mama not to change anyone's recipe. It was just what she did.

"Well, it doesn't matter. What you made is still better. You have that special touch. Any dish you make just tastes more delicious. I don't know why," I said after tasting her salad. Daddy looked up and I winked at him. I knew he understood. Our salads tasted the same but for the second time that day—I didn't steal Mama's thunder.

"You know, not a soul asked this morning why it had been a year since we'd been to church. I'm glad. I wasn't sure what I was going to say if they did," Mama changed the subject.

"Not a one of 'em said anythin' to me about it either. Guess their Mama taught them like mine taught me. You know, *if you caint say, or in this case, ask nothin' good, keep yer mouth shut.*"

"Asa, I think you might have twisted that a bit. My mother taught me the same thing. But it goes. *if you can't say something good about a person, don't say anything at all.* Here's the catch though. Saying nothing isn't our only alternative. We can always say something kind or encouraging instead. That congregation chose kindness over prying. As far as I'm concerned, kindness wins every time," Theodore added.

"Yes, but like I told you would happen. Scarlett gained their attention. They couldn't keep their eyes off of her. That could be another thing to make 'em plum forget about everythin' else too." Daddy never missed a chance to praise Scarlett. He was a smitten Grandpappy for sure.

"Well, I'm mighty impressed with that group of church people. I think that showed real Christian love. It was more important to the Good Lord and them too, for us to be there. They didn't need to know why we stayed away. And of course, the Lord already knew."

I hadn't thought of it that way before, but Mama was right.

"I'm convinced today went the way it was supposed to. It was the way God wanted it to go. And I am glad," Theodore said.

Chapter Twenty-Seven

I WENT FORWARD at church the next Sunday, renewed my faith, and was baptized. Only then did I understand what Theodore was talking about when it came to the heaviness being lifted.

After that day, the Bertram and Dalton families were regulars at the little church on the left between Muddy Ox and Kennett. If anyone in the congregation wondered about the timing of mine and Theodore's wedding, Scarlett's birth, or my growing belly it was never expressed to either my parents or us.

We each found our niche. Of course, Theodore's beautiful voice was put to use. Mama fell right in where she left off in the baking department, Daddy was and always had been the ultimate handyman, and I discovered I had a way with children along with being quite handy with making crafts.

FESTIVALS CAME WITH the fall. The holidays brought

potluck dinners. After that, a new year was on the horizon. We tried to be as involved in church activities as possible. But although many things were similar about my two pregnancies, there were differences as well. I was larger this time. And instead of just leg cramps, I also had backaches. By mid-December I was getting around at what felt like a snail's pace.

Theodore kept his promise. He was a great help. But this being Scarlett's first Christmas, I probably worried about making it special for her, more than I should have. So, I pushed myself. Also, she had two more months of undivided attention before having to share a nursery, grandparents, and—us.

Mama and Daddy agreed to celebrate Christmas morning at our house, so we didn't have to expose Scarlett to the cold. I had biscuits in the oven and country ham frying in the pan when they arrived.

The sweet aroma of cinnamon rolls, not long out of the oven preceded Mama as she entered. Daddy, a pouch flung on his back and bearing a close resemblance to St. Nick himself, shadowed her. All he needed was a pudgier belly and a white beard.

Theodore took Daddy's pouch and placed it under our Christmas tree. Then he poured them coffee. They pulled their chairs on each side of Scarlett's play pen to be near her.

"I just caint get used to seeing a baby put in a cage," Mama remarked.

"Don't think of it as a cage, Mama. It's a playpen. She plays with her toys in there. She actually loves it."

"Well, I never put you in a cage."

"There was only one of me. In two more months, we're going to have two babies. It will be almost like having twins. Only, Scarlett can crawl now. Try to think of it as a way we can keep her safe."

"And we always have her where we are. She can see us at all times. And we can see her," Theodore addressed Mama while smiling at Scarlett.

"It's a full-time job keeping her away from the Christmas tree. You don't want her pulling it over on her or getting choked on a strand of tinsel, do you?" I asked.

"Aww look at her, Emmy. She aint fussin.' She's grinnin' big. Did she cut another tooth? I swear, that baby gets more beautiful ever time we lay eyes on her," Daddy gloated.

"Yer right. If she aint mindin' it, guess I should hush about it too."

I wasn't sure if I had won Mama over about the playpen or she only conceded but I let a sigh of relief either way.

"Alright. The biscuits are almost ready. The ham is done. I'm going to fry up some eggs and we can make our own sandwiches. The rolls can be for after we open presents." I was happy to move on.

"Sounds good to me. You know Scarlett doesn't

know what to expect this year. But next Christmas she's probably going to want to open her presents before breakfast." Theodore smiled.

"Are you sure it's not you that doesn't want to wait until after breakfast?" I teased.

"Guilty as charged," he confessed.

"Scarlett won't even be two years old by this time next year. We may get by with making her wait until Christmas after next for that.

We pulled the playpen closer to the tree to give Scarlett her presents, one at a time. Mama had crocheted her the sweetest little hat, sweater, and mittens to match.

"I made them to fit her now. But, if she out-grows them, and if the other baby's a girl, she can wear 'em. I'll make Scarlett new ones. Far as that goes, I'll just make 'em both new ones."

Having talented and crafty grandparents abolished any worry I had about making Scarlett's first Christmas a memorable one. She had rattles made from dried gourds, blankets and quilts, a personalized rag doll, wooden push-and-pull toys with wheels, and dresses, with pinafores galore, all crafted and perfectly smocked by hand. Once they were all opened, she couldn't decide which toy to grab first.

"Lucretia, can you put on coffee while your dad and I get a few things from his truck?"

"There's more?" I questioned.

"You'll love this," Theodore said.

"Do you know what they are up to?" I probed Mama once they were gone.

"Yes, but I aint about to ruin that man's surprise for that little girl."

Her jaw was set. There was no cracking her. Mama and I laughed to hear the bungling and bumping coming from outside. Santa, his reindeer, and all the elves couldn't have caused any more commotion than my dad and Theodore were at that moment.

They finally flung the door open, and the proud pair came in carrying the most beautiful little wooden rocking horse. Theodore rocked her proudly after setting Scarlett on its hand-carved saddle.

She smiled and jabbered with approval as Theodore sang his *horsey* song he'd composed for her. To make the entire scene complete, Scarlett said, "Horsey, horsey, horsey."

Theodore and Daddy both wiped tears.

"Oh my, that is the cutest thing I have ever seen. So, this is what you two have been so secretive about? And it's the project Daddy has been working with you on for months? I love it."

"More important, that baby loves it. Look at her smile." Mama beamed.

"And I can tell you now, we are working on one with wheels and a handle she can hold onto when she starts trying to walk," Daddy said proudly.

Well, you all have certainly made her first Christmas a special one. That's for sure." I dropped into a chair to rest my feet and back.

"It's not completely over with yet." Theodore said with a huge boyish grin.

"There's more? You've made her more toys?"

"No. The next gift is for you—well us. Sit still a second while we get them."

"Them?" I questioned.

Theodore and Daddy made another trip to the porch and returned with two beautiful, matching, padded, rocking chairs.

"Oh my," I exclaimed.

"We didn't make these," Theodore began.

"But we probably could have," Daddy interrupted. They laughed.

"I went where we got the Jenny Lind baby bed and had the man order us chairs to match the bed as closely as he could. There is one for both of us if our babies need to be rocked at the same time."

Several thoughts brought a smile to my face. I could vision us rocking our babies together. How sweet.

I could also imagine the perplexed look on the store owner's face when Theodore gave him the difficult task of finding chairs to match beds that we gave him a headache about before deciding on the one we wanted. Also, that we would be needing two rocking chairs, instead of just one. That's okay. I am sure when all was said and done, he appreciated another sale, especially to a man that was more concerned about what he wanted than he was about the price tag.

One more reason to love Theodore Xavier Dalton.

Chapter Twenty-Eight

NEW YEAR'S EVE brought us cherished memories. We laughed reminiscing about how we'd forgotten to bang pans, shoot the gun or yell to the neighbors because we were so shaken from our first kiss. He loved it when I confessed I wanted him to kiss me every night for the rest of our lives from then on.

"And I promise to never let a night pass until I've done just that."

Then, in the fashion I had grown accustomed to since our very first New Year's Eve—he kept his promise.

THE ENTIRE MONTH of January,1945 was brutal. It brought a mixture of cold rains, ice storms, and snow to the Bootheel of Missouri. Being only days from giving birth, the conditions pretty much isolated me. I couldn't chance slipping and falling on the ice—nor could Mama. Theodore carried messages back and forth and truthfully, at that point, I would have settled to hear her fussing at me just to hear her voice.

"I'm back from town. I stopped by to check in on Asa and Emmy. They're fine and send their love. Your Mama said to keep your eye on the calendar. There's a full moon these next few days." Theodore placed several heavy bags and a big pot of something on the kitchen table.

"Does the weather show any sign of letting up? I haven't seen Mama and Daddy for over a month. Since it's into the second week of February, I was hoping it would get better so they can come over."

"If not, I will go pick them up myself for a visit one day," Theodore promised.

"That would be nice. But you shouldn't risk being out on the slick roads either unless it's absolutely necessary."

"If getting her over here is because you need her, that's necessary. She sent some turnip greens and cornbread for supper. How does that sound?"

"Sounds good to me if it's okay with you."

I hadn't felt good all day. I'd had a very restless night and a lingering back pain since early morning. I wasn't up to cooking and for that matter, much of anything else.

"Oh, and she sent a peach cobbler too," he added.

"Well, that settles it. Mama's peach cobbler is the best."

When I stood to waddle toward the kitchen, he said for me to sit.

"Turnip greens are easy to warm up. I can handle that. You just stay where you are."

"Thank you. My back has been hurting a lot today. I must have slept wrong or something."

"Is there a chance it could be labor?"

"I don't think so. It feels different than when I went into labor with Scarlett."

"Well, does labor always feel the same every time?"

"Since this is my second baby and I haven't had it yet, I really don't know."

"True. I obviously am not any help in the labor department, but I can handle heating up the greens. Do you want anything else to go with…?"

"Oh…oh…" The second groan was louder and drawn out.

"What's wrong? You okay?" Theodore looked per-plexed.

"This might be one of those absolutely necessary times to be on slick roads. Maybe you should go get Mama and Daddy and contact Dr. McFarnz on the way."

Theodore grabbed the playpen, set it in our bed-room, and put Scarlett in it with ample toys to keep her occupied, before helping me into bed. I cautioned him to drive carefully up until he closed the door behind him.

Then I prayed.

In answer to his question earlier, if this was labor, then no it wasn't the same as with Scarlett. I ached with her a couple of days before actual labor set in. These back aches only started this morning. And the sharp pain I felt that set him running for help didn't come until closer to delivery before. What if I had this baby all alone? What if something went wrong? I wouldn't know what to do. What if…

"Lucretia?"

"I'm in here. In the bedroom."

"When did your pains begin?" Doctor McFarnz questioned, pulling a stethoscope from his bag.

"They were only light pains this morning. But they got real bad, real quick," I moaned.

"Sometimes that happens with your second delivery. Okay, let's see what's going on." His voice was calming and reassuring.

"Where's Theodore and Mama? How did you get here before them? How did you know I needed you?"

"Deke McCrady came running into my office. Said Theodore flagged him down and asked him to tell me to get here as soon as I could. I'm guessing your man and your Mama and Daddy will be here any time now."

"Good. Mama and Daddy haven't been able to come for a long time because of this weather."

"Alright, looks like you're well on your way to having this baby. But I'm pretty sure your Mama will be here for the grand…"

The sound of Mama's voice made me smile, even if she did sound like a drill sergeant. "Theodore, fill a couple of the biggest pots y'all got with water and get 'em boilin.' Asa put 'em greens in the refrigerator 'fore they sour. Theodore, after you get that water on, round up those old heavy blankets we used on the bed when Scarlett was born."

Theodore and Daddy followed Mama's directions completely.

"How's it look, doctor? Sorry it took us so long to get here." She took a long breath as if she might have run the entire way.

"I understand. The roads are pretty bad right now. Looks like it's not going to take near as long to get this grandbaby here as it did the last one, Emerald. Glad y'all made it here when you did."

"Here are those blankets you wanted, Emmy," Theodore said entering the room.

"Good. Now, can you help us raise her up so we can get 'em in place?"

Before the doctor could get in position to help, Theodore had me in his arms. Mama quickly had the blankets in place. He gently lowered me to the bed, kissed my forehead, and said he would be right in the other room.

After handing Scarlett to Daddy, standing just beyond the bedroom door, he grabbed the playpen on his way out.

"Come to Grandpappy, sweet little girl. Let's go in here and wait for your mother to get yer baby brother or sister here," Daddy said as they left.

I tried to keep my moans and whimpers to a low. I didn't want to upset Scarlett. She was too young to know what was going on.

"Okay, push Lucretia. Push hard. Give us one big last push," the doctor instructed.

I gripped one of Mama's hands, while she kept wiping my face and forehead with the other.

"Yer doing great, Lucretia," she encouraged.

I bit down hard on the rolled cloth Mama gave me. I couldn't stifle my high-pitched screech as I gave one last forceful push.

"She's out. It's another girl," the doctor exclaimed.

"I had Scarlett a best friend for life," I muttered before succumbing to exhaustion.

"Here she is. Another beauty," the doctor said as he laid my new baby girl across my chest.

"Oh, my goodness. Look at that sweet face. I'll go tell Asa and Theodore we've got another girl," Mama gushed as she left the room.

"Lucretia, you brought that little girl into this world like a trooper. And this baby was a bit bigger than the last one. But you did good. Well, I'm finished with my part. I'll go send her daddy in to meet her," the doctor said.

Theodore's eyes repeatedly brimmed with tears, replacing the ones that wouldn't stop rolling down his cheeks. It took him a few minutes to gain enough composure to speak.

"Another beautiful baby girl. I couldn't be happier."

"Then I don't have to ask if you're disappointed that we didn't have a boy."

"I am not disappointed one bit. I already had a fine boy," he said proudly.

"Yes, you did. Well, truthfully, I'm not disappointed either. I like it that we have two girls to grow up together. Billie Kay brought that up the day I told her we were having another baby. She said if we had another girl, Scarlett would have a baby sister and a best friend too."

"Like you and Billy Kay are best friends, right?"

"Yes. We're like sister-friends."

Theodore smiled.

"Have you thought of any names?"

"What about Melanie. Scarlett's best friend in *Gone With the Wind* was Melanie," I suggested.

"I like that. Melanie Dalton. It has a nice ring to it."

"Melanie Annella Dalton, after your mother. Remember, we said if we had another child and if it was a girl, we would name it after your mother?"

"My mother would be so proud and honored to have our daughter be her namesake. Lucretia, you have made me a very happy man." More tears rolled.

"Can Scarlett and her Grandpappy meet that baby sister now?" Daddy appeared at the door with Scarlett in his arms.

"I got Dr. McFarnz taken care of with a hot cup of coffee, so I'd like to witness this introduction too," Mama said. She was the one trailing behind Daddy this time.

Theodore lifted the baby so they could see her better as they entered the room.

"Meet Melanie Annella Dalton," he proudly announced.

Chapter Twenty-Nine

MAMA TAUGHT ME the ways of motherhood so well when Scarlett was born that she decided only a couple of days after Melanie's birth I could be on my own.

"Are you sure you don't need to stay at least one more day?" I didn't share her confidence.

"No, if y'all keep on like yer doin' you'll be fine."

Mama had always delighted in being in charge. For her to step back and push me forward was overwhelming for me and strangely out of character for her. I was wishing she would see how inadequate I felt. If she did, she dismissed it.

"I worry I can't produce enough milk to nurse both babies," I confessed.

"Lucretia, women with twins do it all the time. Look how healthy Scarlett is. You've always had plenty of good milk for her. It'll be there for Melanie too. The more you nurse, the more the milk comes. You'll get the hang of it."

"But what if my milk runs dry?"

"Healthy eatin' and nursin' regular is the trick. Set a schedule fer them babies and stick to it. The Good Lord thought of everything when He created us mothers. If we do our part—He does His. Don't worry. Muddy Ox aint that far away. I can be here in no time if you need me. But from what I've seen so far, yer doin' good."

"Scarlett's eleven months old and pulling up to things. The way she's going, she'll be walking soon. I suspected it would be harder after the baby came but it's worse than I imagined."

"You got that cage…uh playpen. I've come around to seein' how them things can be mighty handy. And you got Theodore. I been watchin' how he does with Scarlett. Some men are as useless as a wooden skillet when it comes to handlin' babies. Not that man. You got a good 'un there. You may have to shift it into second gear sometimes with two babies pullin' at you, but y'all can do it."

"Theodore is not only a big help, but he also calms me when I get panicky. He has that way about him."

"Guess I might as well tell you. You know how I can just have a feelin' about some things? Well, I got this strong feelin' like I need to get on home. We aint seen nothin' of yer Daddy since he left here yesterday. That aint like him. And now, it's way past dinner time. That aint like him neither."

There it was. She hadn't said anything as to not alarm us, but Mama was worried about Daddy. I had been so consumed with my own woes; I hadn't given his absence a lot of thought. Knowing his obsession with the babies, she had a right to be concerned by him not showing up. And now, so was I.

"Scarlett's down for her nap and Melanie's cradle is right here next to you. Will you be okay until I get back from taking your mother home?" Theodore asked as he and Mama stood at the door to leave.

"I'll be fine. Go on and get her home to Daddy. And be careful on the roads." I cautioned.

"The roads are clear now. I won't be gone long," he assured.

"Thank you for all your help, Mama. I hope Daddy is safe. I love you. Tell him I love him too."

"I will. I am so proud of y'all." She smiled and quietly closed the door.

For the first time in a week, other than an occasional cooing from the nearby cradle, and the rhythmic swinging pendulum on the eight-day wall clock—there was only silence.

Melanie was sleeping sweetly. She and Scarlett were both beautiful babies. Although they had prominently different features, they favored enough that it was obvious they were sisters. Scarlett had my dark hair, green eyes, and Theo's dimpled chin. Melanie's hair was sandy blond. Her dimples were at the corners of her mouth.

I had so much to be thankful for. Our babies and I were healthy. The doctor's watchful eye was on Theodore. The house was warm, our pantry was full, life was good. Surely, there were valid reasons we hadn't heard from Daddy.

Please God—Daddy has to be okay. He just has to be, I prayed silently. In my entire life, Daddy was always okay.

Had I not drifted off to sleep, I would've been concerned about how long Theodore had been gone. His hand on my shoulder startled me awake.

"Daddy—is Daddy okay?"

"Yes, but…"

"Oh no, but what?" I tried to brace for the worst.

"He slipped on the steps after feeding the chickens this morning. When we arrived, he had pulled himself up next to the wall for protection from the cold. Your mother and I managed to get him to Doctor McFarnz's office."

"How bad is it? Did he break anything?"

"I'm afraid so. The Doctor is pretty sure Asa's shin bone is fractured. His knee is badly bruised and swollen and his ankle was so big his boot had to be cut off to even examine it. Doc can't tell if his ankle is broken until after the swelling goes down a bit."

"Oh no. Poor Daddy."

"He was given something for pain and is warmed up now. The doctor said had your mother and I not arrived when we did, your dad could have suffered from hypothermia—maybe even died.

"That's scary. Mama had a feeling something was

wrong."

"Yes, she was on pins and needles all the way there. She said she could feel his distress in her spirit. She didn't want to let you know how worried she was. But she also said, she felt sure we could handle what we had going with the babies."

"Now, we have to. Mama will have her hands full taking care of Daddy. It's not going to be easy either. He'll be fit to be tied that he can't get out in the field. Spring planting is only a little over a month away."

"Asa is likely to be out of commission for some time. I wish I knew about farming so I could help—but I don't. I will try to hire someone who does though. I can do that," Theodore promised.

"Daddy's going to hate every part of this. He won't like being waited on. He'll really be out of sorts that he can't tend his own field. And he was so looking forward to bouncing the girls on his knees."

"He can still bounce them. But until his damage gets repaired, he'll have to bounce them on his good knee one at a time. Also, would you believe that with all his injuries, he was worried that they had to cut off his boot? I promised him another pair as soon as he could get around again."

"Daddy loved those boots. I'm not surprised at all, knowing Daddy. Do you have anyone in mind to hire to work his crops?"

"Deke McCrady is the person who has always been

available to do what I need done. I'll start with him."

"He may be able to drive a tractor and hitch a plow, but you may have to keep Larson Strom on hand to fix things if and when they get broken," I said, remembering how Deke was always getting Larson to help with his car. Remembering also, how frequently Daddy's equipment would break down.

"I'll hire them both then. If that is what it takes." Theodore said with certainty.

Chapter Thirty

THE AROMA OF spring flowers tickled our noses, and our faces were kissed by the April sun. I sat holding Melanie on the porch while Theodore chased thirteen-month-old Scarlett as she ran through the fresh, green, grass. A soft breeze tossed the leaves of the willow tree as its branches swayed to the song of the birds nested above. Had this scene been a family portrait, the peace of God could have been its frame.

"Scarlett is going to have so much fun hunting Easter eggs this year." An out-of-breath Theodore wrestled the giggly toddler to join us on the porch.

"She's going to make every one of our holidays more fun from now on. They both are. Do you want to hold Melanie while I chase Scarlett for a while?" Scarlett was content for the moment pulling the petals off the dandelions she had picked. But I knew she would be squirming to get down again soon.

"I may take you up on that. The little one isn't mobile yet," he joked.

"It could be Scarlett has run herself ragged enough that after she eats, she'll be ready for her nap. Then I can nurse the baby while you're gone to pick up Mama and Daddy for supper."

"Sounds good to me."

As soon as he stood for us to take the girls inside, Deke McCrady and Larson Strom pulled in the yard.

"Hang on a second. They are probably coming by to get paid," Theodore said before sitting back down.

"Those are two fine looking babies you got there," Larson said as he approached.

"Pretty as little dolls," Deke echoed.

"Thank you, they get their looks from their mother," Theodore teased.

I smiled.

"They sure do. I mean…ah…yer not bad lookin' either. But you aint pretty like their mother is. No disrespect intended to you Mr. Dalton or you either, ma'am." Deke spoke too quickly. He kept looking for the right words to dig himself out of his awkward ramble.

I didn't know how to respond until they all, including Theodore, laughed.

"Thank you again. I need to get *this* little beauty down for her nap."

I started to swap babies with Theodore before I remembered he would need both hands to get his wallet and pay them. They had come directly from the field. Neither of their hands were clean enough that I wanted them holding my baby. I automatically shifted Melanie to one arm and held Scarlett on the opposite hip while

Theodore paid them their wages.

"Thank ya, Mr. Dalton," Larson said before turning to walk away.

"Yes, thank you. Just wanted to let you know we may need to get that plow sharpened before long," Deke said.

"Okay, I'll be seeing Asa in a little while, I'll ask him who he usually gets to do it and get back with you.

"Sounds good. Y'all have a nice rest of the weekend," Deke tipped his hat to me as he turned to leave.

"You two fellas do the same," Theodore replied.

We remained seated until they drove away.

"Those are two hard-working men right there. I've never asked anything from either of them that they weren't willing to do."

"They sure have been a help during Daddy's recovery."

"I wish you could have seen the look on your face when you realized one of them could be holding the baby while I got the money from my wallet to pay them. You did some fast thinking there."

"I wasn't snubbing them. I wouldn't want you or even me holding either of the girls with hands that dirty," I justified.

We swapped babies once inside. I took Scarlett to the nursery. He found a comfortable position on the couch to hold Melanie.

As Scarlett's eyes went from partially to completely

closed, I heard Theodore softly singing to Melanie from the living room.

Eyes of hazel,

Blond Ringlets galore,

How could this Daddy,

Love you one heartbeat more…

"Sounds like you've written Melanie her own song," I said after getting Scarlett in her crib.

"When it comes to our girls, all my songs are interchangeable. I love them both more than I can say."

"That's so sweet. Want me to nurse her now while you go get Mama and Daddy? All I have to do is whip up some biscuits after they get here, and supper will be ready."

"I'll be ready when it is. I've worked up an appetite, chasing Scarlett. That little girl might be a track star when she grows up."

"The doctor said you needed plenty of exercise. But he also said not to overdo it."

"I have a check-up with him pretty soon, don't I?"

"It's the Tuesday after Easter. That's still about two weeks away," I replied.

"I'll be fine until then. You worry too much," he consoled.

"You would tell me if something was wrong, wouldn't you? Remember the doctor said you didn't have to wait until your appointment to let him know."

I scanned his face for any warning signs. There was nothing alarming. He looked a little tired but that was understandable these days.

"No new problems that I can think of. But maybe he needs to increase the Digitalis now that Scarlett's training to be a track star." He joked on his way out the door to go pick up my parents.

If his joking was to keep me from worrying—it wasn't working.

"Alright, baby girl. It's your turn now. Let's get your little belly full so you can go to sleep," I whispered to Melanie.

Her big hazel eyes met mine and she smiled as though she understood my every word before starting to nurse. She was such a pleasant baby. I needed to ask Theodore if anyone in his family had dimples at the corners of their mouth like she did.

Chapter Thirty-One

"I ALWAYS GET Jake Walby, over in Doodlum Switch to do my blacksmithin.' Matter a fact, he's my brother-in-law. His wife Effie is Emmy's sister. I got a runnin' account with him. Just have yer man take whatever needs workin' on to Jake and he will add it to my tab. I sure do appreciate you takin' charge like this. Don't know what we'd do without you." Daddy was visibly humbled by Theodore's effort.

"I'm sure Deke knows Jake. I think he knows about everyone in these parts. I'll tell him Monday where to take it when the time comes. He just said the blades may need sharpening before long. Didn't sound like anything urgent when he mentioned it to me."

"The biscuits are ready," I announced. "Let's eat while the babies are sleeping."

"Won't be long 'til Scarlett will be wantin' to eat at the table with us," Mama remarked.

"Emmy, remember how you use to grab yer bites 'tween feedin' Lucretia while you tried to hold her still on yer lap?"

"Oh yes, I remember that well," Mama replied flatly.

"Scarlett needs a highchair." Theodore had a lightbulb-moment.

"She'll be needin' one soon. That's fer sure." Mama agreed.

"We're going to need two highchairs eventually. Might as well get two while we're at it and save ourselves a trip," Theodore added.

"Scarlett is still nursing but I've been giving her a few things off the table here lately too. She loves gravy and biscuits."

"She has to. She's my grandbaby aint she?" Daddy laughed.

"How's the leg and ankle doing, Asa?" Theodore questioned.

"Doc said I shouldn't put my full weight on it for another month or two. Said a break like I caused needed plenty of time to heal if I wanted to walk the rest of my life without a serious limp."

"Doc McFarnz knows what he's doin.' He's been the doctor in Muddy Ox fer a long time. Why, he delivered Lucretia. Let me back that up. She come 'fore he got there but he finished things up after he finally made it," Mama clarified.

"I think that is special. The same doctor that delivered Lucretia, delivered our girls too," Theodore said.

"*Almost.* I said he *almost* delivered Lucretia," Mama stressed.

"Was him that signed the birth certificate, anyway," Daddy added.

"Well, I hope y'all let him catch his breath 'fore he has to deliver another child fer you two. You got yer hands full with these babies for now."

"You're right about that. Our hands are full. I agreed."

Theodore helped Daddy to the porch for some fresh air while we did the dishes.

"Didn't Daddy ever take turns with you to feed me when I was little like Scarlett, Mama? You know, to let you finish your meal, after he finished his?"

She stopped washing dishes and faced me. "Have you been gone from our house so long that you forgot who and how yer Daddy is? Remember me tellin' you about how some men are? Yer Daddy is one of the best farmers and one of the hardest workers in Muddy Ox. There aint much that man caint do when he sets his mind to it. But he's of the opinion that there's man's work and then there's woman's work. And as far as he's concerned, takin' care of and feedin' babies is all woman's work."

"What does he think about how Theodore helps me?"

"Guess it's different with him when its yer daughter on the receivin' end. He don't say nothin' against Theodore for helpin' you."

"That's good to hear."

"Don't take this wrong cause yer Daddy thinks a whole lot of him. But since Theodore don't seem to know how to do much of anything else, he might as well do womanly things. Now, yer Daddy didn't put it just like that, but I'm readin' tween the lines."

"Well, in his defense, Theodore is a very manly man. He makes sure the truck is serviced before winter, keeps the porch, and walk shoveled all winter long, and provides for us very well. That's manly."

"Now don't get all riled up. Like I said, yer Daddy is crazy about him. But, to tell you the truth, I think Asa probably learned how to walk holdin' on to a plow. He aint never known nothin' but hard work in his life. He caint even imagine what a life without hard work would be. Anyways, like I said, don't take it wrong."

"Mama, is that what you think of Theodore too?"

"Aint I made it clear to you what I think of him? I admit I was worried when y'all first got together 'bout him being so much older than you. But like that preacher said at the church last time we were there; God's got His own idea how things ought to go. I see now that Theodore and you are exactly what you needed a little over a year ago and yer still what you both need now. Don't ever tell yer Daddy and I'll deny it if you do, but I'd a give anythin' if Asa had a helped me just a little bit when you was a baby, like Theodore helps you."

"I'm sorry you had it so hard, Mama. I know you love Daddy and no doubt he loves you. He just has his own way of showing it."

"Oh, I wouldn't know what to do without him. And havin' it hard has made me the strong woman I am today. I aint complainin.' God had His own idea 'bout me too. I'm thankful for that."

Scarlett cried as Theodore and Daddy were coming back into the house. Within seconds Melanie whimpered.

"I'll get Scarlett. You get Melanie," Theodore said to me on his way in.

"Why don't you let me get Scarlett this time so I can feel useful. Besides, I'm glad they're both awake. I've been waitin' to show y'all what I made for 'em. I snuck the bag in the nursery when we first got here," Mama said.

"Okay, then. I'll put on a pot of coffee. I know for a fact you had a cake with you when you got in the truck," Theodore replied.

"Now, aint this the cutest little thing? She's all ready for Easter come next Sunday. And there's one to match for the baby too."

"You made the girls matching dresses and bonnets for Easter? Mama, you've been busy."

"I been hangin' on to this flour-sack material for a while now. It being yellow with purple flowers, it was ideal for their Easter dresses. Purple always was yer favorite color, right?"

"Yes, I love purple. Mama, they are adorable."

"Yes, and them dresses and bonnets aint bad either.

My lap is a waitin' for that little one now that I got situated here on the couch. But make sure she aint wet first." Daddy laughed.

"Here you go, Daddy. She's dry and ready for you."

"I've been meaning to ask y'all. Since Melanie Annella is such a mouth full, can we call this baby Melly Ann?" Daddy asked as I placed her on his lap.

I looked at Theodore to read his reaction.

"I think Melly Ann is cute, don't you Lucretia?" he agreed.

"Yes, I do. Melly Ann, you be a good baby now and don't spit up on your Grandpappy," I teased.

"I forgot. Babies can get you from both ends, caint they? Maybe you better hand me a bigger spit-rag—just in case." Daddy said it as a joke, but we all knew he was serious.

The room roared with laughter.

Chapter Thirty-Two

"HOW MANY EGGS did Scarlett find?" Theodore asked once we were in the car after church.

"I haven't counted. But her basket Is full. What about hiding them again, after we get to Mama and Daddy's. Then after dinner, she can have another hunt and they can watch since they missed it the first time."

"My plan exactly." He grinned.

"I'll have to tell Mama how everyone went on about the girl's outfits. I hate they had to miss the Easter service, but Daddy still can't get around good enough for that."

"He should be better by the end of May. That's another month from now. I will ask the doctor at my appointment on Tuesday."

"I pray you both get a good report."

"I'm praying for the same thing," he agreed.

"I overheard you and Daddy talking the other day. Does he know you are paying Deke and Larson every week and that you took care of his account with Jake Walby?"

"He knows Deke and Larson need money to live on and I am paying them weekly. But he doesn't know I paid Jake. And I asked Jake to keep it between the two of us for now. Asa keeps saying he will settle up with me after the crops are harvested. Of course, I have no intention of letting him. He can't afford that. But I don't have to tell him about that now. We will have that discussion when the time comes."

"One of these days, you need to let me in on where all the money is coming from. I've never asked before."

"Remember I told you how my mother made secret investments for me?"

"She must have invested a lot. You are very free with it as far as I can see."

"She did. But I learned you have to let the money work for you too. So, I used most of that invested money to purchase stock in a company in St. Louis called Small Arms. They are one of the largest suppliers of arms and ammunition in the United States. I never fought but Theo did. It was my way of helping him and supporting our country too. The contract with them is huge. It has done well for us."

"That's good to know."

While we rode the rest of the way in silence, my mind went back to Mama's and my conversation. I wished I could tell her that Theodore didn't have to know how to pull a plow as long as he was wise enough to pull the right financial strings. But that line of conversation would open up a whole new can of worms that I didn't want to waste our day with. It was Easter

Sunday and we needed to enjoy it.

"OKAY, TELL ME what they all said about the babies' outfits," Mama began right after Theodore finished saying Grace over our meal.

"Well, as you probably already expected, eyes turned the second we walked in. And we were surrounded as soon as church was dismissed. Everyone loved the outfits and went on and on about the girls."

"And from the pulpit, the preacher asked that everyone pray for Asa's complete healing, and for you while you're nursing him back to health," Theodore added.

"That group of church people really does love you all, Mama."

"It's good to be thought well of. We love them too," she replied.

"Sure is. Sure do," Daddy agreed.

"Oh, I forgot to tell you, Asa. I ran into Effie the other day at the Big Store. I invited her and Jake over later to have some cake with us since it's Easter. They're always so busy with their church and their family I don't get to see much of my sister anymore."

I looked at Theodore to get his reaction. Even though he had asked Jake to keep their agreement confidential, the subject of Daddy's account at Jake's shop could accidentally come up. Theodore had shared with me only moments before how he wasn't ready to discuss that with Daddy.

"Well, good. I aint talked to Jake in a while now. Maybe we can catch up on a few things," Daddy said.

"I haven't seen Aunt Effie in a while, either. And they have never met our girls," I said, trying to lead the conversation in another direction.

"It should be a fun time then. They'll enjoy watching Scarlett hunt Easter eggs." Theodore sounded unconcerned about Uncle Jake spilling any beans. So, I shouldn't worry either.

Dinner was interrupted by a wail from Scarlett. As usual, her crying woke Melanie.

"Lucretia, bring Scarlett to me so you can nurse the baby," Mama yelled as I rushed to answer their calls.

"But you're still eating, Emmy. Go on and finish your dinner," Theodore said, pushing back from the table to help me.

"I don't mind a'tall. Sit back down and finish yer dinner. I'm experienced with holdin' a young'un on my lap and eatin' too. Lucretia, bring her to me after you get her diaper changed," Mama insisted.

"Are you sure?," Theodore asked Mama again.

"I'm positive. I bet she'll love some of these taters and gravy. Let me have that little girl," Mama repeated as I placed Scarlett in her lap.

In true character, Daddy continued eating, oblivious to our entire exchange.

"Asa, I have your chair ready for you out on the porch. Can I help you get to it?" Theodore offered after our meal.

"I've been getting' around pretty good with this cane. But you can steady me if you see me a wobblin.' Lucretia, you can bring Melly Ann to me after I get sat down, if you want. I caint handle that other little firecracker though, not yet anyway."

"She's a firecracker alright," Theodore agreed. "That's why we brought the playpen. It definitely cuts down on the amount of running I have to do to keep up with her."

"Here's the baby, Daddy. Thank you. I can take her back if you get tired of holding her after Mama and I get the dishes done." I said, carefully placing Melanie in his arms.

"She may get tired of me, but I won't get tired of her, unless she starts spillin' over from somewhere. I don't know what to do with 'em when they start doin' all that," I heard him say as I left to help Mama in the kitchen.

"I'll be out here with you, Asa. I'm so experienced by now with them spilling over as you put it, I can handle anything she does," Theodore said while unfolding the playpen and searching for a shady spot to set it in.

"I never said it before but, it pleases me to see how much help you are to our daughter with these babies. And it makes me ashamed that I didn't help Emerald like that with Lucretia."

I flinched when Mama dropped her iron skillet on the floor.

"Everythin' still in one piece in there Emmy?" Daddy yelled.

"Yes, I dropped a skillet when I felt a cold chill run up my back. And the devil just put on his over-coat cause his fiery lake froze over. Other than that, everything is fine."

I heard Theodore snicker. And I held my hand tightly over my mouth to stifle a laugh.

Mama did too.

"SCARLETT, BE CAREFUL. You're about to spill all your eggs out of your basket," I cautioned from the porch while Theodore helped her find Easter eggs.

"Lucretia, y'all got two of the prettiest babies I seen in a long time," Aunt Effie said, watching Scarlett run from one corner of the yard to the other.

"Look at those little legs go. That baby girl can really run," Uncle Jake remarked.

"Yes, Theodore said the other day he thinks she's going to be a track star when she gets in high school."

"Whoops! Lucretia, I think I need another spit-rag. This uns' spillin' over again." Daddy held Melanie in the air while drool ran down her chin.

"I'll take her," Aunt Effie said. "A little spit-up don't scare me none."

Mama pitched her a fresh rag. Aunt Effie had Melanie cleaned up in one swipe.

"Here's a wet one for you, Lucretia. Yer gonna need it when Scarlett finds all those eggs and starts diggin' into that Easter candy."

"Aww…Emmy. I think that's one of the times they look the cutest, when they have their faces all smeared with chocolate," Uncle Jake said, then laughed loudly.

"That's cause you aint the one washin' them up or tryin' to get chocolate stains out of their clothes," Aunt Effie quipped sharply.

"So, I want you to know I'll be settlin' up with you at yer shop, Jake, as soon as my crops are done," Daddy cut in.

"Uh…," Jake began.

Theodore reached the porch in time to clear his throat loudly to interrupt.

"Oh…oh…now Asa, you know I aint worried about that. Besides, I know where you live," Uncle Jake joked.

When Daddy heard Scarlett ask for candy, he forgot

where he was going with his conversation with Uncle Jake and addressed Mama.

"Emmy. Don't we have some more candy somewhere for this little girl?"

"Sure do, Grandpappy. I'll get it right now. Are the rest of y'all ready for cake and coffee?" Mama asked on her way inside.

"Sounds good to me. What kind of cake you got Emerald?" Uncle Jake asked.

"Coconut," Mama replied.

"Umm…Umm. Asa, we lucked up when it comes to gettin' wives that can cook," Uncle Jake remarked.

"That we did. So, where was I? Oh yeah, 'bout that account…I"

"Daddy, did you tell Uncle Jake about your slow smoker?" I interrupted.

"What slow smoker?" Jake questioned.

Getting Daddy talking about his smoker filled the remainder of the conversation that day. That and how good Mama's cake was.

Before they left, Uncle Jake had an order in for a smoker too as soon as Daddy was able.

Chapter Thirty-Three

I COULD TELL by how Theodore plopped down on the couch he had not gotten the report from the doctor that he hoped to receive.

"You don't look very happy. What did the doctor say?"

"Evidently, the Digitalis isn't helping." Theodore confessed.

"Does he think Mama should drag out the sassafras tea root?"

"Not as long as I am still taking the Digitalis. He's hoping it will start making a difference over time. Let's let the sassafras root idea stay in the cellar as long as your Mama doesn't bring it up or out."

IT WAS FOUR months after Daddy's accident. His shin and ankle were healing nicely but the doctor all but forbade him to try to get on and off a tractor. He described it as a near miracle that he was able to repair

Daddy's breaks as well as he did. And he feared that if he injured himself again, Daddy's quality of life, as far as getting around or tending his farm, could be greatly compromised.

The doctor got through to him. Daddy agreed for Deke and Larson to continue working his crops the rest of the year.

There was also a glimmer of hope that the war was winding down. Hitler committed suicide on April 30th. Germany formally surrendered on May 8th. We only needed Japan to get on the peace wagon too.

We—I tried to remain hopeful on all fronts. But, although he had been more careful with his diet and continued to take the Digitalis religiously, I couldn't see any improvement in Theodore's health or energy level. He did his best to keep up with fifteen-month-old Scarlett and bounce four-month-old Melanie on his knee every chance he got. But as much as he tried to hide it, I saw how quickly he became overly tired and winded.

"I can't believe that yesterday was already the fourth of June. It's only a month until the 4th of July again. Your dad and I never got that smoker built for us. We forgot all about it after his slip and fall in February."

I handed Theodore a cold glass of tea after he had sat down to rest for the second time in an hour. "Daddy built his in one weekend. There is still time," I replied.

"Asa is moving a lot slower now. Guess maybe I am

too. I'm worn out from trimming a few low-hanging limbs from that willow tree. And the walk from the shed to here on the porch after putting the cutter away finished me up. I'll be glad when that *wonder cure* I'm taking finally does its job."

"Me too. I've been wanting to bring that up for a long time. I'm glad you said it first."

Before Theodore could reply, Deke McCrady's car whipped into the yard. "Do either of y'all know where Mr. Bertram keeps his key to the shed? He said he had some extra cans of oil in there for his tractor."

Theodore looked at me, I suppose hoping if I knew I would speak up. Instead of answers, I had questions.

"Isn't he at home? He's stayed pretty close to home since his accident. Didn't Mama tell you where Daddy keeps the key?"

"No ma'am. Sorry, guess you hadn't heard. He was backin' out of their yard just as I was pullin' up. Woulda' backed right into me if I hadn't seen him first. Said he had to get yer mother to Dr. McFarnz's office in a hurry. I didn't have time to ask him nothin'."

"What was wrong with Mama?"

"I don't know, ma'am. Like I said. He didn't take time to talk."

"He used to keep the key up under a water bucket he let sit by the corner of the shed. Theodore. We need to go!"

"Thanks. I'll go look under that bucket. Y'all run on

to the doctor. I hope yer mother…"

I didn't stop to hear Deke finish. Theodore grabbed Scarlett from her playpen. I was out the door with Melanie in seconds. We left a trail of dust as we sped to Dr. McFarnz's office.

"Whatever is wrong with Mama, please God let her be okay," I prayed silently. I had whispered those same words in a prayer for Daddy only a few months before. What was happening? My world suddenly felt tilted.

We rushed into the office like mad people, each of us holding a wide-eyed child. I heard Daddy's muffled voice beyond the slightly cracked door to the doctor's examining room. Theodore sat down, shifted Scarlett on his lap, and with his free arm, reached for Melanie. I started toward the door, but Daddy's next question stopped me in my tracks.

"Is she goin' to make it Doc?" Daddy's voice was quivering.

"Yes, but only because you got her here so quickly. Time is of the essence with stroke victims. You saved her life, man." I detected a slight quiver in the doctor's voice as well. After all, he and Mama went way back.

"So, she's goin' to be okay. Thank God. That is such good news."

"Asa, I said she's going to live. But…"

"But what Doc?"

"It is according to what your definition of okay is. Emerald will come out of this, but she will suffer some paralysis. Whether it's long term or short term remains to be seen.

I winced. Daddy and the doctor turned to face me.

"Lucretia, yer Mama's had a stroke." Daddy's voice broke again.

"I heard. How bad is her paralysis, doctor?" My question was barely audible.

"She's partially paralyzed on her left side. But these things can get better with time. As I told Asa, she's a lucky woman he got her here when he did. He saved her life."

"Can she walk? Talk? The left side of her face and mouth is drooping. Will that stay that way, doctor?" I asked after joining them.

"I'm going to have her transferred to the hospital in Dyersburg. There are tests they can do to determine the extent of her damage. Again, time will tell."

"I will stay with her until she gets to come home. If I can't be in her room, I'll stay in the lobby. If I have to, I'll sit out under a tree in the yard of that hospital. But I aint leavin' yer Mama 'til we find out something or until I can bring her home."

Daddy's unwavering determination calmed me some. I knew he would do what he said. I also knew he had every intention of eventually bringing Mama home.

Chapter Thirty-Four

AFTER A WEEK, Mama came home as Daddy had promised. He also never left the hospital until she could leave with him—another kept promise. Theodore took him clothes and food, trying to be as supportive as possible.

There was some improvement for Mama's paralysis. She could walk behind a wheelchair for a short distance, by dragging her left foot slightly. The drooping in her face and mouth had lessened. And although her speech was somewhat impaired, she could talk. Luckily, her right arm was not affected by the stroke so she could feed and somewhat bathe herself.

Because of the babies, I didn't get to go see them as often as I would have liked. However, Theodore checked on them practically every day.

MELANIE WAS KICKING and cooing in her cradle and Scarlett was playing with the rag doll Mama made her for Christmas. I stood to clear the breakfast dishes.

"Before you get busy with the dishes, could we talk a minute?" Theodore's tone got my immediate attention and I sat back down.

"Sounds serious." I replied.

"Actually, it is," he said, reaching for my hand.

"Theodore, is something wrong?" I shifted in my chair and tried to prepare for what he had to say.

"Everything that has happened with your parents here lately has made me realize how fragile life can be."

"I know. Daddy could have died in February from hypothermia. Or his fall could have been even worse. And now, Mama has had a stroke. The doctor clearly said had Daddy not got her to him when he did, we would have lost her. I can't bear to think about that."

"Lucretia, I feel like I need to make you aware of our finances and how to take care of things if something unexpectedly were to happen to me. I hadn't seen the need before, but I do now."

"Why now? Has something changed with you?"

"I'd like for you and the girls to go with me today when I go check on your mother and dad. Also, I'm sure it would perk them up to see you and their grandbabies. But I'd like for us to stop by the bank first. You need to have a signature card on file so you can withdraw funds without me being present. What if I suffered a fall like your dad? Or had a life changing event such as your mother?"

"Theodore, you're scaring me."

"It's just a precaution. My intention is not to scare you. It's to empower you. You've never met Mr. Caldwell at the bank. More importantly, he has never met you."

"Well, if it would give you peace of mind. We can do it. You are right. I'd be lost if I had to take over things like my dad has had to do."

"That's what this is all about. I want peace of mind to know you and the girls will be okay if, God forbid, a catastrophe should happen. If so, Mr. Caldwell will know exactly what you all need."

"It won't take us long to get ready after I get the dishes done. I only need to brush my hair and wash the girls faces." I was excited to see Mama and Daddy. More so, for them to see the babies. It had been a while because of Mama's stroke.

Theodore offered to wash the girl's faces and pack the diaper bag while I finished up. His willingness to share in caring for the girls, especially now that Mama couldn't help me at all was immeasurable.

Poor Mama. Her having little to no help from Daddy, compared to being entirely dependent on him now, must be devastating. Especially for such an independent woman as she.

"OH, MY WHAT sweet children you all have," a lady gushed as she joined us in Mr. Caldwell's office.

"I'd like you to meet our head teller, Mrs. Thatcher. If you should ever need anything and I'm not here, she can take care of you."

"How do you do," she extended her hand.

I greeted her cordially.

"Just sign here on the line, Mrs. Dalton. After this, all you need to do is come in and get whatever you need." Theodore was right. Mr. Caldwell had a way of putting us at ease.

However, Mrs. Thatcher, put me on the defensive. Perhaps because she eyed me a bit longer than necessary.

"I'll sleep better now." Theodore gave a sigh of relief after we left the bank.

"I think I feel better too. At least, if I ever should need help with our finances, I'll know who to ask. My hope is that I never do. They were so accommodating. We were treated like royalty."

"Lucretia, we are royalty, in a sense. Banks rely of dividends like the ones they get from my Small Arms Factory investments. Believe me when I say, they are happy to accommodate us."

"Look Theodore, I know you want me to know all the ins and outs of the business. And I'm glad I went with you to the bank today. But I'm happy to leave that up to you. I'm not a businesswoman."

"But you could be," he debated.

"I wouldn't know how," I replied.

"Remember, I told you one time, you're smart enough to be anything you set your mind to be? I honestly believe that." He smiled.

Daddy was sitting in his favorite porch chair when we arrived. A pile of wood shaving lay between his feet.

"What are you doing out here Daddy? Where is Mama?"

"She's takin' a nap. I know, you don't have to remind me. I'll have to get this mess cleaned up before she sees it. But whittlin' helps to settle my nerves a bit these days."

"I'm sorry, Daddy. I know this is hard on you." I kissed his forehead before sitting in Mama's empty chair next to him. Scarlett squirmed, wanting to get down from my lap.

"Lucretia, can you manage this one too until I get the playpen out of the truck?"

"Let me lay this whittlin' aside and I can hold that one for you," Daddy said.

Daddy laid his knife and stick on the floor beside his chair and wiped his hands on the leg of his overalls. I appreciated his attempt to clean his hands before taking

Melanie. I would have rather he washed them with soap and water first. But I let it go.

"Did you hear that Melly Ann? Grandpappy wants to hold you?" Theodore sat her on Daddy's lap and dashed to get the playpen.

"How you doin' sweet girl? And how you doin' little firecracker? Grandpappy's missed you two somethin' awful." He spoke with a voice saved only for them.

"How long as Mama been sleeping?" I asked.

"This is her second nap today. I wasn't markin' the time for this one, but judgin' from this mess I made, it's been 'bout an hour now. She should be wakin' up pretty soon. When she's awake, we'll know it. She'll holler for me to come and help her get up."

Theodore reached for Scarlett as soon as he unfolded the playpen. "Okay, Scarlett. Here's your baby doll and her blanket." Then he sat on the edge of the porch beside her pen.

"Want me to take her now, Daddy?"

"No, I'm happy as long as she is."

"She looks happy enough to me," Theodore observed.

"A.a.a.s.s.s.a.a.a,"

"There's yer Mama, he said, handing Melanie to me on his way inside.

"Let me take her so you can go help your dad with your mother." Theodore took the baby and I hurried inside.

When I returned to the porch, Melanie was lying in the pen with Scarlett and Theodore was sweeping Daddy's wood shavings into a bag.

"Asa forgot all about this when your mother called. I thought I would get rid of them so they wouldn't distress her."

"That was thoughtful of you. She may want to come out here later, but for now, we have her sitting on the couch in the living room. Want to take the girls inside now so she can see them?"

"Oh…there's my sweet babies. I've missed you so much," Mama said in her new, slurred voice.

"It's only been a few weeks, but young'uns like this can grow and change a lot in that much time," Daddy said.

"Are you all hungry? Daddy do you want me to cook something for you all while you visit with the babies?"

"That refrigerator is full of food. The ladies of the church have took us under their wings. Why, there aint a day goes by they don't bring a dish of somethin' to us. We've been eatin' high on the hog. That's fer sure. If you want to, you can look to see if there's somethin' you want to warm up. We can always eat."

Daddy was right. There was food galore for them in the fridge. *God bless the sweet women of that church*, I prayed silently.

"I see potato salad, tossed salad, and fried chicken.

There's even a plate of tomatoes, already sliced. We won't have to warm any of that and mess up the kitchen. It's all good cold," I announced.

"Well, let's eat then," Daddy said.

I prepared the table while Daddy led Mama to her chair. After we ate, Theodore helped her get to the porch.

"Mama, you all enjoy being with the kids and Theodore while I do the dishes. I won't be long."

While standing at the sink, I loved hearing all their laughter. It was distorted but Mama even managed a chuckle now and then. Both girls squealed when Daddy tickled them. The scene was so different from the last time we met. Mama had dropped the iron skillet after hearing Daddy confess he hadn't helped her when I was a baby. And she had expertly fed Scarlett and ate her meal too, while I nursed Melanie. Bless her heart. Would she ever be able to do that again? Now, feeding herself was difficult enough.

Theodore was so right this morning. Life is fragile.

Chapter Thirty-Five

O UR HEARTS WERE heavy after leaving my parent's that day. Daddy's injuries from his fall were better but we could see how he struggled to care for Mama. Aunt Effie volunteered to help him with the house, at least once a week. That was something. We decided we could go on the weekends and do what we could also.

The next morning, Theodore made his usual sweep by the field to see how Deke and Larson were doing so he could give Daddy a report when he went by to check on him and Mama.

I had just gotten both babies down for a nap when I heard Theodore's truck pull back in the yard. I poured us a glass of tea and met him on the porch so our voices wouldn't wake the babies. In addition to his usual tired appearance, he looked troubled.

"Oh no, has something else happened to Mama and Daddy?"

"No. Your Aunt Effie was there when I left. She had the house looking spiffy. She said she knew your mother would be stressed to see it any other way."

"Then why is that wrinkle across your brow? Were Deke and Larson having trouble with the equipment again?"

"No, I drove by there first. They have everything under control. Asa is pleased with the good job they are doing."

"Well, something is definitely wrong. What is it?" I knew him well.

"It's the war. When will this terrible thing end? Used to when I'd go into the Big Store in Muddy Ox, you could hear people talking about farm equipment or their crops or even the weather. Today, all I heard was about death, and bloody battles, and lost loved ones. I want a more peaceful world for our girls to grow up in."

"Theodore, you can't fix world leaders any more than you can fix the health issues my parents are dealing with. Don't stress yourself so much. It's not good for your own health."

"I know. I didn't let things get to me as much before you and the girls became a part of my life. But now, it's hard to lay everything aside."

"The girls and I will be okay as long as you are," I promised.

"And you all will be taken care of regardless. Remember?"

"I know that. But I don't—I won't give that a thought. Because nothing is going to happen to you. It can't. It just can't. Theodore, you are scaring me. Why are you talking like this?"

"Is that Doctor McFarnz's car pulling into the yard?" he interrupted.

"I'm not expecting him—are you?"

"No, I'm not. Wonder why he's coming to see us?" Theodore questioned.

"Oh…no…I hope nothing is…" His visits usually meant something was wrong. Of course, my first thoughts were that something else had happened to my parents.

"Well, what do we owe the honor of this nice visit?" Theodore asked.

"Nothing, just stopping in. Was on my way back to the office from Muddy Ox. When one of the McDougal's neighbors flagged me down. They found Minnie collapsed in her back yard in pretty bad shape. So bad, they were afraid to move her until she could be checked out. She's claiming she fell. Her injuries say otherwise. Her run-ins with her son, Nate, are common knowledge. But with no witnesses and her sticking to her story, all I could do was bandage her up and let it go."

"That's terrible, Doctor," I said.

"Yes, it is. But if or when it happens again, the truth will come out. Anyway, I saw you all sitting on the porch. Thought I'd stop and see how Theodore was doing."

"Dr. McFarnz. I was afraid you had more bad news of some kind for us." I might as well admit it. Panic wasn't easily hidden.

He smiled. "That's one of the perils of being a doctor. Even if it is just a friendly visit, people see you coming and automatically think the worst."

"As for Theodore, can you give us a clue as to when the Digitalis will start working?" I questioned.

"Well. it's not a miracle cure. But I was hoping it would help in time. Are you having more problems, Theodore?"

"Just the usual ones, I guess. But I am going to have another birthday in a couple of days." He joked and downplayed his condition, as usual.

The doctor smiled.

"Anyway, we're glad you stopped by. Can I get you some tea, Doctor?"

"I'd like that very much, Lucretia. Thank you."

"Bring us a plate of those cookies you made last night. She has become quite a cook, Doc," Theodore boasted as I walked away.

I don't remember setting the glass of tea or the plate of cookies down when I stepped back onto the porch. All I remember was seeing Theodore lying on his back and the doctor crouched over him.

"Theodore!" I cried.

"Lucretia. Get something to put under his head. And if you have any, bring me an aspirin," the doctor ordered.

I ran back inside, grabbed a blanket from the playpen, the bottle of aspirin we kept on the windowsill over the sink, and rushed back to the porch and knelt by

Theodore.

"When I lift his head, place the blanket under it. Now, hand me an aspirin."

After doing as the doctor asked, I held Theodore's hand and kissed his forehead.

The doctor slipped the aspirin under Theodore's tongue. "Come on Theodore. Stay with us. You hear?"

"Please Theodore. Please," I begged.

Theodore turned his face toward me. "Lucretia, listen to me." His voice was weak.

"Please God let him be okay. He has to be okay," I prayed. God answered that prayer when I prayed it for Mama and Daddy. Surely, He would hear and answer me again.

"Theodore, please be okay," I sobbed.

"Listen to me," he repeated. I put my ear close to his lips to hear more clearly. "Bank…. Caldwell… remember?"

"Yes, Theodore, I remember but don't worry about that now. Just get better. We need you. The girls and I need you."

"The girls. Do what… have to do. Take care… them… yourself… Do what have to do…for Theo… girls… and me."

"Theodore! Theodore!" I screamed.

The doctor put his ear to Theodore's chest but couldn't hear a heartbeat. He searched for a pulse. There wasn't one.

Theodore was gone.

"SHE'S IN SHOCK," Doctor McFarnz's words sounded distorted as though he was speaking through a thick fog.

"You get some rest now, Lucretia. We'll see that the babies are taken care of," Aunt Effie said while leading me to bed.

Everything after that was a blur. If I thought my world had tilted because of Daddy's fall and Mama's stroke, it had now spun off its axis. I'd lost all bearings, stuck in slow motion in the center of a whirlwind. My brain no longer controlled my senses. I could see but not focus, touch but not feel. Hear only roars. Smell only stenches. Taste nothing but the bitterness of death.

Chapter Thirty-Six

"**A**RE YOU AWAKE enough to nurse this baby now?" Aunt Effie stood in the door of my bedroom trying to console a wailing Melanie.

"Yes, bring her to me. How long have I been asleep?"

"A little over five hours. You were exhausted after all you'd gone through. You needed every minute of it, I'm sure."

"No wonder she is crying. I never go past four hours without nursing her."

"Here's yer Mama now sweet baby girl," Aunt Effie said, placing Melanie in my arms.

"What about Scarlett? I still nurse her too."

"I've been feeding her table food. That child loves biscuits and gravy." Aunt Effie laughed.

"I know. Daddy says she takes after…

I couldn't finish my sentence for a fresh flood of tears.

"Now, honey, don't go gettin' all upset again. A baby, especially if they're still nursin,' can tell when its mama is comin' unraveled, and it gets them in a tizzy too." Her well-meaning hand on my shoulder was for comfort. But it only caused me to sob harder.

"Daddy and Mama. Has anyone told them about? Do they know Theodore...?" The word *died* just wouldn't pass through my lips.

"Doctor McFarnz drove over to tell 'em. Said considerin' the shape they're both in, it'd be better to hear it from him. If they took it too hard, he'd be on hand to doctor 'em."

"That's good. They both thought so much of Theodore. No doubt, they'll take it hard. Where is Scarlett? I don't hear her?"

"She's keepin' her Uncle Jake busy right now. He's watchin' her play in the yard. But I'll go check on 'em."

As I gazed at the innocent face of my nursing baby, I wondered how different her life would be from now on without her daddy—how different all our lives would be.

"Melanie is finished nursing. If you want to take her and bring me Scarlett, I'll nurse her too. I imagine Uncle Jake will be glad to get a break by now."

"Alright." She took Melanie but paused at the door. "Honey, I aint tryin' to tell you what to do but as good as Scarlett eats table food, you might think about weanin' her. Yer gonna have yer hands full now, more than ever. It'd be easier with only one baby a nursin,' I think."

"You're probably right. But I don't know where to begin. Mama always knows when the signs are right to do things like planting and cutting your hair and weaning babies. But she can't…"

"Oh, I can help you with that. I know how to read the signs too. If you start weanin' a baby when the signs are in the thighs, then by the time they get out of the foot, they're weaned. I'll look it up for you so you can do it right." She sounded confident. After all, she was Mama's sister. They were taught by the same person— my grandmother.

"There's a Farmer's Almanac in the bookcase by the Victrola." Aunt Effie probably wondered why the mention of a Farmer's Almanac would bring me to tears again. But it was too painful at the moment to have explained how Theodore bought a new one each year so he could talk almanac with Mama.

Scarlett wanted down to run as soon as she finished nursing. However, I was able to confine her in the playpen in the living room for the time being.

"I can hold Melanie while you try to find what you are looking for, if you like."

"Good idea. I am havin' a time tryin' to read it while this baby keeps pullin' at the pages." She laughed.

"Can you grab a diaper on the way? She's wet."

Within minutes after handing me Melanie and the diaper, Aunt Effie found what she was looking for.

"Now, accordin' to the almanac, it is about three and a half more weeks until the signs will be in the thighs again. So, if you start her on July the twentieth, she should be weaned by the twenty-fifth," Aunt Effie said with surety.

Suddenly, a surge of overwhelming, unexplained, anger hit me. Why was I being robbed of everything familiar? Theodore had been ripped from me. Now Aunt Effie wanted to wean Scarlett away from me too? I couldn't face another change in my already unrecognizable world. I wanted to lash out at something or someone. She was the person in front of me at the moment. Why was she trying to make another change for me? Why?

"Horsey, horsey. Go to town." Hearing Scarlett singing sweetly to her doll help to calm me and deescalated my rage.

"Aunt Effie, I guess you are right." Actually, I knew she was right. "Weaning Scarlett will be one less thing to juggle. And by your calculations, I'll have about a month before the signs are right to get used to the idea. So will Scarlett. Maybe we will be more settled by then."

"Lucretia, just take one thing, one day, at a time. You can get through this. You can—because you have to."

"You 'bout ready to go, Effie?" Uncle Jake stepped inside the door. "I gotta go by the shop, feed the stock, and get my other night chores done. I'm sorry, Lucretia. Wish we could stay longer."

"I know, Uncle Jake. I know. It's okay. You all have been such a help. I don't know what I would have done without you."

"Thank you, Aunt Effie. I appreciate you and Uncle Jake coming over so much."

"We were glad to do what we could. If we could do more, we would. But right now, we need to run on. We left a lot of things undone. Jake has to go shut down his shop. I left a mess of cucumbers ready to pickle. When we heard what happened, we dropped everything to get here. Also, since it's on our way home, we thought we'd stop in and check on Emmy and Asa."

"I understand. Yes, go by and see them if you can. Tell them I love them too. I'm stranded here for now. I can't drive. Theodore was going to teach me but…" I stifled another flood of tears. I could cry another time— but not then. They were leaving and I had to hold it together for my babies.

After they left, I was thankful Melanie was sleeping and Scarlett remained content for the moment, playing with her toys. Not knowing how to feel or what to do, I curled on the couch, hugged my knees to my chest and allowed another quiet cry.

For a second, my mind lied to me. I thought the footsteps I heard on the porch were Theodore's. That he was back and none of this was real. A knock on the door was startling. Theodore wouldn't have knocked.

I couldn't move.

"Lucretia," Doctor McFarnz spoke through the partially opened door.

"Oh, Doctor. It's you. Come in." Reality jolted me again.

"I met Jake and Effie as they were leaving. They said you were in here with the babies."

"Yes, they had to get back to their own things. They were so good to help. I don't know what I would have done without them."

"When they said they would stay for a while, I left to break the news to your mother and dad. I worried how they would handle it," he said.

"How—how did they handle it?"

"Of course, they cried. Theodore had won over both of their hearts. But as parents, they were more concerned about you and the babies than they were themselves. Probably some of their tears were because they knew they wouldn't be able to help you now like they wanted."

"Poor Daddy. He hasn't completely healed from his accident. And now he has all he can do to take care of Mama. He is over-loaded already."

"Lucretia, I can't even begin to tell you how much I hate this for you. No doubt everyone will pitch in and do what they can. But I am still, so sorry. Theodore was one of the finest men I have ever met."

"Thank you Doctor. Yes, he was so good. I couldn't have asked for a better husband or father for the girls."

"That's another reason I wanted to stop by today. I thought you should know that we had discussed how his condition had worsened during his last office visit. I suggested he tell you so you could be at least a little prepared. But he didn't want you to know. He knew how much it would worry you."

"He downplayed it all the time. But I could tell he wasn't getting any better. It was all he could do to keep up with Scarlett since she is getting around so well now. But he insisted on trying anyway." I was remembering the many times I offered to let him sit and hold Melanie while I chased Scarlett.

"You and those little girls brought so much to his life. You all were his sole priority. Even as he was having his heart attack, while you were getting the blanket and aspirin, all he worried about was leaving you and those two babies."

"It's sad to think that he only had four months with Melanie." I wanted to cry again but fought it.

"I kept hoping the medicines and changing his diet would make a difference."

"And it did, Doctor. Just not enough," I said.

"But no amount of time would have ever been enough. It never is for anyone," he replied.

"I have a question, though. Why give him aspirin? What was it supposed to do?"

"It was a long shot. My brother is a doctor in St. Louis. He told me about a trial they were doing with aspirin to treat heart patients. My plan was to start Theodore on it as soon as they could prove it worked.

There wasn't anything else we could do for him when he was having his heart attack. I knew it couldn't hurt him. And if it helped at all—then good. Who knows, it might have given him a few more minutes to talk to you before he passed. We can only hope."

"It could have, we will never know. Anyway, I thank God you stopped by today when you did."

"I thank Him too, Lucretia. I hadn't planned to stop. Even when I saw you all on the porch, I was just going to wave. But I turned into the driveway before I knew it. Maybe God had a hand in that too." He looked away to wipe a tear.

"I can't imagine watching him have a heart attack alone."

"It was all God's plan and timing for me to be here with you, Lucretia. I honestly believe that."

"Me too, Doctor. Me too."

"I want to say one more thing before I have to leave. Let Theodore's last words sink in and guide you in the days ahead. He told you to do whatever you had to do to take care of yourself and the girls. Life goes on, Lucretia. Theodore died—you didn't.

"Live your life to the fullest. I'm not sure what he was referring to about you not having limitations, but you probably know. He was right though. I've known you all your life. You are resilient. The only limitations I can see you having are ones you put on yourself."

"I can't even think about what our future will hold

right now. But thank you, Doctor McFarnz. I appreciate you so much. You are more than just a doctor to our family. You are a friend."

"Well, at that, I have to go. Is there anything else I can help you with or do for you?"

"If you don't mind, will you ask Pastor Abrams to stop by? We need to plan Theodore's funeral."

"Be glad to, I'm sure he will come as soon as he can."

I thanked the good Doctor again as I walked him to the door, gave him a hug, and he was gone.

As I lay in a fetal position with my knees curled to my chest again, I wished to be a child once more. If only but briefly, I had a lap to climb on and arms holding me so tightly that no pain or sadness could penetrate their shield of protection. Instead, I was the lap, and my arms were the shields and protection for my babies from whatever lies ahead.

AUNT EFFIE AND Uncle Jake volunteered to watch the girls for me during Theodore's funeral. Doctor McFarnz was kind enough to take me and offer a strong arm of support. It broke my parent's hearts, but Mama was in no condition to attend, and Daddy had to stay home and care for her. Besides, in true Bootheel fashion, it rained. Not just a summer shower but as Uncle Jake would have put it, a drenching, toad-strangling, rain.

Theodore's funeral was fitting for a man so well thought of in the community. Those in attendance, filed by one after another to give their condolences, offers of help, and regrets for not going to the gravesite because of the rain. I told them I understood and was sure Theodore would have as well.

Mr. Caldwell assured me that he and the bank were at my service. All I could decipher from Mrs. Thatcher, through her sobs and wet handkerchief, was poor, poor babies.

Once the church was cleared, I along with Doctor McFarnz, Pastor Abrams, Deke and Larson and the other pallbearers, and Larson's mother, headed to the cemetary.

As soon as Pastor Abrams finished with the graveside service, he, and the soaked-to-the-skin pallbearers, quickly offered last words of comfort before leaving.

Larson and Deke were drenched too but stayed behind.

"Miss Lucretia, I am so sorry. Mr. Dalton was a good man. Don't you worry. Deke and me will keep on workin' yer Daddy's farm, just like we always did. I'm gonna' go now. I told my mom you'd understand if she stayed in the car so she wouldn't get wet," Larson said, shielding his face from the rain by his over-sized hand.

"Thank you, Larson. I'm glad you told her to stay out of this rain. Please thank her for coming."

"I sure will. You take care now, okay?" Then he patted my shoulder before leaving.

"And you know I will be there if you need me too," Deke struggled with his words. I knew how much he thought of Theodore.

"I know, Deke. Theodore thought so much of you and Larson. He really did." I managed. He lingered, as though he had more to say, but bowed his head and walked away in silence.

"I'll get the car, so you won't have so far to walk in the rain, Lucretia," Doctor McFarnz said as he scurried away.

Standing there alone by Theodore's casket, I couldn't separate my tears from the raindrops running down my face, When I was a little girl, I use to think rain was angel tears falling from heaven. Maybe the angels are crying now because Theodore died.

That thought gave me a slight measure of comfort.

Chapter Thirty-Seven

AUNT EFFIE GAVE a full report of when Scarlett was fed and how hard she played before surrendering to a nap. They both hugged me, offered their services again if I needed them and went on about how Melanie was such a pleasant baby. Uncle Jake remarked about hating to see it rain so hard when people were trying to have a funeral.

I cautioned them about standing water in the roads and urged them to drive carefully on their way home before they left.

Uncle Jake and Aunt Effie's offers of help were all well and good, but if they had any help to give, I wanted Mama and Daddy to have it. They would need them more than ever now that Theodore was gone.

The rain continued to pound outside, while my heart pounded within my chest. My mind replayed the funeral, graveside service, the many well-wishing promises, the prayers, pats, hugs, and kisses. But the most painful burning memory was how the unforgiving rain hammered down on Theodore's casket as we drove away.

He was all alone there—my babies and I were alone

here.

The girls eventually woke from their naps and busied up the rest of my evening until it was bedtime again.

I suffered a fitful, restless night, only to rise to a new day facing the same challenges and more. A bright, shining, belied sun gave the appearance of hope and life. But I could only see and feel the emptiness of death covering me with clouds of reality.

The pain in my heart numbed any pains of hunger I might have felt. But I knew I had to eat for my own strength and to produce milk for Melanie. After putting on some coffee, I began rummaging through the refrigerator and pantry for food when I heard a knock.

"I hope I'm not botherin' you Miss Lucretia."

"No, it's alright, Deke. Come in."

"I wanted to tell you again how sorry I am about Mr. Dalton."

"Thank you. I appreciate that."

"I would like to talk to you a spell if you don't mind."

"I don't mind, Deke. But can we sit at the kitchen table. The baby is sleeping," I said softly.

"The kitchen table is fine." He glanced towards Melanie in her cradle, lowered his voice, and quietly took a seat.

"I think the coffee is done. Would you like a cup?"

"Okay, I'll drink one with you."

As I poured our coffee, the thought struck me that

if Deke needed money for anything to do with Daddy's farm, I never carried any. Then I remembered, the doctor gave me Theodore's wallet after he died. I still hadn't brought myself to look inside. I didn't know how much money, if any, was there.

"What did you need to talk to me about, Deke?"

"Now, that Mr. Dalton is gone, and yer Mama and Daddy are ailin.' I thought you might need some help. I'll do anything I can for you and them babies if you need me."

The independent side of me wanted to tell him we would be fine and could make it on our own. My sensible side knew better. I also knew how committed he was about caring for Daddy's crops.

"Thank you. But don't you already have your hands full with the farm?"

"The farm's doin' fine right now. So…

"You know Theodore handled all of the farm business. I don't know what he paid you and Larson each week. Or even how much he gave you to pay the hired hands." I knew anxiety was causing me to speak out of turn, but I couldn't stop myself.

"He paid me and Larson ten dollars a week to oversee and work the farm. The adult hired hands got a dollar a day for chopping. Kids fourteen and under got fifty cents. If they are over fourteen, they got adult pay. But…"

"Well then, Deke. I'm glad you offered. You're

right. I am going to need your help with a few things in the days ahead. Theodore was going to teach me to drive, but well… I'll need to go to the bank and the Post Office in Muddy Ox as early as tomorrow. How many adult hands and kids are working for you?"

"Right now, we have twenty-three adults and fourteen kids. But…"

"So, let's see, that's twenty for you and Larson. A hundred and fifty for a full week for your regular workers. I figure I need to have at least one-hundred and ninety dollars on hand for each week. A hundred and seventy to cover you all and the hired hands. And twenty extra for incidentals."

"You did that in your head that quick Miss Lucretia? Mr. Dalton was always braggin' how smart you are. Guess he didn't stretch it none. But…"

"Could you take me to the bank once a week, so you will have money to pay your hands and to pay you and Larson too."

"I said I'll take you where you need to go. But…"

"But what, Deke?"

"You only need to pay us for what we worked this week. Choppin' is done for now. You won't have to worry 'bout payin' nobody anymore 'til pickin' starts."

"Oh…When do you think picking season will begin this year?"

"It may not be the same fer ever body. But I'm guessin' our field will be ready somewhere 'tween the first and second week of August, since we were able to plant earlier than usual."

"I know a lot of workers will follow the harvest elsewhere until we need them again. But what will you and Larson do? With Daddy not well yet, I may still need you all. Maybe just not as much."

"Me and Larson will still be around. We can pick up odd jobs here and there until the cotton's ready to pick. I can let the hands go after I pay them at the end of this week. But the tractor needs tunin' up a bit and there's a few other little things we been puttin' off doin' until we had the time. It may take Larson and me another week to get it all done."

"Of course. And I'll continue to pay you as long as you're still working. I'm sure that is what Theodore would want me to do."

"That's mighty nice of you, Miss. Lucretia. And there's a chance it won't even take us a week to get things wrapped up. If we can do it sooner, we will."

"However long it takes."

"You sounded just like Mr. Dalton right then." He grinned.

"I could hear him saying that too. I want to do by you the way he would have if he were still here. Like I said, Theodore handled the farm business. Actually, he handled everything."

Saying that out loud reminded me again how alone I was and caused me to shiver.

"You okay, Miss Lucretia? Are you sick? Looked like you were havin' a chill."

"I'm okay. No, I'm not sick. Deke, from now on, you can drop the Miss and just call me Lucretia?"

"If that's what you want, ma'am," he replied.

"You don't need to call me ma'am either. If we're going to do business together, we can call one another by our first names. If that works for you, it does for me."

"Works fer me," he agreed.

"Also, I'll need to go to the grocery ever so often. Can you take me there too?"

"I'll take you there or any other place you need to go, Ma'am—I mean Lucretia." He smiled nervously.

AFTER MY TALK with Deke, I didn't feel as hopeless as before. Talking with him about the farm business sort of pushed the clouds aside and gave me a new reality to deal with. I even amazed myself how quickly the money part came to me. Theodore had trusted and counted on Deke. I would too. He was to pick us up around eight-thirty the next morning. I made a list. Stopping by Mama and Daddy's was at the top of it.

I couldn't avoid going through Theodore's wallet

any longer. I had to know how much money was there before I went to the bank. When I opened it, one hundred and ninety dollars fell on the table, along with Theo's baby picture. Had we followed through and had gotten pictures of the girls and us, I'm sure they would have been there too. I quickly pushed that regret aside and felt relieved as I crossed going to the bank off tomorrow's list. Ironically, he had just the amount of money in his wallet, that I had calculated.

Deke arrived promptly at eight-thirty. The girls and I were ready and waiting.

"Lucretia. Lucretia. Lucretia. Not Miss Lucretia. Remember. Call her Lucretia." I heard Deke mumbling as I opened the door.

"Good morning Deke."

"Oh…mornin' Lucretia. It may take me a few times to get the hang of calling you that."

"You'll get used to it, eventually." I couldn't help but smile.

"Larson said tell you not to worry about the time. He's got everything under control in the field today."

"That's good. I appreciate the both of you helping like this. But today may not take as long as I thought. Theodore had money in his wallet, so we won't have to go to the bank. At least not this trip."

"That's good. But it doesn't matter to me how long it takes. We will do whatever you have to do." He walked over next to Melanie's cradle. "Want me to carry this one or the other one?"

"You can carry that one if you like. Her name is Melanie." I picked up Scarlett and shifted her to my hip before reaching for the diaper bag.

"Let me get that bag for you." He took Melanie in his arms, slung the bag over his shoulder, opened the door for me, smiled and said, "We're ready."

Scarlett took her place in the middle. He sat the bag in the floorboard after handing me the baby. The only difference was it was him behind the wheel instead of Theodore.

"Where to first?" he asked.

"I'd like to go to my parent's house. I need to let Daddy know I will be handling things now."

Daddy was on the porch in his chair whittling. Mama sat beside him. It took them a few minutes to figure out who we were since we were in Deke's car and not Theodore's truck.

"Do you want me to stay in the car with the baby?" Deke asked.

"No, if you don't mind, I'd like for you to go with me. They'll want to see Melanie too. And it's a little hard to manage the two of them alone. We won't stay long. I didn't bring Scarlett's playpen. She's a challenge to keep up with right now without it."

"You shoulda' said something. I'd a got it fer you," he almost sounded apologetic.

"Honestly, I forgot. Theodore, always thought

ahead for things like that. Guess I'll have to think for two from now on."

"I'll try to help you. You got a lot on yer mind." Bless Deke's heart. He clearly aimed to please.

I hugged Daddy first.

"I'm sorry child. He was a good man."

"Yes, he was, Daddy. Are you all okay? I know how much you and Mama thought of him."

"We're okay. It's you we worry about. You got them young'uns. And everything is piled on just you now that he's gone. It would be different if we could help you. But…well…you understand."

"I do, Daddy. You have a lot to handle too."

"It'd be a heap easier if you didn't live so far away. I know you got a nice place in Bragg City. And it wouldn't seem that far if things were different right now. But they aint. They're a mess."

"I feel just as bad that I can't be here for you and Mama too. Fortunately, Deke has offered to take me wherever I need to go while Larson Strom covers the field."

Deke tipped his hat to Daddy.

"We appreciate you helpin' our little girl…uh daughter, Deke. Guess I can't call her little girl anymore since she has two little girls of her own." Daddy said.

"I'll do what I can, sir," Deke replied.

"I don't want you to worry about the farm business, Daddy. Theodore told me what and how to do. I can take care of it for you."

"How are you goin' to do that, run a household, and manage two babies all at the same time? That's a big bite for a woman." Daddy replied.

"Woman or not. I can do it. Trust me, Daddy."

"But…" Daddy persisted.

"She's got a good head on her shoulders, Sir. I've already seen that head in action." Deke confirmed.

Daddy seemed to surrender, at least for the time being.

"How are you feeling, Mama?" I went to hug her and held Scarlett close so they could share a kiss.

"Doin' better. Lovin' fresh air on porch." Mama hadn't completely regained her speech. She spoke in parts. She didn't have to say anything about Theodore. The tears running down both cheeks and the sadness in her eyes spoke for her.

"Okay, Scarlett. Kiss Grandpappy before we go." I sat her in his lap, and she wrapped her arms around his neck. Then I took Melanie and let them each kiss her too.

"You go so soon?" Mama asked.

"Yes, I have a list of things I need to take care of today. And even though Larson promised he has everything under control, I know Deke won't want to be gone from the field any longer than he has to. I mostly wanted to tell you not to worry about things, Daddy. And to see how you all were taking the news about Theodore."

"Well, we're handlin' it best we can, like I can tell you're tryin' to do. That's all a body can do when things happen beyond our control," Daddy said solemnly.

"I'll be stopping in as often as I can. Don't worry. I'll—we'll be okay."

"Caint help but worry, Lucretia. But understand. We'll make it okay here too," Daddy assured.

Deke picked up Scarlett, nodded to Mama, and shook Daddy's hand before we left.

"I guess we should go to the post office next. Then to the Big Store," I said once we were settled again in the truck.

"Whatever you say," Deke replied.

"I thought of one other thing I want to ask you to do for me, if you don't mind."

"I already told you. I'm willin' to do anything you need."

"It would take up some of your weekends. And I know you and Larson look forward to them." I continued.

"It doesn't matter. Just ask. Anyway, Larson has a lady friend now. He spends most of his weekends with her these days. Guess what I'm sayin' is my weekends are free. Weekdays will be too, 'til I pick up a odd job, anyways. What is it you need?" Deke asked.

"Can you teach me how to drive? Theodore was going to, but he never got around to it?"

Chapter Thirty-Eight

DEKE CHECKED ON me every two or three days, as he said he would. And as Theodore had said of him, he was willing to do anything I asked. He objected, but I continued to pay him his weekly ten dollars as though I was one of his odd jobs.

Six weeks had passed since Theodore's death. I missed him terribly, but the house, the girls, checking in on Mama and Daddy and everyday tasks consumed my days. The only idle time I had was at night while the girls were sleeping or rare times when I had a few minutes to actually sit down during the day while they were napping. I didn't cry myself to sleep as often anymore. I was exhausted, and even too tired to cry.

I took Aunt Effie's advice and weaned Scarlett. As she had promised, by the time the signs were out of the foot, I only had one baby to nurse. I hadn't thought of it before, but maybe I needed to ask Aunt Effie if there was a sign to follow for breaking a child from their diaper too.

I had always been aware of Theodore's help. But I was finding out firsthand, just how much he actually had done to help with the girls in addition to things he'd kept up with around the house. Changing light bulbs, taking out the trash, a loose board on the steps, destroying a wasp's nest built under the eve of the porch, yard work, were only a few things on an endless list. Theodore had effortlessly done things I hadn't even known needed to be done before.

Thankfully, Mama was getting stronger and had regained more mobility and most of her speech. Other than a slight limp, Daddy was healing as well.

I changed Melanie's morning diaper, finished her six o'clock feeding, and had gotten her back to sleep. By filling the washer and rinse tubs the night before, I hoped to get the washing done as early as possible to beat the heat.

As soon as I stepped onto the porch to put the diapers in the washer so they could start agitating, I heard the steady thrashing of the push mower. Obviously, Deke had also decided to get a jump on the heat.

I waved to him and rushed inside to start breakfast. Scarlett would be waking soon. I decided to ask Deke to join us and added a few more biscuits to the pan. We needed to talk about when he thought the cotton would be ripe for picking anyway.

Catching a glimpse of my straggled hair in the windowpane made me gasp. I pinned it up best I could, before stepping back onto the porch. Guess it really didn't matter. He'd already seen me look my worse the day Theodore died.

After accepting my offer, he parked the mower and paused by the pump in the yard to wash up before coming inside.

"Thank you, Lucretia. I usually grab a bite before leaving the house, but I wanted to get as much done as I could in the cool of the morning. This first day of August came in as hot as the devil, like it usually does."

"Yes it did. Me too. I wanted to get the wash..." Scarlett whimpered. I stopped mid-sentence and ran to get her before she woke Melanie.

Deke automatically raised the tray of the highchair for me to sit her down.

"Looks like you've done this before," I said. I was amazed how he seemed to know what to do to help before me asking.

"My sister has a couple of little ones too. They're not as close together in age as these two are but almost."

"So that's why you're so in practice." I smiled.

"Here you go, girlie. You ready for breakfast too?" Deke teased.

Scarlett giggled.

Once we had her settled and he sat back down, I set two eggs in front of him like I had Theodore, many times. I just took for granted he liked his sunny-side-up too.

"Looks good," he said.

"I assumed you like your eggs like that. But I guess

maybe I should have asked."

"I aint picky. I can eat 'em any way they're cooked. Those biscuits and gravy look good too. That was another thing Mr. Dalton bragged on you about."

"I got better after I went along. Poor man, he never complained but I'm sure he had the right to many times."

I laughed and went on to explain how patient Theodore was while I was learning. Deke thought it was funny but wasn't surprised about the cookbook and how Mama didn't like it at first.

"Now, getting down to business. I was wondering when you think the cotton will be ready to pick," I asked.

"I drove by the fields yesterday. I think we should give them about another week and a half. That'll be Monday, the thirteenth."

"How much money do you think I will need for that first week?"

"It's hard to know. It'll depend on how many hands we end up with. I can always leave Larson in charge while I run you to the bank after dinner time to get what we need. After that first week, we'll have a better handle on it."

"When we go by to see Mama and Daddy on Friday, I want to put Daddy's mind at ease that I am still taking care of things."

"He should be proud of you," he said handing Scarlett another biscuit crust where she dropped her first one on the floor.

"Don't worry about that crust down there. I'll clean that up after she gets through making her mess. She wants to feed herself all the time now. She's an independent little girl. That's for sure."

"Like her mother," he added. Then smiled.

"Well, I want her to be what she needs to be to get by in this world." I might have replied a little too sharply. He apologized immediately.

"I'm sorry. I didn't mean that like it was a bad thing. I really meant it like a compliment."

"I know, Deke. Guess I'm still a little on edge and don't realize it. I'm sorry too," I clarified.

"Well, thank you for the breakfast. Guess I'd better get to work er me startin' early was just a waste." Although we both said sorry, he sounded and acted uncomfortable.

"Me too. As soon as I get this mess she's made cleaned up, I need to get on with my washing."

"Is there anything else you want me to help you with before I get started back on the yard?" He slid his chair back under the table and grabbed up his dishes to put them in the sink.

"Yes there is. Do you mind grabbing the playpen and setting it up on the shady side of the porch as you go? Maybe if Scarlett is out there, she will let the baby sleep a little longer."

"Sure thing," he replied.

He folded the playpen to take outside, while I cleaned the floor under the highchair. Then with Scarlett on my hip and a wet washcloth in my hand, I followed him to the porch. Again, as if by instinct, he took Scarlett from me, lowered her into the pen and handed her a toy.

"Alright. I need to get busy," he repeated.

As he turned and started to walk away, Larson Strom's truck stopped by the edge of the road. He and a woman walked toward us hand in hand.

"Hey Deke."

"Mornin' Larson. Where y'all headed? How you doin' Miss Edna?"

Edna nodded and said fine.

"We're headed to the courthouse in Caruthersville. This sweet lady here has said she'd marry me." Larson was grinning larger than life.

"Wh…why…that's great. Guess congratulations are in order. Lucretia, this is Edna…uh… Sorry, don't think Larson ever told me yer last name."

"Madden…Mary Edna Madden. But everyone calls me Edna. How do you do?" She extended her hand and I met it with mine.

"Pleased to meet you, Edna. Yes, congratulations."

"Glad to meet you too, Lucretia. Larson told me about…about your husband. I was sorry to hear about that. I've heard over and over about what a good man he was.”

“He was the best,” Deke chimed in.

“Yes, he was,” Larson echoed.

“We were just talkin.’ Think the cotton will be ready for pickin’ on Monday, the thirteenth. How does that work for you, Larson?” Deke asked.

“Sounds good. I’ll be glad to get back to makin’ some steady money again.”

“Y’all should be over yer honeymoonin’ by then, I reckon.” Deke smiled.

Edna blushed and smiled sweetly.

“Oh yeah. We’re just goin’ over ’round Caraway, Arkansas. Edna’s got family over there she wants me to meet. We’ll only be over there a few days though. I’ll get back in plenty enough time to get the tractor and other equipment in shape.”

“I know you will.” Deke said with confidence.

“We’re gonna get goin’ now. Just wanted to tell you the news.” Larson put his arm around Edna’s shoulder to lead her away.

“Congratulations again. And maybe a few weekends from now, you all can come over and we will celebrate with cake and coffee. Deke, you can come too, if you like,” I offered.

“We’d love that. Wouldn’t we Larson?” Edna asked.

“I ain’t never turned down cake and a cup of coffee in my life. Just say when.”

“I wouldn’t want to miss out on one of Lucretia’s

cakes neither," Deke said.

"Good. I'm looking forward to it too. Deke can let me know when you all are back in town, and we'll pick a time."

Chapter Thirty-Nine

"Now, Daddy. I said I'll take care of this. And besides, you can't leave Mama here at the house all day alone," I argued.

When we stopped by to see them again on our next trip to town, I was met with a very defiant father.

"Doc says I can drive since I can get in and out of the truck now. He just don't want me climbin' up on a tractor or a wagon."

"But what about Mama?" I protested.

"We got that covered. I built her some steps to get in and out of the truck. And I made this lean-to with a cover here that she can sit under. It aint gonna hurt either of us to be out in a cotton field. Especially if we're under a shade and in a chair. We mostly sit out here on the porch all day anyways."

"But Daddy. I don't want either of you to overdo it until you are completely ready."

"That's what I been tellin' you. We are completely ready. I can weigh the sacks for people. I can sharpen hoes too. And yer mama has come to herself enough to write down ever body's totals. And we both can still figure purty good."

I looked at Deke for backup. However, he didn't say a word. Finally, I asked him. "Deke, what do you think? Do you think they can do this?"

"Not meanin' any disrespect here, but it ain't his decision." Daddy was even more defiant.

"I'm not asking him to decide. I'm asking him if… well does he think…Can he see you all…"

"Yer a puttin' him in the middle of this. I can tell by the look on his face that ain't where he wants to be." Daddy spouted.

"But Daddy…" I began.

"Lucretia, your dad said the doctor gave him the go ahead." Deke interrupted but kept eye contact with me as if he wanted me to finish his sentence.

"Yes, he did," Daddy sassed.

"The doctor. If the doctor said it was okay…" Again, he paused and held eye contact.

I finally caught on. He was telling me without saying, that I should talk to Doctor McFarnz. Daddy would listen to him.

"Oh…okay, Daddy. But will you promise that if it is too much for either of you to do that you will say so?"

"That…I will do." He said staunchly.

I might not have been able to get through to either of my parents. But the good doctor, a long-time friend of theirs could and would. If he didn't think Daddy or Mama could or should be out in the field all day, then he could talk to Daddy.

Deke was smart.

"THANK YOU FOR what you did in there," I said once we were in the truck and leaving.

"I could see you weren't gettin' anywhere arguing with him."

"You're right. Doctor McFarnz can straighten Daddy out if anyone can. His office is on the way to Muddy Ox. We need to go there first."

"Yer not thinkin' yer dad would say the doctor gave him the go ahead to get back in the field if he didn't are you?"

"No, I don't think Daddy would out and out lie. But everyone is capable of taking what someone says and turning it into what they want to hear instead. Also, I need to know when the doctor last saw them." Deke nodded as a sign he understood.

Although I didn't think my dad would lie. I do think he could have taken something the doctor told him and stretched it out of shape enough to fit his way of thinking.

"You saw first-hand, just how stubborn my dad can be sometimes."

"Don't take this wrong. But I kinda' get it." Deke

said cautiously.

"You do? How?" I questioned.

"It's his cotton field. He wants to be in control of it. He's your dad. And he knows what you've been through and what all you have on your plate right now."

"Well, yes. I see all that too. But he had a terrible accident, and my mother had a stroke. They both could have died. I've learned the hard way how someone can be with you in the morning and be gone from you forever before suppertime."

"I'm sorry you had to learn that so hard, Lucretia."

"Thank you. But I can't get all bogged down in that again right now. Theodore wouldn't want that either." I couldn't allow myself the luxury of self-pity.

"Alright. To the doctor's office we go."

"Then to the bank. I need to get enough money to cover wages and expenses for the first week. Maybe after a few weeks, what we're paid when we sell the cotton at the gin will cover expenses the rest of the time."

"True," he agreed.

"LUCRETIA. DEKE. GOOD to see you all. How can I help you?" Dr. McFarnz asked once we were settled in his office.

"I wanted to talk to you about Mama and Daddy. He thinks he can go to the cotton field every day and do the weighing when picking starts. And he wants to take Mama out in the hot field with him. Doctor, do you think they both are well enough for that?"

"I told Asa he couldn't climb onto the wagon or up on a tractor, but if all he was going to do was weigh the cotton and keep totals, he would be okay. He said he had come up with something for them to sit under to block the sun. If he has, then knowing Emerald, she would probably be happier there than anywhere else."

"So, they did see and talk to you about this?" I questioned.

"Yes, they did. There's a lot to be said about feeling useful. It goes against Asa and Emerald's grain to just sit around and do nothing. Besides Lucretia, they worry about you as much as you do about them. They know what all you are dealing with right now."

"But Doctor, are you sure Mama is up to it?" I pressed on.

"Your mother has made great strides toward her recovery. Her speech has improved. She can get around better. Yes, she still has a way to go. Emerald may never get back to one hundred percent, but we will be happy with the part of her we have for now."

"I know it kills her not to be able to help with the babies."

"I'm sure it does. But it looks like you have some-one who's stepped up to help here. Good to see you, Deke."

"Tryin' to do what I can, Doc."

"If you say Mama and Daddy can do this, then I trust your judgment.

"I think we have to at least let them try. Now, if either of them begins to push beyond their limits, then we may have to reel them back in. But for now, let's give them a little line and see how it goes."

"Sounds about right." Deke picked up on the fishing analogy right away.

He probably pictured a calm day of fishing for perch along the bank. I knew my parents well. They were like crafty catfish that were always looking for a way around getting caught. But Dr. McFarnz had never steered me wrong yet. Like I said. I trusted him.

Scarlett immediately became fidgety and wanted down. This triggered Melanie and she began to whimper.

"We need to go now. I still have to stop at the bank and the Big Store."

"It was good to see you, Lucretia. You too Deke," he said, giving him a pat on the shoulder.

"Thank you again, Doctor." I stood to bounce Melanie in hopes to calm her whimpering.

Deke did the same with Scarlett.

"Y'all have your hands full there."

"We sure do, Doc." Deke smiled.

Chapter Forty

"IT'S GOOD TO see you again, Mrs. Dalton. How can we help you today," Mr. Caldwell stood to greet me as soon as we entered the bank.

"I need to make a withdrawal." I replied.

"Certainly. Mrs. Thatcher, can you help Mrs. Dalton with this transaction?"

"Yes. I would be glad to. There are those sweet babies again. Mrs. Dalton, you have the most beautiful little girls," she said patting the girls on their heads as though they were puppies.

"Thank you," I replied.

"So, how much money will you be needing today?" She spoke to me but was looking curiously at Deke.

"I'd like to make it an even two hundred. I'm not sure yet how many hands we will have until after picking begins. Do you think that will be enough, Mr. McCrady?" I figured by addressing him as Mr. McCrady, she would see him as the business associate he was.

"Yes, I think that will do, Mrs. Dalton." Deke followed my lead.

Mr. Caldwell reappeared as we stood to leave, and they both thanked me again. I felt four eyes piercing our backs as we walked to the door. Surely word had gotten out about my parent's health. They had to know I needed help with the girls. However, their glares made me feel like a specimen under a microscope.

When we walked down the street to the Big Store, we received much the same glares from others we passed. Deke, carrying Scarlett and following me closely, showed little to no reaction to the eyes casts upon us after we walked inside.

I gathered my list as quickly as possible and was making my way to the counter when I heard a familiar, loud, high-pitched voice. "Lucretia dear, how you doin'? Just look at 'em sweet young'uns," Mrs. Grimsley said.

"Hello, Mrs. Grimsley," I responded quietly.

"How's yer mother and daddy doin.' That was such a awful thing that happened to 'em. And yer husband dyin' right after? But it's good you got this young man here to help you these days. How you do, Deke?" Her words seem to bounce off the walls and magnify throughout the entire store.

"They're better. Matter of fact, Daddy and Mama are going to be out in their field after picking starts. I'll tell them you asked about them," I replied softly.

Scarlett chose that time to start squirming and said she wanted *down, down, down.* Melanie was already fretting a little. It was time for her feeding, but I wasn't sure how or where I could make that happen.

If there had been that one person whose eyes

weren't already following us through the store, they certainly were after all of that unfurling.

"You want me to take them both to the car while you pay up?" Deke asked under his breath.

"Yes, that would be good," I whispered.

He shifted Scarlett to his right arm. When I handed him Melanie, a big wet spot appeared on my dress where my breast milk had leaked. Fortunately, Mrs. Grimsley didn't see it or I'm sure she would have brought that to the attention of the entire crowd as well.

I paid quickly, said my good-byes, and hurried to the car. Both babies were crying and kicking when I arrived. Deke looked a bit flustered but somehow remained composed.

"Well, that was certainly embarrassing," I said.

"Aww, people are used to her. I wouldn't worry about it." Deke started the car and was about to turn in the direction of home.

"I'm sorry but I have to find a place to nurse the baby. You know, some place private and out of sight. I can't put it off any longer." By now, my strutting full breasts were making me miserable. To worsen the situation, Melanie's fretting had progressed to a loud cry.

I didn't know where, but I needed privacy to nurse Melanie away from the eyes of passersby—and Deke's.

"I know a place." I was glad Deke chose to be a man of few words at the time. I wasn't anxious to go into detail about leaking breast milk.

Before I knew it, we were pulling in the Strom's yard. Larson, Edna, and Larson's mother were sitting on their porch. After a brief interchange with Larson's mother, Deke returned for Scarlett and said I was invited to nurse Melanie in the privacy of their home.

Edna stuck her head in the door of the bedroom after Melanie was fed and quieted down. "Want me to hold the baby so you can wipe that milk off your dress?"

"That would be nice. I was so embarrassed. We were getting groceries in the Big Store. I was trying to run in and rush out, but Mrs. Grimsley stopped me to talk. Scarlett was tired and acting up. Melanie was hungry and her whimpering made my breast start leaking. Mrs. Grimsley kept asking about my mother and dad. And everyone was gawking at us…" There was no more holding back the tears at that point.

"It's okay. They are babies. That is what babies do. Mrs. Grimsley is lonely. She will talk to and drill anyone she can pen in a corner. It didn't take me long to figure her out. And don't worry about people gawking. That's what people do too. Let them gawk. If they were in your situation, wonder how they would handle it? Here, let me have her so you can get that milk off before it stains." She took Melanie and handed me a warm rag to wipe my dress.

"Thank you. You're right. Babies cry. People gawk.

Breast milk leaks," I forced a smile.

"Nursing a baby is also a natural thing. Of course, I never did. My milk wasn't good. My sister had also just had a baby. She had good, rich, milk and plenty of it. She was able to nurse mine and hers too."

"You have a baby?" I asked, not thinking how awkward that question was since she and Larson had just gotten married.

"He's almost grown now. But I had him when I was fourteen."

"Fourteen! I thought I was young having Scarlett at seventeen. You got married that young?" After seeing her face, I realized I had just asked another awkward question.

"I think it is wonderful how Deke is trying to help you. Don't pay any attention to people. Just look them straight in the eye and go on about your business," she continued, ignoring my question.

Her tone and undaunted expression told me she knew what she was talking about from first-hand experience.

"Theodore was going to teach me to drive but…well he never got a chance. I asked Deke to teach me, but it is impossible with two babies. I will learn someday. I can promise you that. But until I do, I have to rely on him to get me where I need to go."

"I'll help you. I'd be glad to watch the girls so he can teach you. I've been driving for years. I learned for the same reason you want to learn—to be independent. You can do it. Driving is really not that hard."

"That would be so good. Deke is going to be tied up at the field when picking time starts. Think I could learn before then?"

"Larson was just saying it will start in a little over a week. Sure. You're smart. With enough practice, I think you could be driving yourself around in no time at all. I'll even watch the girls this afternoon if he wants to get started giving you lessons. The sooner you start—the better."

"Let's go ask him now," I said.

"DOES THEODORE'S TRUCK have enough gas so you can use it for my driving lesson?" I asked Deke once he returned later that day.

"Yes, I filled it up the other day when I picked up chicken feed for your parents."

"I'm excited. Edna and Larson should be here soon."

"Well, I'm excited for you. Not a lot of women can drive around these parts."

"It seems to be catching on. Billie Kay learned to drive after she moved out of her parents' house and in with her sister. Edna was telling me she learned when she was about my age, like me, out of necessity. Did you know she has a son?"

"Yes, I did. Actually, he's a year older than you are. I heard she had him when she was just a kid herself. He lives over in Arkansas with his grandpa. At least that is what Larson told me."

"Wonder why he doesn't live with her?" I found Edna's story intriguing.

"Larson said she moved to St. Louis to take a job at the Small Arms Plant. She left him with his grandpa while she was up there working. Larson never went into detail about why her son stayed with his grandpa instead of going back to live with Edna."

"Small Arms? Theodore's inves…" I stopped abruptly. Something just didn't feel right about sharing Theodore's personal information. "I mean Theodore told me about that place. He said it is a huge supplier of ammunition."

"That's what Larson said too. He got hired to haul several loads of copper and brass up there for a while. That is where he met Edna. Next thing I hear is Larson convinced her to quit her job there and move to Muddy Ox. He said he fell hard for her right after they met."

"She seems like a very nice lady—smart too. I can see how Larson would be so taken with her. We talked a little when she came into the bedroom after I finished nursing Melanie. I did notice one thing about her though."

"What's that?" Deke was curious.

"There was a sadness in her eyes when she spoke about her son. It didn't last long. I can't explain it. But it was real. She's evidently been through some hard things in her lifetime too."

I managed to get Scarlett and the usual mess she made around her highchair cleaned, the table wiped, and the dishes soaking in a pan minutes before Edna and Larson arrived. I had the rest of my life to do dishes and only a week and a half left before Deke would be spending most of his time in the field again.

Besides, I was thrilled to be learning to drive.

Chapter Forty-One

"LET'S START WITH you getting the feel of the wheel," Deke said.

"Okay. How do I do that?"

He started the truck and put his arm over the back of the seat. "Scoot over here so we can see how good you are at keeping on your side of the road."

I was nervous. But before long, I felt comfortable managing the stirring wheel. Being comfortable sitting that close to Deke took a bit longer.

"Are you ready to take the next step now?" he asked after a while.

"Yes, I am."

We swapped places with him remaining close enough to handle anything that could go wrong.

"This is the clutch. This is the brake. And this is the gas pedal. Here is the gear shift. You begin by pushing the clutch down to the floor to put it in low gear. Let up on the clutch real easy while you press lightly on the gas. After you gather a little speed, take your foot off the gas, press the clutch in again to go to second, then finally, after you get more speed, let off the gas again, and press the clutch down once more to go into third.

After you get the hang of going forward, I'll show you how to back up."

"This is more complicated than I imagined. It's a lot different being the person in control than being the one watching someone else do the driving," I said after watching him maneuver through all the gears.

"Yes, but I promise, after a while, it'll be like second nature to you. Now, let's give it a try. Push the clutch all the way to the floorboard with your left foot. Then let it up slowly while barely pressing the gas with your right."

The truck jumped for several tries. Deke even pressed the brake a time or two to stop it. But as soon as I got the feel of the clutch and the gas pedal working together almost as one, it started to fall into place.

"Well, how did I do?" I asked.

"You did real good. Especially for it bein' yer first time ever to drive."

"So, you think I'll be driving well enough to go it alone by the time you have to be in the field full time?"

"That's what we're aimin' at. That buckin' and jumpin' will get better after a few more lessons." He smiled.

It became obvious to us that he was still sitting close to me. However, he didn't move over right away. "You did real good," he repeated. Our eyes remained locked.

"Mommy. Listen. He sounds like my horsey," Scarlett's squeal from the porch broke our stare.

Scarlett was jumping up and down in her playpen

while Larson was entertaining her. Melanie was on Edna's lap.

"Looks like Larson brought his harmonica. He can make all kinds of sounds on it. Seems like he's learned a new one," Deke said, moving over quickly to get out of the truck.

"How was the lesson?" Edna asked after we reached the porch.

"She did good. Real good for the first time ever under the wheel."

"At first it was a little like taming a bucking horse," I said. "But I got it tamed down before we got back to the yard."

"Sounds like y'all been horsin' around too," Larson teased. "This little girl here sure loves her horsey. So, I was makin' it talk to her."

"Horsey, horsey go to town..." Scarlett began to sing.

Edna saw me tear up, so she broke in. "Larson has a way with kids. He loves them and they're crazy about him. Also, it was the best way we could keep up with this little bundle of energy."

"She's a firecracker, alright," Larson chimed in.

"That's the name my dad has for her. He calls her his little firecracker."

"You came back into the yard a lot smoother than you left it," Larson said.

"She'll do fine after a few more lessons. Want us to

come back over so y'all can go out again tomorrow?" Edna kindly offered.

"I would really appreciate that. I didn't want to ask but yes if it isn't too much trouble."

"It's no trouble at all. Shoot, I can come every day if you want me to. If Larson has something he has to do, he can drop me off. Although, I think he enjoyed it as much as I did." Edna smiled.

"Every day you can come would help. I'd love for her to have as many lessons as we can squeeze in before she gets out in the truck by herself. And especially when she's out with those babies."

Deke had just brought up something I hadn't thought of before. How was I going to drive with those two girls? How did other people do it?

"I can go with her the first few times she's out without you. That is, until she gets more practice."

"That would be wonderful, Edna. Thank you," I said.

"So, same time tomorrow?" she asked.

"If y'all can do it," Deke replied.

"We can do it 'til the field starts callin' us," Larson said, standing to leave.

"Larson and I are glad to help y'all out if we can. I know how hard things can get sometimes." Edna had that look again for a second. Besides, we need the practice. We hope to have a baby of our own before long.

She and I shared a look at the same time Deke and Larson did. This time, I didn't say anything awkward. If Edna wanted to speak about her past or present for that matter, I wanted it to be her idea.

Edna handed me Melanie. Deke picked up Scarlett and we took the girls inside after they left. I figured I'd have to shift into high gear to catch up after allowing myself a few hours of personal time. Melanie needed to nurse; the dishes needed…

"Oh, my goodness, Deke. Edna must have washed the dishes too. How kind of her to do that."

"She is a good woman. Larson did good for hisself when he got her."

"You don't think she did well to get Larson too?" I asked.

"Larson's got a lot of good things goin' for hisself. He's one of the best mechanics in these parts. He's not lazy. He's funny and would give you the shirt right off his back."

"Then again, didn't she do well getting him?"

"He's got a temper. And yes, he'd give you the shirt off his back, but heaven help the person who'd try to take it. He has the strength of an ox and the temper of a bull. Also, Larson loves his drink."

"That's hard to imagine. I've never seen that side of him," I replied.

"Well, you've never tried to take his shirt," Deke joked.

"Have you?" I teased.

"No. And I ain't ever gonna try. I've seen him bend a tire tool in half to make it work for a job he was tryin' to get done on a car. And one time he twisted a bolt right off a tractor. Nope. I think I'd just give him my shirt first."

We laughed.

It ended up easier for Edna to watch the girls at my house than to try to take them to their place. So, every day she and Larson showed up like clockwork for my driving lessons.

And every day. Deke said I did good.

Chapter Forty-Two

WE MANAGED TO go by and see my parents either at the beginning or the end of each of my lessons. They weren't happy that they didn't get to see the girls but understood. Mama had reservations about me driving. But she warmed up to the idea when I explained about how I wouldn't be dependent on Deke or anyone else to get me where I needed to go. And it also meant that later on, I could come and see them on my own more often. She was glad that Deke was so much help to me. But I think she might have had a few reservations about him too.

Daddy was thrilled that I was learning to drive. He was also thrilled that I wasn't challenging him about going to the field and taking Mama with him any longer. I never told him about mine and Deke's trip to talk to Doctor McFarnz. I wouldn't deny it if he asked, but I didn't see the need to ask for a tongue lashing either.

After a full week of lessons, I felt pretty good about my driving abilities. It was Saturday. Picking season started in two days. After this lesson, Deke only had one more day to make sure I was ready to drive on my own.

"When I gave Daddy money today so he could pay

the hands, he said after another week, he should have enough profit built up that he can pay them himself. He also wants to start paying me back. But since Theodore wasn't going to let him, I don't think I should either."

"You need to do what you feel is right," Deke agreed.

"I'll go to the bank Monday and withdraw enough for him to cover the next week's wages. Then if he wants to be on his own for a while, I will be there to help if he needs me."

"Maybe we should practice you backing up again. You'll have to back up after you park at the bank. I think you've only tried using reverse a couple of times."

"Good idea. Where do you want to go to practice?" I asked.

"Let's go to Five Points. You can stop and back up five or even ten times there if you want to." He teased.

We didn't talk about it but the reason we didn't go to Muddy Ox a lot was to avoid gawking and gossip. A part of me worried about it since this was only August and Theodore died the end of June. But my circumstances called for help. And since my parents had problems of their own, Deke was the available one.

Another part of me wanted to look at it like Edna said. What would people have done if it were them? I would have lied if I said it didn't bother me. But looking back. I did what Theodore had told me. I did what I had to do.

Lord, how I missed Theodore.

Before we left Five Points, I felt very qualified to back up in any given situation. I suppose the only thing I worried about was if I drove by myself with the girls. I would have to give that some thought.

"I think I will make a jelly cake and invite Edna and Larson to stay and have cake with us tomorrow. We can celebrate it being my last lesson. And it will sort of be a thank you for how much they have done for us." I felt a little strange saying '*us*' so often here lately. Deke turned and looked at me. Then quickly looked away. I wondered if he had the same thought.

"A jelly cake. That's nice. They'll love that." Deke's mind didn't seem to be on what he said.

"And maybe Monday instead of staying and watching the girls, Edna may want to ride to the bank with us."

"That might not be a bad idea. You know—since it will be your first time driving on your own." Was worrying about me driving alone the reason he was so preoccupied?

"Do you think you will ever feel like I can drive anywhere on my own?"

"Guess that's not for me to say. But I'll admit I'll worry about it for a while. You know. Since you'll have the babies with you," he tried to justify his concern.

"Okay, I'll ask Edna. To be honest, I guess I worry a little about it myself."

"CAN Y'ALL STAY a little while after the lesson today? I made a cake for us to celebrate my learning to drive and to thank you for all your help?" I asked Edna and Larson when they arrived.

"Sounds good. What kinda cake?" Larson joked.

"Oh, don't pay any attention to him. He don't care what kind it is as long as it's cake." Edna smiled.

"We won't be gone long. Oh, and I left coffee in the pot for y'all too if you want it."

"But stay away from that cake, Larson," Deke teased.

"Oh, don't worry. I'll save you a little." Larson teased back.

"Take your time. We will be okay here. And so will the cake." Edna promised.

"Alright," Deke said once we were seated in the truck. "I will just sit here and let you do on your own. Just pretend I'm not here."

"So, this is like my final examination?"

"If you want to call it that. But you already passed the class. Just you wantin' to drive and havin' yer jaw set like you did, let me know you could do anything you put yer mind to."

"Really? That's what Theodore always said."

"Well, I agree."

"I can't believe this is my last lesson."

"You use words like final and last and…well, it's not like yer done with me. I'll still be around." Deke looked almost offended.

"I know that. I just won't be such a burden to you if I can drive myself to the store, the bank, or the Post Office. And most of all, over to my parent's house. Although now, they'll be out in the cotton field with you."

"I can still go with you to those places, if you ever needed me to go, that is," Deke offered.

"Well, if you wanted. But only if you want to and not because you have to."

"Let's get something straight. Anything I done for you or with you this last month and a half, wasn't 'cause I had to. I wanted to. Matter of fact. I'll miss takin' you 'round town. It felt good to be needed."

"Even with all those judgmental eyes on us?"

"I don't care 'bout what people think they see or the notions in their heads."

"Honestly, Deke. I don't believe you do. And that's a good thing. I'll miss going those places with you too. And not just because you help me with the girls. I love my girls. And believe me, they fill my day. But it's good to have another adult around to talk to—and do things with."

Suddenly, a couple of chickens ran across the road. I

swerved to miss them. Deke was by my side in an instant, grabbed the wheel, and brought us to a stop.

It scared me so badly, I was shaking. Deke held me, until I was calm. We sat there for a few minutes, me crying against his shoulder and him silently patting me.

"You okay?" he asked hoarsely.

"Yes, but I don't know if I would be if you weren't here."

"Next time, hit the chickens. We'll invite Edna and Larson for dinner."

My sobs immediately broke into laughter.

"You think I'm jokin.' But I'm not."

Then he started laughing too.

"So, did I fail? Guess you want to drive us home now?" I asked.

"No, it's kinda like gettin' stung by a cotton worm out in the field. You shake the thing off, stomp it in the ground, duck yer head and pick on down the row. If you don't, you'll be afraid of cotton worms the rest of yer life."

"You do have a way with words, Mr. McCrady."

"Why thank you Mrs. Dalton."

Chapter Forty-Three

"YOU MEAN YOU had a chance to bring home a chicken dinner and you passed it up?" Larson teased.

"It's Lucretia's fault." Deke chimed in.

"Next time, run over 'em chickens and bring 'em home. Edna can cook us up some fried chicken that'll make you smack yer lips."

"See, Didn't I tell you, Lucretia?" Deke played along.

"Want me to get the cups and saucers for you?" Edna offered while I made a fresh pot of coffee.

"Yes, they're in the cabinet to the left. The silverware is in the drawer under that cabinet if you want to get that too."

"So, Deke since this was her last lesson, are we all safe to be on the same road with her?" Larson smiled.

"As long as yer not a chicken," Deke teased.

"Will you two jokesters leave this poor girl alone? I think I can safely say everyone at this table has either swerved to miss a chicken in the road or in Larson's case, purposely ran over a few in their lifetime." Edna said, coming to my rescue.

"I'd say yer right about that," Deke agreed.

"Hey, you can run up on a lot of suppers on the highway. You caint go from here to Caruthersville, without seein' a big old soft-shelled turtle tryin' to cross the road in front of you. They make the best turtle soup. And raccoons don't have a lick of sense. They'll try to dodge a car every time they see one. Edna's famous for her baked coon and sweet taters."

"Not everyone loves baked coon, Larson." Edna gave him a kiss on his forehead.

"Well, the man you married sure does. Hey Deke, want to step on the porch a minute? I can grab a smoke while they get the coffee on?"

"Grab it quick. This pot doesn't take very long to brew," I said as they stood to leave.

"Edna, would you like to ride with me to the bank in Muddy Ox tomorrow? Deke is worried about me driving alone for the first time. Especially with the girls in the truck," I asked once we were alone.

"I was going to offer to watch them for you. But going with you would be nice too."

"That's good. I've been trying to come up with a plan how I can keep them safe with just me and them. I could lay Melanie in a basket in the floorboard. Sometimes Scarlett will sit still in the seat. But most of the time—she won't."

"A friend of mine in St. Louis had a little boy about her age. She found this thing they call a booster seat made by Bunny Bear Company. It's like a chair that hooks over the back of the car seat. Her kid can sit next to her and see out the window while she's driving. It even has a toy steering wheel on it for them to play with to keep them busy. She ordered hers from Sears and Roebuck Catalog. You might want to look into that."

"I will. That sounds like it might be what I need."

"It was for her," Edna said.

"Deke says you worked at Small Arms Plant in St. Louis?"

"Yes, my job was to sign for the shipments we received. That's how I met Larson. I signed for a truck load of brass and copper he delivered there."

"You must have fell quickly for him to quit your job like that," I said.

"We started seeing one another after he made a few more truck runs. It wasn't long before he started talking marriage. He can be pretty persuasive when he wants to be. Rumors began circling around the plant that Small Arms would be losing their government contracts as soon as the war ended. When he heard those rumors, he wanted me to quit and move here so we could get married. I figured I could be out of a job soon anyway if those rumors were true, so here I am.

"I know Larson has made a reputation for himself around town. There could be truth to some of it I guess. And a whole lot of it is pure speculation. Anyway, people don't know him like I do. He's not perfect, for that matter neither am I. But he is a good man and with the right woman, he could be even better. I'm going to try my best to be that woman."

"That's so sweet. Edna, I see a very kind and special lady when I look at you. Deke said the same thing. He said Larson did good when he got you."

"I think Deke is a good man too. There isn't one ounce of pretense about him. He's the same every time I see him." Edna held eye contact as though she had more to say but the men stepped inside. I figured we could talk more tomorrow, woman to woman.

"I smell coffee," Larson said as soon as he and Deke walked inside.

"It's ready," I said while putting the cake on the table.

"That looks delicious. I'm gonna need your recipe." I took that for a real compliment coming from such a good cook as everyone said Edna was.

"I got it out of a cookbook I found when Theodore and I first got married. But Mama added her touch and it's even better now."

Larson shared some of his coon hunting stories while we ate. He was quite the storyteller. Deke had a few tales to spin as well. Edna cleared the table while I nursed Melanie. Of course, she did the dishes also.

"Well, we need to run along, Mom will be wonderin' what happened to us. We told her we'd only be gone a couple of hours," Larson said.

"My mother thinks so much of your mom. Why don't I send a piece of cake for her home with you?"

Larson and Edna both beamed when I spoke of Mrs. Strom.

"I couldn't ask for a better mother-in-law. She is one of the sweetest, Christian women I've ever known."

"She's pretty fond of her new daughter-in-law too," Larson added, standing to leave.

"What time should I be here tomorrow?" Edna asked.

"The bank opens at nine o'clock. If you can be here around nine, we can get there a little after it opens."

I WAS UP, nursed the baby, fed Scarlett and myself, got the girls dressed and ready to go by the time Edna arrived at precisely nine o'clock. She could have driven us, but that would have defeated the purpose of me trying so desperately to learn to drive.

I could do this. I knew I could.

It helped that Edna didn't seem a bit worried about riding with me driving. I had gone over the steps several times in my head before she arrived.

"Scarlett, can you be a good girl and sit there and hold your baby doll while Mommy drives us to the bank?" She looked at me with her big blue eyes, like she understood.

"I'll hold your little sister and you hold your baby. And we will both be good girls, okay Scarlett?" Edna definitely had a way with kids too.

Hearing Deke's instructions in my head, I took a deep breath and backed out of the yard as if I'd done it all my life.

"I'm glad you decided to go with us today. It would be harder to concentrate my first time driving without Deke if I had to worry about the girls too."

"I was happy to do it. I like being around you and your babies. I always have loved children. And like we were talking last night, I think a booster seat like the one my friend got her little boy will really be a help to you, once it's just you and the girls. If and when I ever have another baby, I want one of those seats too."

"So, you and Larson want a baby right away?"

"More than anything. Larson has never had any children of his own. He's crazy about kids. And as far as right away, I am not getting any younger. Even if I got pregnant now, I'd be thirty-six by the time she was born."

"She?" I asked.

"I'd love to have a little girl. You know, since I've already had a boy. It doesn't matter to Larson. He'd be happy with either one."

"It must have really been hard having a baby at

fourteen. You were just a child yourself. And the father? Was he…?" I immediately felt sorry to have asked that question. Her body stiffened and her countenance fell. The silence was heart-rending.

"I…I was molested. When I was thirteen. I've always said I let a stranger have his way with me and never saw him again. That was a lie I made up for everyone else. But for some reason I wanted you to know the truth. Please keep it between us, okay?"

"Oh, Edna. I won't tell a soul. I promise."

"Good. I appreciate that. I just felt like you'd understand and wouldn't judge me."

"I would never judge you, Edna. But why didn't you tell about being molested? Instead, you took it upon yourself—like you were willing for it to happen?"

"I was protecting those I loved. I didn't want people digging into it. Someone I trusted molested me. Let's just leave it there, okay?"

"Alright. I get it now. When you said look people straight in the eyes and not worry about their gawking, that's what you did—had to do?"

"Yes. When you're not married, pregnant at thirteen, and have a baby when you're fourteen, people gawk at you and whisper about you, it makes you grow up fast and tough. Those kind of people don't know what to do when you stare them down."

"I know my Mama could stare people down to shut them up really fast."

"We girls can learn a lot from our Mamas." Again, Edna seemed to be speaking from experience.

My heart broke for her. Of course, she had to have gotten pregnant when she was only thirteen to have given birth at fourteen. How awful. And to be molested by someone she trusted? That was even worse. I decided not to bring it up to her again. If she wanted to talk about it, she could be the one to bring it up.

"Yesterday, you mentioned rumors going around that the Small Arms Plant might shut down. Do you think there was something to those rumors? Or did Larson use them to convince you to quit and move here?" Not only had what she said troubled me, I thought it was time to lead the conversation down another path.

"It's been my experience rumors like that usually have some merit at least. And, they had already cut everyone's overtime. Guess we'll have to wait and see. Anyway, Larson didn't have to work very hard to convince me. I'd already made up my mind to marry him." She smiled.

Edna offered to sit in the car with the girls while I ran in the bank to make the withdrawal. I was glad. That way, we would have more time to look around the Big Store. If the girls cooperated, we might even grab a burger and fries at The Green Fly—maybe even a Coca Cola too.

"Good morning, Mrs. Dalton. It's good to see you

again." Mr. Caldwell greeted me in his usual manner. "How can we be of service to you today?"

I was sure he already knew the service I needed. The only reason I would ever come to the bank would be to withdraw money.

"Oh hello, Mrs. Dalton. You didn't bring the girls today?" Mrs. Thatcher asked.

"They are in the truck with a friend," I replied.

"Mr. McCrady?" she questioned.

"No. Mmm…no…another friend," I said. I started to tell her Mrs. Edna Strom, but what business was it of hers who the friend was out in my truck?

"It's good you have a lot of *friends* willing to drive you to town. That's nice," she continued. She made the word friends sound dirty or questionable.

"Yes. I have a lot of good *friends*." I mocked her. "But actually, I drove myself today. I won't be needing anyone to drive me around any longer."

"Mrs. Thatcher, I can take care of Mrs. Dalton this time," Mr. Caldwell broke in. My tone of voice might have told him she was getting on my nerves. And he would be right.

"Thank you, Mr. Caldwell." He pulled out a chair for me at his desk and I sat down. "Thank you again."

"You are welcome," he replied.

"I would like to withdraw two hundred and twenty dollars today, please."

"Alright." He cleared his throat. "But that's twenty

dollars more than you usually withdraw."

"Is there a limit? I have need of twenty extra dollars. Am I limited to only two hundred?"

"No ma'am. I'm sorry. Of course. Let me process your withdrawal right away." He was back in minutes and counted out my money to me as usual.

"Thank you, Mr. Caldwell."

He clearly had something else he wanted to say but hesitated in order to weigh his words.

"Mrs. Dalton."

"Yes, Mr. Caldwell."

"Ah…I just wanted to say thank you for your business here at our bank."

"You're welcome…"

We sat for a second, waiting for the other one to speak. I didn't feel like thanking me for my business at his bank was what he had on his mind. But when he stood and wished me to have a nice rest of the day, I took that to mean our business was finished.

However, as I walked out of the bank, I still had the feeling he was going to say something more. Something that evidently he figured I wouldn't want to hear. Maybe he would come up with the right words when I made my next withdrawal.

Chapter Forty-Four

EDNA AND I got our staples and walked around the store for a while. We decided to come back to the Green Fly with Deke and Larson. Neither of us felt right to have burgers and a coke while the men were sweating out in the cotton field.

"Isn't that Deke's car coming toward us?" Edna asked after we had turned off the blacktop onto the gravel road leading home.

"Yes, it is."

"Guess he had to make a run to town for something," Edna said.

"Or something is wrong." After the turns of events, I had experienced during the last few months, I automatically thought a catastrophe was lurking somewhere.

Deke pulled over and parked to the side of the road, waiting for us to reach him.

"What is wrong?" I asked even before bringing the truck to a complete stop.

"Nothin.' I left Larson to help Asa so I could come and…uh…we needed some bailin' wire. You know how bailin' wire comes in handy out in the field. See you made it to the bank, since yer headin' back this way."

"Yes. We went there first and then to the Big Store. How's Mama handling the heat out there? Daddy hasn't been trying to climb up on the cotton wagon, has he?"

"Yer Mama's farin' fine. That lean-to Asa come up with is doin' the trick for both of 'em. And no, he's behavin' hisself so far." For Deke to answer so quickly, told me he'd been keeping an eye on them without me asking.

"I appreciate you looking out for them."

"Glad to do it. Well, I need to hurry back. If I don't run by this evenin' I'll run by in a day or two unless you're needin' somethin'?"

"I don't need anything that I can think of," I replied.

"Hmm...well...let me know if you do." He sounded almost rejected.

"In case you're wondering, she's driving like she's been doing it all of her life. You must be a good teacher." Edna smiled.

"No problems backin' up?" he asked.

"Not one," I was happy to report.

"Good. Figured you'd do okay. Gotta go now." He grinned, and the worry wrinkle disappeared from his forehead.

"Tell Larson I said hi and I'll see him at supper." Edna yelled. We saw his hand wave through the dust, signaling he had heard, as he sped away.

"Baling wire. Who does he think he's fooling? Daddy always has baling wire in his truck. I'd be willing to say Larson does too."

"You're right. Larson can fix most anything with a screwdriver and some baling wire. He wouldn't be without it," she confirmed.

"I know, and you know too, Deke was coming to check on me. He was worried about my first time driving without him."

"Aww…Don't be mad at him. That's sweet. It's clear that he cares about you—and these girls too."

"Deke was who Theodore hired to help him do anything he needed done. And he hired Larson for anything mechanical. Mama and Daddy couldn't help me after Theodore died because of her stroke and his accident. They still can't. Mama has only regained partial strength in her arms. And Daddy is still moving pretty slow. I kept Deke employed for that reason. I knew I couldn't make it by myself. I still can't. I'm not mad."

"Deke's a decent man. I think he would have done anything you needed him to do if you had never given him a red cent."

"Yes, Deke is a good person. And I appreciate all he has done. And I'm a decent person too. I would never let him do for us like he has without paying him."

"Yes—you are decent, Lucretia. I know you would never take advantage of Deke's kindness."

We didn't do much talking on the way home. I was

thinking about Edna's observation about Deke. Were people at the bank and in town seeing the same? There was no denying when he sat close to me during my driving lessons, I felt a certain energy between us. Was it more than just nervousness?

But wait. I had only been a widow for less than two months. I couldn't bring another scandal for Mama to have to deal with, especially in her condition, even if it was an innocent one this time.

What was wrong with me? Maybe I wasn't the decent person I thought I was. It was understood there was an acceptable time of mourning that needed to be done before a widow even allowed herself to have thoughts of...

"Lucretia, I just remembered seeing a Sears Catalog at Larson's mom's house. Want to drop by there on our way home so you can look to see if that car seat is in it?"

"Well, it is on our way."

"It might be smart to stop and look at it now, before it ends up in their toilet."

I never thought about it before. Mama and Daddy may have even gotten one too. If so, it probably went straight to their outhouse. They were barely getting by with Theodore's generosity and the church helping them. They definitely didn't have money for catalog orders.

But since we were closer to the Strom's than to Mama and Daddy's house. We might as well stop there.

Besides, Melanie would need to nurse again soon.

Mrs. Strom was walking toward us when we pulled into the yard. From the bonnet on her head and the hoe she had flung on her shoulder, I assumed she had been weeding her garden.

"Whew, it's mighty hot today," she said, throwing her bonnet back and resting her hoe against the porch post.

"Let me get you a cold glass of water, Mother Strom. Your face is as red as a beet," Edna said as we approached.

"Thank you dear. I shoulda stopped sooner. But I caint hardly quit a job 'til it's done." She was clearly over-heated.

"I'll bring you a cool cloth to wipe your face with too." Edna added.

"My daughter-in-law takes good care of me." Mrs. Strom smiled as she dropped into the porch swing.

"She's a good person," I replied.

"Y'all get yer runnin' done? How'd you do drivin' yer first trip to town?"

"She did real good. I just rode along for moral support—and to help her with those babies her first time out," Edna said handing her a glass of ice water and a washcloth and Scarlett a cookie.

"How's yer Mama and Daddy doing since his fall and her stroke?"

"They're both better. Matter of fact, they are both

back in the cotton field today.

"Oh my. Are they well enough for that?"

"I was worried about them too. But Dr. McFarnz gave them the go ahead as long as Mama stayed in the shade and Daddy didn't do any climbing on the wagon or tractor. They both promised to follow doctor's orders."

"Larson and Deke are keeping an eye on them, I'm sure. Lucretia, it's just us women here. You can go on and nurse that baby now if she's hungry," Edna suggested.

"Chickie, chickie," Scarlett said, pointing toward the chicken pen.

"You want to go see the chickens? We're gonna go see the chickies while you nurse baby sister." Edna announced as they left hand in hand.

I covered myself with a diaper for modesty's sake to nurse Melanie even though it was just us ladies present.

"Deke must a taught you real good for you to learn to drive so quickly," Mrs. Strom said.

"He did. And he was very patient with me. But it couldn't have happened if Edna and Larson hadn't come to watch the girls though."

"From what they said, it was a pleasure for them. They both love children. Sometimes, Larson acts like a big kid hisself when he's around them. And Deke. Well, he's just a mighty fine man. I'm proud how he's stepped up to help you like he has."

"Oh yes. Deke has been right there every time I needed anything. I know people are saying things about us since it hasn't been that long since Theodore died. But Mama and Daddy were in no shape to help. And I needed someone. Besides, Deke is still on the payroll."

"It's clear to see how fond Deke is of you, dear. I think him being on the payroll doesn't have a thing to do with him stickin' by yer side. Let people say what they will. They'll give you a rest when the next person gives them somethin' jucier to chew on. You have to do what is best for you and those babies."

It was as though she had heard Theodore's last words to me. I knew she hadn't. Only Dr. McFarnz and I heard his last wishes. I hadn't told anyone what he said. And the doctor wasn't one to repeat private matters like that.

Her calm voice and soft brown eyes put me at complete rest. I knew in an instant why Edna was so fond of her and why my mother referred to her as one of the finest Christian women around. She reflected a peace that could only come from God.

"This little doodlebug loves to watch chickens," Edna said as she arrived with a giggling Scarlett.

"She loves you too," I replied. "Are you about ready to go? They will be ready for their naps by the time we get them back home."

"Mother Strom, why don't you sit there and cool off until I get back. I won't be long," Edna said.

"I think I will. Lucretia, stop by and see me anytime. I'm most always here."

"Thank you, Mrs. Strom. I've enjoyed talking with you."

"Oh, I almost forgot. Mom, do you have a Sears catalog?"

"Why, yes, I do. It's on the bottom shelf of the end table by the couch."

"Can Lucretia borrow it? There is a car seat she wants to order for this little wild child. I will bring it back when she's through with it."

"Sure. I was just going to put it out in the toilet anyway when I was sure Omar didn't need anything else out of it. Go on and get it for her."

Scarlett followed Edna inside to get the catalog and reappeared with another cookie. I probably wouldn't have given her another one, but I knew it was Edna's way of showing her love.

"Thank you Mrs. Strom. I'll see that you get it back," I said as we headed to the truck.

"I can see why you are so fond of your mother-in-law. She is a precious soul," I said once we were back on the road.

"That she is," she agreed.

EDNA HELPED ME into the house with the girls then scurried on home. I fed Scarlett something other than cookies, changed their diapers, and got them down for naps. I took advantage of the quiet time to find and order the car seat for Scarlett. Even though she was kind enough to offer, I couldn't keep asking Edna to ride with me every time I had to go anywhere. I needed that seat as soon as possible. The order sheet said it should arrive by Friday, August seventeenth. That worked out perfectly. I would need to go to the bank again on Friday.

After wearing mostly maternity dresses for the last two years, I enjoyed thumbing through the ladies' section of the catalog. The last thing I remembered thinking before drifting off to sleep, was how much the styles had changed.

I was awakened from an exhausting dream by a constant rapping. My heart was still pounding when I opened the door to Deke.

"Lucretia, are you alright? I've been knocking for a while now. I knew you were home because the truck was here. What took you so long to come to the door?" Deke looked distraught.

"I'm fine. Well, I guess. I fell asleep and was having a very disturbing dream. Oh, Deke. It was awful."

"It must have been to have you so shaken like this. Do you need to talk about it?" He asked, ushering me to the couch.

"Things were being sucked out of the house by a big, black, whirlwind. I was helpless to hold on to anything. Things went right through my hands like I was a ghost or something. Theodore's books and music. The gold star his mother got for their Christmas tree when he was a child. Everything that was Theodore's was being sucked away. The louder I screamed for it to stop, the harder the winds blew. Then a thunderous voice spoke to me from inside the whirlwind."

"Well now, I've had some bad dreams in my time. But I aint ever dreamt of a talkin,' whirlwind. What was it sayin' to you?"

"It shouted. *Let go. Get out. Leave.* Then the voice became Theodore's voice, only it was kinder. He said the same things. *Let go. Leave. Get out. Find what is important.* I took it to mean not to fight the whirlwind. Then it dawned on me that I hadn't seen the babies during the storm. When I ran into the nursery, they were there, sleeping peacefully, beautifully.

"It was as though I immediately understood what the whirlwind and Theodore were saying. Those babies were what was really important. Nothing being sucked away counted as long as I had them, and they were safe. Then Theodore's voice said, *Do what you have to do.*

"Deke, that was the last thing Theodore's said to me the day he died. Now, I am afraid of what lies ahead of me. What will I actually have to do to keep my promise to him to make sure the girls are taken care of? I thought I was already doing all I could for them. Mrs. Strom even said earlier today that I should do what is best for my babies."

"I think you have been under a lot of strain these days. You've been worried sick about your parents. Then Theodore died. You've pushed yourself to learn to drive. I'm sure that was stressful. It looks to me like you're doing a wonderful job of taking care of everyone, including your parents and the babies." Deke's voice was soft, soothing, and understanding. I hadn't realized until then he had both my hands in his.

"Was that dream a scary warning? Or was it what you just said, a result of all the stress I've been going through? I hope it isn't a warning of worse things ahead for me. I don't know how much more I can take."

"Lucretia, I feel like you've only scratched the surface of the strength you have inside of you. I'm like you. I hope there isn't something worse ahead of you. But I will promise you this. If there is, it won't be just you facin' it. I will be beside you all the way. We will face it together."

"Oh Deke." I cried, falling against his chest. He wrapped his arms tightly around me. And I felt safe.

SINCE DEKE HAD to pick up some axle grease at the Big Store anyway, he offered to go to the bank with me on Friday. I drove to get the practice and he corralled the girls.

Fridays were usually busy in town but for some reason, today was especially busy. Deke offered to stay in the car with the girls while I ran into the bank to make my weekly withdrawal. This would be the last large one I would have to make since Daddy said he was getting paid top dollar for cotton this year.

"Good morning, Mrs. Dalton," Mr. Caldwell's greeting didn't sound the same as usual.

"Good morning," I replied.

"Are you here for your withdrawal?" he asked.

"Yes, I am but…"

"Will you step into my office, Mrs. Dalton. We need to talk."

"I don't have a lot of time. Mr. McCrady is in the truck with the girls."

"This won't take long. But I have something very important to talk with you about."

"Okay, Mr. Caldwell. This sounds serious." His face was drawn. His usual toothy smile was not there.

"I guess you heard that last Wednesday, the fifteenth, the Japanese issued a statement declaring they would accept the terms of the Potsdam Declaration to end the war. Now, they haven't actually surrendered yet, but it will be settled as soon as President Truman accepts it to make it final."

"That sounds like a good thing, Mr. Caldwell. Why do you look so worried? Don't you want the war to be over?"

"Yes, I do. But it has its consequences as far as your account here at the bank is concerned."

"What consequences are you talking about? Theodore assured me that all I needed to do was come to you and we had plenty of money here in the bank."

"You do—well, you did."

"What do you mean I did?"

"You have some money here, but it's not a plentiful amount any longer. With the war over now, Small Arms lost its contract with the Government to purchase weapons. Weapons aren't needed if there isn't a war going on. Your account was being fueled by dividends from that Small Arms contract. All that is going to eventually cease."

"Well, we—I still have money in my account right now don't I?"

"You have some money left, like I said. But it will slowly diminish now that nothing is going to be added to it from Small Arms. And unfortunately, Mr. Dalton invested everything he had in just that one source."

"What are you actually telling me, Mr. Caldwell?" I knew what he was telling me, but my mind couldn't accept it. Theodore thought he had the girls and me securely taken care of. He never counted on this.

Neither did I.

"Mr. Dalton was a generous man. Actually, he was too generous. And his generosity was not a problem until now. I'm afraid he took more out than was going in for a long time before he died. I know he thought it would even out. But now, there is no way it can."

"Are you telling me I am broke—or soon will be?"

"It saddens me to say it but yes. At the rate you are taking money out of your funds, you only have about a month and a half of withdrawals left in your account."

I was pretty sure most of the blood had drained out of my face at that point. I felt as though I would faint if I stood. So, I sat quietly until my head stopped spinning.

"Mrs. Dalton, I will be glad to meet with you in the near future and try to help you manage what assets you have and try to get you on a workable budget. You have your house and grounds and if you liquidate…"

For a brief moment, his voice sounded like the thunderous one I heard in my whirlwind dream. He didn't say the words *get out, go, or leave* but everything he had said up to that time meant the same.

"Mrs. Dalton. Lucretia. Are you hearing me?"

"Yes, I hear you. Yes, I hear what you are saying. But…but I need one hundred and ninety dollars today. I was going to tell you that I think my father's yield will take care of him for the rest of the season. But now…today…I need one hundred and ninety dollars."

"If you are sure you need that much after everything

I have told you just now, then I will get it ready for you."

"Yes, Mr. Caldwell. I am sure. I need one hundred and ninety dollars. Now…today."

"I will draw it out for you then. Do you want to make an appointment for me to go over your assets like I suggested?"

"An appointment? Ah…I'll have to get back with you about that. Right now, I need what I came here for and then I need to think about all of this."

"Suit yourself. But I am here if you…"

"My girls are out in a hot car. I need to go now. I'll thank you to get my money so I can go." All I knew for sure at the time was I had to go. I had to get out of that bank and go.

Chapter Forty-Five

I FELT LIKE a different person walking out of the bank than the one who entered minutes before. My brain was spinning from what Mr. Caldwell had just said? Was the money that let Theodore die thinking my babies' and my future was secure really almost gone? Did he see this happening the last few seconds of his life? Was this why he gave me his final request? I wasn't sure now if it was a request or a warning. Had I only assumed he died in peace?

"Lucretia, do what you have to do to take care of our two babies." If Theodore had some kind of premonition into this shattering crack in my world, if he had seen the whirlwind I was going to be caught up in, then why didn't he go beyond the request to tell me how? I was so confused. How was I going to do this? I couldn't work at any job with two babies. Mama and Daddy were barely getting by. They couldn't help me now. What was I going to do?

Melanie was cooing. Scarlett was singing one second and merrily jabbering the next when I returned to the truck. Of course, they were, they didn't know their very foundation was crumbling beneath them.

"What's wrong Lucretia? You look like you're going to faint," Deke said as I slid into the truck beside him.

What was it he had promised me only two days ago after my terrifying dream? If something worse was waiting for me, I wouldn't have to face it alone? He'd face it with me. Sweet Deke. How was he going to help me face financial ruin? He was on MY payroll. The payroll that depended on the money that was dwindling a few withdrawals at a time.

"I'll—I'll be alright. Here is one hundred and seventy dollars for you to give Daddy. Let me know if that isn't enough."

"Are you ready to go to the Big Store now?" He was still looking at me, confused and concerned.

"Do you need more money to get your field supplies?" I responded with a counter question, extending the remaining twenty dollars toward him. He didn't move.

"No, yer Daddy sent enough money for that. Lucretia, what's wrong? Something happened inside that bank. What was it? Did they say more stuff about us? About me being with you?"

"No. They never said anything about us—you today."

"Then tell me what's wrong. Something must have gone on inside that bank to make you act and look like this. I wish now I would have gone in with you."

"I'll tell you on the way back home. Or maybe it

could wait until later? Go on and get what you need in the store. I'll sit here with the babies this time."

"Thought you had things you needed too. I saw you pick up a list before we left your house."

"Oh, yes. I need a couple bars of Ivory Soap to wash the babies' diapers and to give them their baths. I can make do without the rest of my list until—until another time."

I extended the twenty dollars to him once more. But he said he had money enough for a couple bars of soap. Any other time, I would have insisted he take my money. But I didn't have the stamina to protest at the moment. Deke glanced back at me a few times as he walked toward the store. I knew I would have to tell him about Mr. Caldwell's and my conversation. But I needed time to process it myself before I could go into it with him or anyone else.

Who else would need to know? Daddy—I would have to tell Daddy. He'd been wanting to go back to taking care of his own business for weeks. He just got his wish. Now, he'd have to be on his own for certain. I—my money was almost gone.

Deke had said he saw me pick up a list before we left my house. My house? How much longer would I have something—anything, I could call mine? Right now, my two greatest treasures were my babies. And they were depending on me—for their every need.

"Before we leave town, are you sure that's all you

want from that list?" Deke asked after pitching his supplies in the bed of the truck and handing me the two bars of soap.

"Yes. I have what I need for now. Let's get back to the house. I'll get the girls down for their naps. If you have the time, maybe I can explain everything then. Or if you need to rush back to the field, maybe you can come back at the end of day. But for now, I just need to think."

"Tell you what. I'll drop y'all off at your house and come back after I take these supplies to Larson. That'll let you get the girls settled. When I get back we can talk. Maybe then, you can tell me what's going on. Is that okay with you?" Deke asked.

"Yes, that'll be fine," I agreed.

I needed to try and sort things out in my head and heart. I welcomed the time alone to do that before having to go into it with him. Starting the girl's day earlier than usual played in my favor. They were ready for their naps.

After quietly closing the door to their nursery, I curled up in the corner of the couch, hugging my knees close to my chest, which had become my *I-don't-know-where-to-go-from-here* position.

My mind raced to think of possible jobs I could do. Every possibility ended with the dilemma of what to do with the girls. For a brief moment, I thought maybe I could get Edna to watch them for me while I worked.

But I read through the lines of our many conversations that she saw a move for her and Larson as soon as picking season was over. Deke had sort of confirmed that. He spoke many times of Larson's itchy feet to get out of the Bootheel. Farm work was not for Larson. Apparently, it wasn't for Edna either by the way people described her *one-elbow-on-her-knee-technique* of picking cotton. I knew she would have gladly watched the girls. I also knew it would have been a temporary job for her and a temporary fix for the girls and me. Temporary was not my answer.

Maybe I could take in a boarder? But who? I didn't welcome the idea of a stranger living with us. Now, if Billie Kay was still around, she would be perfect. Or would she have been? Billie Kay tended to lean toward the wild side of life. She was that way as a teenager and hadn't changed. But wait. She still was a teenager. So was I. Although, the carefree life of a teen was gone from me forever. So many things were gone for me forever. My youth, dreams of furthering my education, having my parents as a safety net, and now Theodore, plus the financial security he died thinking we had, was gone.

My parents. Maybe I could move back in with them. I could help them and… Before finishing that thought, I knew moving back home with Mama and Daddy was not and never would be possible. They loved the girls and me wholeheartedly. But their lives had changed too.

They were older, neither was in good health, and…well, one thing had not changed. Mama's world remained spotless, orderly, and controlled—even in her present state of health. Babies were messy, disorderly, all over the place, and loud. Disrupting my parent's routine and my babies' schedules was not the answer either.

Maybe I could work at home? But doing what? Taking care of two babies was a full-time job. The term full-time was self-explanatory. There were only twenty-four hours in a day.

Maybe…maybe I…

"Lucretia." Deke whispered, peeking around the door.

"Come in," I whispered back.

"I was afraid to knock and wake the babies. I've been so worried about you. I couldn't get back here fast enough. Please tell me what's going on," he pled.

I went into detail about how the dwindling returns from our bank investments coincided with the war ending. As precisely as I could remember, I repeated my conversation with Mr. Caldwell. Then, I told him about all the brick walls I had bumped into trying to figure how I could make it work to keep things going. I summarized with how afraid and helpless I felt before breaking into tears and shriveling into a pile of nerves.

Deke listened patiently, taking it all in before responding. "There is one solution I don't think you even thought of."

"If you have another one, please tell me. I'm at my wits end." I sobbed.

"Don't reject the idea before you give it a chance. And don't take what I am about to say the wrong way," he replied.

"I won't take any idea you have wrong, Deke. You've always tried to help anyway you could."

"Marry me, Lucretia. Marry me and I will work until my last breath to take care of you and those babies."

I stopped in the middle of a sob, sat back to look at him face on, and tried to speak but couldn't form the words at first. His willingness to sacrifice his own life to make one for me and the girls humbled me shamefully. Finally, I was able to respond.

"Oh, Deke. That is so sweet. For you to offer to marry me out of the pure goodness of your heart is beyond kindness. I couldn't expect…"

"Lucretia, I'll just lay it all out here for you. I have a confession. I think I have loved you all my life. I was the boy that got the grasshopper off yer back the day our mamas sat us under the cotton wagon together when we were kids. You were scared and crying. I had to raise the back of yer shirt to get it off of you. Yer mama saw my hand under your shirt and went crazy."

"I was so young. I can barely remember. So you were that little boy?"

"Yes, that was me."

"Mama yelled at you and whisked me away so fast, I

never had time to look back." I had almost forgotten the entire incident until now.

"You bet she did. She grabbed you up and took off with you like I was a criminal or somethin.' Yer Mama almost scared me to death that day."

"I'm sorry, Deke."

"I was in the eleventh grade when I dropped out of school to join the Army. You were in the tenth. But I think I loved you even back then. I had it in my mind to try to date you one day when you were old enough. But word was yer Mama was so strict with you, she wouldn't let you out of her sight. I also feared if she realized I was that little boy under the cotton wagon that day, she would never let me get near you.

"But right after I got out of the Army, I heard that somehow you showed up pretty often down at the dance hall in Muddy Ox. So, I hooked up with Billie Kay that night in hopes of getting close to you and maybe get to talk with you. When I saw how you and Theo were looking at each other. I didn't think I had a chance, so I never tried."

"Deke, do you remember the day Theodore got you to help move the stove into our house? I asked you about being there with Billie Kaye that night. I wondered why you acted so strange about it."

I sat quietly for a moment, trying to piece together everything Deke had told me with the scattered memories in my own mind. After thinking about it, I could see what he was saying was true. Deke had been a constant presence in my life, and I never realized it—until now.

"I'd heard you married Mr. Dalton and how much older he was than you." Deke continued. "Then, when I saw you that day, I knew you were too pregnant for it to be his. I put it together that the baby had to be Theo's. I figured it was just a marriage of convenience. But as time went on, it was clear y'all loved each other. Any fool could see how much he loved you."

"Actually, it did start out as a marriage of convenience. Mama was going to send me away when she found out I was pregnant with Theo's baby. Then when Theodore came to tell us about Theo's death, he saw how insensitive Mama was being toward me and his future grandchild. So, he offered to marry me to give my baby the Dalton name. I took him up on his offer just to get out of the house and not be disgracefully sent away. As time went by, I saw what a wonderful person he was. How could I not love him?"

"I get it. I really do. I loved the guy too. Mr. Dalton was one of the finest men I ever knew," Deke agreed.

"Everyone he ever met felt the same way about him."

"If you don't mind me asking, with yer Mama bein' so strict and all, how in the world were you able to go to the dance hall as often as you did like that?"

"Mama embarrassed me to death one day just because Billie Kay and I let a couple boys walk us home from school. They only walked with us as far as where the blacktop met the gravel road. You know that spot, I'm sure. But she found out somehow and was waiting there for us. She switched me all the way home for everyone to see, including two school buses full of classmates that happen to pass by at the same time."

"I was on one of those buses and saw that. If it hadn't a made me look like a pure sissy, I'd a cried like a baby when I saw her switch you that day." Deke actually looked as though he could have burst into tears right then.

"You were on that bus?"

"Yes, that was my last bus ride and my last day of school. I was already a couple years older than the others in my class. I had failed a few grades because my parents kept me out of school so much to work in the fields. I joined the Army the next day."

"Well, that humiliating switching changed me. I had always been Mama's good little girl. But I decided if my mother was going to treat me like a *no-account-daughter*, I was going to live up to her opinion of me. Billie Kay and I would slip out of our houses every chance we could get. Mama knew what we were doing. But she was powerless since she had embarrassed me beyond caring anymore."

"I'm sorry you had to live like that, Lucretia," Deke said softly. "I can't even count the times I thought about you while I was overseas. I've been so mad at your mother and held that day against her all these years."

"Actually, I didn't do anything but flirt and act the part until I met Theo. We thought we were in love and planned to be married but he got killed right after he left.

"Mama and I made amends after I married Theodore. I think she saw how she drove me to do what I did. And I realized she did what she did out of love, even if she went about showing it in such a cruel way. She finally learned to trust and give me the benefit of the doubt before judging me. And I grew up real fast after suffering the consequences of my bad choices."

"I have another confession, Lucretia," he said cautiously.

"Deke, you really don't owe me all these confessions."

"Well, I need to get this one out of the way and explain some things. I don't want any misunderstandin' to get in the way of your decision about marryin' me."

I agreed to listen, after seeing how serious he was.

Chapter Forty-Six

DEKE HAD BEEN standing and pacing the entire time. His next confession sounded as though it might be lengthy and even more in depth than his previous ones. Before he began, I patted the couch and suggested he sit.

He took a long breath, glance at the ceiling then down to the floor. Finally, he looked square into my eyes. "Mr. Dalton asked me to take a ride with him one day so we could talk in private. He told me how sick he really was and that you didn't know the extent of it. Lucretia, he didn't want to worry you. He asked me to look after you and the girls if anything ever happened to him. Of course, I said I would. Then I confessed how I had always felt about you over the years. He respected me for being honest and trusted me where you were concerned. He said it made him feel good to know there was another good man in this world who put yours and your babies' well-being before anything else.

"I felt like I had to tell you this. Now, I hope you understand. I haven't been there for you just because he asked me to be. I love you. I always have. I would have stepped up to help you if Mr. Dalton had never asked anything of me. And I hated being on your payroll, but I realized that was the only way you would have it." Deke took a deep breath as though a heavy load had been lifted off his shoulders.

"I respect you too for being so honest and open with me. But Deke you need to think about what people will say if I married you at this time. Theodore has only been gone not quite three months yet. Why people are already looking us up and down every time they see us together anywhere."

"I don't care what people say about me. Now, I don't want them saying anythin' about you. And nobody better be silly enough to talk down on you in front of me. We know who we are. We don't need people tryin' to pin labels on us. Neither of us are bound by marriage to anyone. We are free to do what we want. Whoever made up that rule about waitin' to get married again after your spouse dies 'til everybody else thought it looked right, aint never been in your situation.

"Lucretia, I'm a poor man but I'm honest. And I work hard and I aint lazy. Like I said, I'd work my fingers down to the nub for you and those babies. I was hoping to ask you to marry me one day anyway. It just seems to make more sense now. How much you have or don't have in the bank means nothin' to me. The money's not important. I promise."

I believed every word Deke said.

"I don't have much left in the bank and Mr. Caldwell made it clear that unless I work and put it there, no more money is coming in. By the time I paid a babysitter, it wouldn't pay me to work at all. Besides, I don't want someone else raising my children so I can work."

"I will do all the workin' so you can raise those babies like you want to. I'm purdy sure you like me. And given enough time, maybe you could even love me. Those little girls already do. Think about it. Will you just think about it?"

"Yes, Deke. I will." How could I not think about Deke's proposal? Today was full of many things I had to ponder.

"I need to get back to the cotton patch now. Since tomorrow is Saturday, we'll only pick a half day. I can come over as soon as I can get squared away in the field, if you'd like."

"That's fine," I agreed.

"Maybe you'll have had time to think over what we just talked about." Deke stood and nervously shoved his hands into his pockets.

"Oh, I'll be thinking about it, for sure. But…"

"I don't want to pressure you. I know I sprung this on you real sudden like."

"Seems like everything happening in my life here lately is like you say, *real sudden like.*" My head was spinning after he left. I couldn't tell if what I was feeling was fear, pressure, shock, or desperation.

The mail man pulled into the yard as Deke was

walking to his car. "This package won't fit in the box. Since you're out here already, want me to just give it to you?" the mailman asked.

"Thank you. I'll take it back up to the house for Mrs. Dalton," Deke replied.

"Appreciate that," he said while pulling away.

Thinking Deke was gone; I was surprised to hear another light tap on the door. "The mailman asked me to give this to you," he whispered again, holding a good-sized box.

"I bet that is Scarlett's car seat. Can you use your pocketknife to open it?"

Had I known my financial dilemma, would I have ordered the seat anyway, I thought as Deke was opening the box? The answer was yes. My babies' safety was still of most importance.

"Scarlett will love this. Look at the little stirring wheel." Deke grinned.

"Edna said her friends little boy sure loved his. I only hope it will keep her safe if I have to go anywhere with just me and the girls."

"I hope so too." A wrinkle of concern creased his brow. "Okay, I really have to go this time. See you tomorrow afternoon."

Deke had no sooner left when Melanie whimpered. She was wet and ready for her feeding. Scarlett heard her and also wanted up.

Melanie couldn't go anywhere yet, so I dealt with

Scarlett first. I prayed I had a little more control of her by the time Melanie was able to run around too. After putting Scarlett in her playpen with her horsey, I tended to Melanie.

Scarlett immediately started singing, *horsey, horsey go to town.* Both girls were such happy children and full of life. I wanted to do everything in my power to keep them that way.

I needed to talk to someone. Edna had been a good listener. Maybe she could help me find some clarity.

"Hey, Scarlett, want to go see Miss Edna and Miss Strom and try out your new car seat?" I said after I got Melanie fed. "I'm going to lay little sister here on this blanket on the floor while I go put your new seat in the truck. Can you sing to her too?"

Grabbing a couple of pillows, my wicker clothes basket, and the car seat, I rushed to the truck.

I could hear Scarlett singing, *Melly Ann, Melly Ann some candy,* as I left. "That's good, sweet girl," I yelled to her. "Sing to your Melly Ann. Mommie will be right back."

After getting everything in place, I ran back in the house to get the girls.

"Look, Scarlett. You have a stirring wheel too. Sit here and help Mommie drive, okay?" After securing Scarlett in her seat and stuffing the pillows around Melanie in the basket, wedged tightly between the dash and the passenger seat, I prayed for our safety should anything happen.

Mrs. Strom was in her porch swing when we pulled into her yard.

"Look at you, driving around with those babies all by yourself," she said as I led Scarlett to the porch.

"Can you let this one sit here with you a minute while I grab the baby?" I asked.

"Yes, I can. You want to swing with me, pretty girl?" I heard her say, as I rushed back to the truck.

"Those two babies keep you a hoppin.' That's fer sure," she said when I returned with Melanie.

"It was easier when Theodore was still alive. He was so good with them."

"I'm sorry you lost him, child. I know you must have it hard in so many ways with him gone. But you seem to be managing purdy well as far as I can tell. I've noticed Deke steppin' in to help you from time to time too. That's good."

"Yes, it is… Where is Edna? I see her car is gone."

"She heard they had an openin' for a clerk at the corner market. She went to apply for the job since she had experience workin' in her daddy's store over in Arkansas."

"Yes, she talks a lot about her family in Caraway."

"Larson said they're a real nice bunch of people. Guess that's where Edna gets it. I'm mighty fond of her."

"Well, it's evident how fond she is of you too. Mrs.

Strom, can I ask you a question?"

"Ask me anything you want, dear."

"The last time we talked, you said I had to do what was best to take care of my babies. Did you have any special reason for saying that?"

"As I recall, you were worried about people gossip-in' about you and Deke. It's plain to see how much help he is to you. It's also plain to see that no one else has stepped up to help you very much. If he's a mind to do it, then isn't it best for you and yer babies to let him? No matter how many people flap their jaws.

"And as for why I said that. Sometimes, things come to me. When they do, I just say 'em. If God lays somethin' on my heart to say to somebody, then I speak it. I think you needed to hear those words that day."

"I did. It's just that the last thing Theodore said to me the day he died was something like that. I didn't understand it at the time, but a few things have happened here lately to make me see it a little more clearly now. I thought it strange you sort of said the same thing to me, that's all."

"It's been my experience that if God wants to get a message out to somebody, sometimes he sends it by more than one messenger." She smiled sweetly.

"Can I get your opinion on something else?"

"Yes," she said curiously.

"A daughter would usually go to her mother about something like this. But my mother is not well. Plus, I'm not sure Mama could give me a fair answer about this."

"Okay, I'll do my best to be fair," she replied.

"Also, can we keep this just between us? That is until the time is right to make it public, if that time ever comes?"

"If anyone ever hears what we are about to discuss, you can be the one to tell it. I promise I will not say anything to anyone." Mrs. Strom folded her hands in her lap and gave me her complete attention.

"Deke wants to marry me. There are many reasons he wants to, but he told me earlier today, that he has loved me for a long time. I worry about what people will say and how Mama will take it. I hate to bring anything else on her right now."

"I can't advise you one way or the other about whether you should marry Deke or not. That is a decision only you can make. But how I see it, is people will gossip until the next best thing comes along. Then they will give you a rest. But people's opinions, includin' yer mama's, have to get to the back of the line until you come to a decision about Deke."

"It's just so soon. And I have so many memories about Theodore and how our life was before he got sick," I said.

"Yes, I'm sure you do. But honey, you caint live on memories. Memories are good to look back on sometimes but other times they bog us down. We all have 'em memories that warm yer heart. But there are also those that are like ice water runnin' in our veins. You caint build a future lookin' backwards on memories. Futures are built on visions."

"Visions?" I questioned.

"What is yer vision for you and those two babies, Lucretia?"

"A few things happened this morning that probably moved most of the visions I had for myself out of reach for me now. But more than anything, I want my children's future to remain as bright and unlimited as possible."

"Then keep yer eyes on that vision. In the Bible, God led those shepherds to Jesus by a vision—a bright star. He led the people through the wilderness by heavenly visions too. Look up, child. God never led anyone forward by their memories. Visions are what kept 'em movin' along."

"I never thought of it that way before, Mrs. Strom."

"Find yer vision. Pray about it. And let God be who helps you decide yer path—not a bunch of waggin' tongues."

"But what about Mama?"

"God is the only one who loves you more than yer Mama and Daddy. Trust Him first. Then trust their love next."

Chapter Forty-Seven

A S MRS. STROM had predicted. Gossip spread. Tongues wagged. And judgments were passed throughout Bragg City and Muddy Ox for way longer than I would have liked after Deke and I were married. But we were too busy trying to make things work and keep things as normal as possible for Scarlett and Melanie to let it bog us down. We had a like-vision for our family's future and were doing our best to follow it.

It was Mama and Daddy's judgment I had most feared—well—Mama's anyway. I'd always felt as though Daddy had a more practical way of looking at things since he wasn't as easily swayed by popular opinion.

Maybe the effects from her stroke kept Mama from realizing Deke and the little boy under the cotton wagon were one in the same. Or could be both she and Daddy had seen how I did what I had to do, after I explained the bank situation to them. But I chose to believe that because I had honored and trusted God first, and their love second, as Mrs. Strom had advised, that God had a hand in the outcome.

Actually, I saw His hand in a lot of things. Miraculously, I was offered close to the same amount for

Theodore's house in Bragg City that was being asked for a larger, much nicer house a few doors down from Mama and Daddy. It took almost everything Deke and I had to buy it, but we managed. I really needed to have been closer to them all along. Besides, my roots had always been planted in Muddy Ox. For that matter, so were Deke's.

Eventually, the end of the war, the fall and rise of the economy, Stan Musial's return to the St. Louis Cardinals after his stint in the military and hopes for winning the World Series next time around had become more interesting topics to the townsfolk than the ups and downs of my life.

Also, the many questionable incidents at the McDougal residence, and several births that didn't have enough days with an X placed on them for the calendar-marking ladies in town, had overshadowed the tittle-tattle about mine and Deke's ill-timed wedding.

As typical of things happening real-sudden-like for Deke and me, I became pregnant with our first child one month after we were married. Thank heavens, the ladies were able to put their pens and calendars to rest.

I couldn't wait to share the news with Edna since she and Larson were also expecting a baby. Edna gave birth to Meryl Jean Strom and five months later, I delivered Tara Gayle McCrady, another girl. If Deke had been wishing for a boy, it never showed through his excitement of having Tara Gayle.

Edna was curious to know if Tara Gayle had been a boy, would we have named him Rhett to stay with the *Gone With The Wind* theme.

I told her I would have been tempted but that Deke would have had a say in it.

Edna was heartbroken to tell me that our hopes of raising our girls together and the idea that Scarlett and Melanie could have looked out for Meryl and Tara when they all got older wasn't going to be. Larson had taken a trucking job in Michigan, and they would be leaving in a few weeks.

We resolved that our girls could still be friends, but they would have to be mostly long distant ones. She said she was pretty sure they would be making frequent visits back to Muddy Ox to visit Mrs. Strom. Also, she shared how much Larson just loved to be on the road a lot.

I hated to see them leave. I didn't understand why it seemed all my close friends had to move away from Muddy Ox. She would be in Michigan. Billy Kay lived in Texas. I would miss them both something awful. However, we knew it had to be a matter of going where the work was. That had definitely been Billie Kay's reason for moving.

Edna confirmed what Deke had always said about Larson's itching feet to get out of the Bootheel and that neither of them never were, never would, nor even wanted to try to be cotton pickers. She said she and Larson loved the Bootheel area, they just didn't love the farming part. I laughed, remembering what I'd heard about both of them.

Their little Meryl Jean was so cute, and I loved her expressions and head full of curly hair. Edna said she was pretty sure she was going to be a singer, since her cries even sounded like she was trying to sing.

Between us we had four beautiful little girls and knew how blessed we both were.

FIVE YEARS LATER, Mama had never gotten back to where she was before the stroke but was much better. I was glad to have been able to move back so close to them. The girls were such bright spots in her and Daddy's days. Although, she still couldn't be much help to me with them.

Deke was right. I did fall in love with him. How could I not have fallen for a man who had loved me his entire life? Because I had been so young and impulsive, I found myself wondering if what I felt for Theo was actually love or lust? I really did love Theodore, but in an entirely different way than I loved Deke. I was sure there were still those who judged me and would have called me frivolous or flighty, but as Deke had said, we didn't need others to place labels on us. We knew who we were.

Edna was right about her and Larson coming back to Muddy Ox for frequent visits. Each time they'd come, we'd let our girls play and bond together. They became close friends just as Edna and I were. I could always tell when they arrived at Mrs. Strom's. The girls would squeal, "Jean is here" and ask to go play with her.

I never understood why they called her Jean instead of Meryl. But one day, I asked Tara, why? She said, "because she likes Jean better than Meryl." I admired that little girl's boldness. For her to actually decide what she wanted to be called at such a young age was impressive. Then I remembered how bold her mother had been to take charge of her life at a young age too. Guess Jean had a good role model.

Because our girls were so young when Theodore died, Deke was actually the only daddy that Scarlett and Melanie knew. He delighted in his role and was a wonderful father to all three girls. They met him at the door each day when he came home from work with hugs and kisses.

That was why the day he came home with the news of a job possibility in St. Louis it presented such a problem for all of us.

I told Deke I wasn't sure about raising our girls in a big city like St. Louis. I knew Muddy Ox wasn't perfect, but the Bootheel of Missouri was all I'd ever known.

He wasn't sure the big city life was best for our

family either. But he felt like it was a great opportunity for, as he put it, a country boy like him to work at a big company like General Motors, with its benefits and better wages.

I reminded him that he had always said money wasn't important. But he said he meant that Theodore's money wasn't important. But any money he could make to provide a better, easier life for our family was extremely important.

When I said I worried about us living separately, He said he could afford to drive home every weekend. And he'd get telephones for us and him so we could call as often as we wanted.

He said our girls wouldn't need to work in the cotton patch to get their school clothes. Remembering how hard he had to work as a child made that paramount for him.

For every argument I had about Deke living and working in St. Louis, he had a counter argument. Finally, he made me realize that we still had the same vision for our family. He just wanted to take a different path to follow it.

He was right. After he got his job at General Motors, our girls never lacked for anything. However, I did insist they work in the cotton field for extra spending money. They weren't expected to make the daily totals that were required of some of the other children, but I wanted them to learn real work ethic. The cotton field was certainly the place to do that.

My learning to drive came in handy later on when the girls and I would take a road trip to St. Louis to visit Deke and shop for their school clothes.

Seven years after Tara was born, I had another baby girl, Suellen. Sixteen months later, we had our last child, Carreen—also a girl. Needless to say, I never continued my education past getting a G.E.D. However, my life experiences had provided me with a kind of *further education* that couldn't be taught or achieved at any institution of higher learning.

Although I had shocked the community by my unconventional choices, I later became a well-respected lady about town. Because I was seen as a person who somehow rose to the occasion when others would have bowed to defeat, I had become admired for my strength and courage. Seeing how I faced my adversary with intelligence and confidence and refused to be denied, I had become a role model to a few. Instead of whispering behind my back, people went out of their way to greet me with a smile. That felt good.

Theodore had been right about many things but most of all he was right about me having no limitations.

With the help of God, a burning desire to succeed, and enough self-confidence anyone can rise above their mistakes and poor choices. It also helps to have the love of a good man.

I had three.

The end

Proverbs 3:5-6 Trust in the Lord with all thine heart and lean not unto thine own understanding. In all thy ways acknowledge him, and he shall direct thy paths.

Special thanks to:

The SKYWriters workshop: Bobbie Falin, Gerry Brown and Kimberly Bartley. Without your help by reading, critiquing, advising, and encouraging, this endeavor would not have been possible. You all are priceless.

Extra thanks to Bobbie Falin for being willing to drop whatever you were doing at the time to come and help me with any and all of the technical problems I had.

Thanks to all my beta readers—you know who you are. Your time, suggestions and all your extra sets of eyes were invaluable in bringing this book to life.

And thank you Rick Ashby for your continuous encouragement.

Special thanks to Marta Denham Brumley (Melly Ann) for being my special advisor for this story. I hope I did you proud.

And thank you Zacchaeus for being so patient with me during the many hours it took to create this story. My lap is yours again, at least until I start working on my next book.

Special thanks to Aaron Hughey for being such a fan of my work and all you do to help me promote my books.

Most of all, thanks to all of you who are fans of my

books. I am truly overwhelmed and humbled by your outpouring of love and continued interest in my work. You make all the writing and rewriting into the wee hours of night, endless research, and picking myself up every time I feel I'm about to crumble worthwhile.

About the Author

Noel Barton spent her teen years in the Bootheel of Missouri.

She now resides in Bowling Green, Kentucky. She is a mother, grandmother, widowed (twice), best friend to her little dog Zacchaeus and a retired travel counselor. Being a devout Christian, she credits God for her writing ability. Lucretia, her third novel, is a spin-off of a character in her first two books. Although, this account is fiction, many aspects of the story are based on actual facts and occurrences. All of Noel's books have a common thread woven throughout them. They each have a love story, a mystery, and many moral and spiritual messages. She hopes you will enjoy this nostalgic journey down memory lane and be inspired by Lucretia as she courageously faces the Whirlwinds in her life—and survives.